# Rediscovery on the French Riviera

## Charlie Hastain

# Chapters

Prologue

Chapter 1 - The Letter

Chapter 2 - Flashback - The wedding day

Chapter 3 - Here I Come France

Chapter 4 - Ladies who lunch

Chapter 5 - Birth of the boys

Chapter 6 - Theresa gets a phone call

Chapter 7 - Going solo

Chapter 8 - Flashback - Mark's Promotion

Chapter 9 - Drinks with James

Chapter 10 - Monte Carlo or Bust

Chapter 11 - Loo or Loire?

Chapter 12 – Flashback – Blown off course

Chapter 13 - Boulangerie and Beach

Chapter 14 – Italian Stallion

Chapter 15 - Flashback - Theresa writes

Chapter 16 – 'Bonjour' Neighbours

Chapter 17 - Is happiness an illusion?

Chapter 18 - Flashback - David's police interview

Chapter 19 - Have a butchers

Chapter 20 - How do you like your steak?

Chapter 21 - Which one was Pascal?

Chapter 22 - Flashback - 9 to 5

Chapter 23 - Problem solver extraordinaire

Chapter 24 - Houses and More

Chapter 25 - Double Trouble

Chapter 26 - Pascal's Picnic

Chapter 27 - Supper with Gino

Chapter 28 – Flashback - Mark's Funeral

Chapter 29 - A "doer-upper"

Chapter 30 - Business or Pleasure?

Chapter 31 - Ménage à Trois

Chapter 32 - Flashback- Empty Nest

Chapter 33 - Dinner with Pascal

Chapter 34 – Too strong?

Chapter 35 - How to solve a problem like Gino

Chapter 36 - Coq au vin

Chapter 37 - Different shades of beige

Chapter 38 - Trip to the Windmill

Chapter 39 - Mothering Sunday

Chapter 40 - Pizza 'dough'

Chapter 41 - Money for your life

Chapter 42 - Cathy falls for the Cote d'Azur

Chapter 43 - Death comes as the end

Chapter 44 - Cash rich

Chapter 45 – Theresa returns

Chapter 46 - Flashback – Mel and the police

Chapter 47 – All mine

Epilogue – A year ahead

To all of us that need a little bit of *rediscovery* every now again…

## Prologue

I have felt for some time that my life was not fulfilled. I don't mean my whole life. I have been blessed with good health, an idyllic childhood, my two wonderful sons and my 21-year marriage to my late husband Mark. I have supported them, and others, did all I thought was expected of me. After two decades of putting others first, as a mother and a wife, I was starting to feel rudderless and powerless to change direction. Until a tragic accident changed all that. I was not at home when it happened.

It had been a bright Saturday morning, but there was a distinct chill in the air, a slight frost was evident on the grass. I had popped out for a couple of hours for some food shopping, to stock up before the boys returned for Easter. Seems silly to have been doing something so mundane.

The paramedic told me there was, 'nothing she could have done'. What an empty phrase. My husband, Mark, had fallen through a roof. The 18th-century storage shed was located towards the back of our cottage. It had once been a store for hay, then later an air raid shelter, but now it needed attention before it was lost. Our grand plan had been to convert it and run a holiday let, and use it for family and friends to stay in. That had never happened.
The fall had fractured Mark's spine, which in turn had transected the Aortic artery. The sheer loss of blood

would have killed him in minutes. Did you know that the Aortic artery was the largest in the body?
*I do now*, reflected Melissa.

## Chapter 1 - The Letter

Today would have been Mark's 47th Birthday, just over a year since his death.

Melissa stared at herself in the mirror. She sat at her tired-looking dressing table, a rather messy selection of toiletries adorned the table in front of her. The reflection that greeted her was equally forlorn and Melissa's messy hair matched the haphazard dressing table. As a woman in her mid-forties, her skin had begun to show signs of ageing, a natural consequence of the day to day rigours of life, bringing up a family and Mark's death. Her mum said that she was "old before her time", even her name "Melissa" seemed to have a ring of *age* about it, though luckily most friends and family simply called her "Mel". Then there were her eyes, big and brown, which she knew showed an inner sadness. She had to admit she felt flat.

*Shouldn't my life be more exciting?* she pondered.

Snapping herself out of her malaise, she suddenly grabbed her phone, and talking to herself in the mirror, she exclaimed.

'Come on Mel, this isn't you, no time for this!'

Walking down the stairs to the kitchen, she strode to the kettle. Grabbed a mug from the cupboard and stood looking out of the kitchen window. The view was one she'd enjoyed a thousand times before, stretching from the back of the house to the fields beyond. Squinting she could make out "Rocky", rubbing his long and thick equine neck against a post.

The thrum of the kettle boiling interrupted her daydream. She took a lemon and cut a slice and placed it into her warm cup of Earl Grey.

Mel pulled up a chair and sat at the kitchen table, putting on a pair of brightly coloured reading glasses, which she also felt aged her. Health-wise things were good, barring not being able to read a book up close without glasses. She knew she had lost her spark, but for how long had she felt like this? Certainly longer than she'd care to admit. She drained her tea and went towards the kitchen door. She wiggled her feet into a pair of large green wellies and exited into the damp day outside.

Once mucking out and feeding duties had been completed, Mel was hungry. This particular morning, partly due to the inclement weather, she craved something warm and comforting, so she decided on porridge. She made her way back onto the avenue, passing different houses, some new, some old. The rain had cleared, and nearing the house, she spotted the mail van, hazard lights flashing, double-parked outside the house. She trudged on, fumbling in a dark recess of her jacket for the old pair of reading glasses she carried around in preparation to read today's post.

'Morning', shouted Mel in a forced cheery manner, that came across more downbeat than she had hoped.

'Do you have anything for Grove cottage?'

'Yes I do, here you are my love', said the postman as he passed the bundle through the window of his van.

Taking her post into the kitchen she flicked on the kettle. There was a parcel which she decided to open first, hoping it was her new walking boots.

*Walking was good to clear the head and put things in perspective,* considered Mel.

Once the layers of bubble wrap, and an unnecessary amount of brown paper had been discarded, she tried the boots on and strutted around the kitchen, imagining she was in the Brecon Beacons or the Peak District, though in reality, it was more likely they'd be used for a local stroll on the South Downs. Moving back to the kitchen table she picked up two envelopes, the top one was brown and inevitably a bill. The second however was not and was handwritten. Reading glasses on, she closely inspected it, noticing that the postmark was for the Cote d'Azur. Curiously she opened the envelope and started to read.

'Dearest Mel,

*I am so sorry I have not been in contact sooner, and this letter will no doubt seem like a bolt out of the blue. The last time I saw you was about a year ago at Mark's funeral. Life must have been tough since and difficult to adjust. If you remember we exchanged numbers at the funeral, but it seems I noted it down incorrectly, I can't find you on social media. I am therefore writing to you in the good old fashioned way.*

*When we chatted a year ago you mentioned you would like to travel more, have you done so? Travelling is so* good for the soul and to get a new perspective on things, I find so anyway. I have a favour to ask, a rather big one.

Chloe, my daughter, is about to open her first retail outlet in Canada, and with my background in journalism and being a creative consultant for Wisteria publications – well she has asked me to help! This means I need someone to house sit, someone I can trust. I appreciate this will come as a surprise, but please say you can. I know you must miss Mark terribly, getting away might be a good thing, a chance to relax and unwind?

I have enclosed some airline vouchers which should cover the flight costs, call me as soon as you can. +33 4 876 74153.

With love

Theresa x

P.T.O.'

Mel thought for a moment recalling Theresa, Mark's sister. A short-ish woman, wild brown hair, a lovely smile and bright billowing clothes. Mel had a pang of guilt too, she hadn't tried to contact Theresa, she had just wanted to get the months after the funeral out of the way.

She turned over the page, Theresa had added a note.

'I forgot to say, it's likely to be a month, ideally from the 21$^{st}$ of May.

X'

Mel looked at her watch, it was the 16th. She couldn't possibly make it in time, what about the horse and her house? A whole month was out of the question, also why hadn't she written sooner? Mel looked at the envelope, the postcode was wrong, BO not PO. Then some vouchers for British Airways and a €50 note fell out.

Grabbing some paper, she began to write.

*'Dearest Theresa'*

*'So lovely to hear from you, sadly I will have to decline your offer…*

She stopped, looked out of her kitchen window and the grey drizzly day outside. She placed her pen down.

'Sod it! Why not?' Mel declared.

Getting up, she walked to the hallway, fumbling in the pocket of her damp rain jacket for her mobile, still in her walking boots, she dialled, she could hear the faint French dial tone…

*

Mel pressed cancel and sat still lost in thought. When they had met she remembered the conversation had flowed easily, as it had on the phone today. Theresa had been friendly and more than understanding, Mel could just not shake off the feeling of excitement mixed with anxiety.

*What did she need to organise?* She considered as she looked across the garden through the drizzle that dripped down the window in monotonous continual steaks. She began to write a list; *passport, driving licence...*

There were only a few days to get herself organised, the horse was the main issue. She knew that Cathy would be more than happy to help out. Cathy was there the day Mark died, she had run up the road as soon as Mel had called her to tell her. Cathy had consoled and soothed, she had even picked Mel up from the police station that same day after questioning. It seemed odd that today of all days she was planning her first trip abroad in years.

Suddenly she was distracted by the doorbell.

As she opened the door Cathy bounded through like an excited puppy. Mel deduced she had just had a yoga session as Cathy was slightly red in the cheeks and sporting some Sweaty Betty leggings and a bright coloured oversized t-shirt. Cathy was slightly younger than she was, a very good neighbour and confidant for Mel, for whom nothing was too much trouble.

Cathy followed her into the kitchen.

'Going somewhere?' Asked Cathy with a wink.

They had known each other since Mel and Mark had moved into the avenue some twenty-plus years previously. Cathy and Chris lived up the road in a detached new build, red brick with a gravel drive and white PVC windows. Cathy was a homemaker. Chris, her husband, worked in London, an accountant for a large retail company in the City.

Turning away from the now boiling kettle, Mel replied.

'As a matter of fact, I am! Do you remember Theresa, Mark's sister?'

'Vaguely the one that always wears bright floaty clothes, lives in the South of France and if I remember rightly, very friendly and excitable?'

'That's the one!' said Mel, sliding a mug of tea towards Cathy.

'Mmmm thanks,' Cathy muttered as she blew on her hot tea, 'so what's the news? I hope she's not unwell...?'

'No no no' Mel interjected, 'she wrote to me, asking a favour'.

She showed Cathy the letter, Cathy sat back, pushed her mug away and looked straight at Mel.

'Please tell me you said yes?'

'I did but...'

'But what?' cried Cathy. 'It's a great opportunity, go somewhere new and get away from here. Have you been away since, umm, since Mark?'

'No, I haven't'.

Mel began to think about Mark. Today would have been his birthday, a comforting hand stretched across the table and rested on top of Mel's.

'I know things have been tough Mel, but I think it's a good thing'.

'I know I know I should feel excited, but I feel like I've lost my spark, do you know what I mean?'

'Come on let's pack and before you ask, yes I'll keep an eye on the house and Rocky', Cathy smiled at Mel.

'Thank you, Cathy, look, help yourself to food…'

'Now stop worrying and let's get you sorted for the south of France, it will be warm, and you'll need lots of loose fitting outfits and a bikini!' She winked at Mel.

'I haven't worn one of those for years!'

'No time like the present', Cathy was already on her way up to Mel's bedroom before she could reply.

Mel wanted to get excited but kept thinking about Mark? Was it guilt? How long since she'd felt a sense of anticipation? Wasn't it about time she put herself first and seized the day? She started to feel the swell of emotion rise up, she swallowed it down, gulped down the remainder of her tea, forced a smile which turned into a real grin when she heard Cathy bellowing from upstairs,

'What on earth are these?! Are they ear-muffs?'

Dashing upstairs to regain some or any of her dignity, Mel tried to ignore Cathy who was now sporting a polka dot bikini on her head. Cathy flung open Mel's wardrobe doors and began to rifle through, pulling out garments, waving them at Mel. Mel sat on the floor cross-legged and tried to sort out her underwear and socks that she would take.

Gradually between them, they made three piles, with the 'take' pile becoming the largest by far. Mel was engrossed in this task when it suddenly dawned on her - *the flights!*

Theresa had said on the phone to check these as soon as possible.

'Cathy!' exclaimed Mel. She stood up, steadying herself on the edge of the bed.

Cathy now watching her friend intently,

'What? You gave me a fright.'

'Not fright, flight!'

'What do you mean?'

'Well Theresa told me to book flights ASAP and in all the excitement I haven't'.

'Quick where's your iPad, I'm sure I saw it just now. Ahh, here it is under the beach towel'. Cathy handed it to Mel.

'OK let me see, B-r-i-t-i-s-h A-i-r-w-a-y-s…' Mel said slowly as she typed into the search engine.

Shortly, after some deliberating, a flight was booked, the 11:05 am flight from Gatwick to Nice in 5 days time. There was a little confusion over how to use the voucher Theresa had included with her letter, but once that was sorted, it was done.

'I can't believe how good value flights are, should I have known I would have been travelling more,' announced Mel

'I know! I'm sure Chris had to fly for work somewhere in Romania once and got the flights for only twenty pounds or something.'

The morning flowed into the afternoon as they both sat crossed-legged on the floor sorting through piles of clothes, shoes and holiday essentials. When Mel announced, 'I'm starving, will you stay for lunch?'

'Thanks yeah, I'd love to, Chris won't be back from work until later this evening'.

Back in the kitchen, the gloom outside showed no signs of abating. Cathy sighed.

'I'm a bit jealous. I would love to get away from this dark damp weather and take a break from my everyday routine.'

'You and Chris had a holiday back in February didn't you?' She had to admit this was a loaded question, knowing fully there had been a holiday.

'Yes we went down to Austria, but you must remember what a skiing holiday is like? You need another holiday to get over it. Plus I'd actually like some time to myself.'

Mel didn't respond. She was thinking about the last vacation she'd been on, when suddenly the toaster brought her back into the present.

'Who knew packing was such hard work!' said Cathy

'Shall we have some wine? I feel like we deserve it after all that packing.' Mel suggested

'Lovely, very decadent drinking at lunchtime, I'm sure you and Theresa will do it all the time next week.' Cathy sat looking slightly forlorn.

'I dare say we might, but don't forget she's off to Canada and I'll be there alone. She said the downstairs neighbours are sweet but that the next-door apartment is rarely used by the German owners, so not really anyone around to drink with.' Pulling the cork out with the satisfying release sound.

As they sat together eating lunch and sipping wine they discussed what to wear up on the plane, and then what Mel should wear to the beach.

'Cathy, I appreciate you being here and helping me.'

'What? Don't be silly I'm more than happy to help you know that'

'No, I mean today of all days.'

'Today?'

'Yes, it would have been Mark's 47th birthday', she looked down at her empty plate.

'Mel, I'm so sorry, I'd forgotten, is it really that long ago?'

'Yes and I feel guilty Cathy, guilty about going away, guilty about enjoying myself, and I have no idea why!'

'Don't think like that. Look Mark would have wanted you to get away I'm sure, and here I am feeling guilty for wanting some *me* time. What are we like?'

'You are right we shouldn't feel bad about it, maybe I've forgotten how to have fun, you know, to be spontaneous?'

'Nonsense, come on you wash and I'll dry, then let's take the rest of the bottle upstairs and continue the sorting. And you're not to worry about a thing while you are away, remember I'll be at the end of the phone if you need me! Unless it's to tell me you're drinking lovely dry rosé and some bronzed hunk is rubbing sun cream on your back, then I'll just hang up!' Cathy said with a laugh and a twinkle in her lovely round blue eyes.

Ensconced in Mel's bedroom, they sipped wine and continued sorting. Later in the afternoon, Cathy said her goodbyes, let herself out and went off to pick up some dinner for her and Chris.

A moment of panic enveloped Mel, she stopped what she was doing dashed to her bedside table, she knew it had been somewhere, where did she put it, when did she last see it? Was it on the side table? Or is it in the bottom drawer of the dressing table? An additional pang of worry came over her. Was it still in date? She did use it about 3 or 4 years ago or was it 5. *Ahh, there it is...*

Pulling down her reading glasses to her eyes from the top of her head she flicked to the picture page, *good, it's in date*, she thought to herself.

She tossed the passport onto the bed, and started to return the scraps of paper back into the drawer.

Picking up a photo she turned it over to see Mark standing outside a church, wearing a 90s beige suit with a white shirt and light blue tie. It couldn't have been that long after this photo was taken that she and Mark had been married.

The packing continued, Theresa had suggested adding hold luggage, as she was going to be away for a month. But the way the *take* pile had built up it looked as if she were going off for years.

The bashed-up old Samsonite suitcase was nearly full and Mel was just arranging some toiletries. When she remembered that photo from earlier, it was funny how the old adage that - *a picture paints a thousand words,* seemed to be true. As she began to think back to her wedding, that wet muggy Saturday in July. It felt like a lifetime ago, *I suppose it was*, thought Mel. The guilt she had felt earlier began to creep over her again, why should she feel guilty?

    The wedding day had been good, but had it been *the happiest day of her life?* She mulled it over. There had been a break in the rain and the obligatory photos could take place without any need for umbrellas. Her thoughts began to wander. She had married the man of her dreams, hadn't she?

    She felt tired, probably the wine at lunchtime. She would just take a little nap. As she began to doze and the memories of the wedding crept in, it had been planned up to the finest detail by her, Mel's eyes closed, she dreamt.

## Chapter 2 - Flashback - The wedding day

The day had started gloomy and damp. *Typical!* Mel thought, *it's July and the weather is rubbish!*

She hadn't slept well. She had tried for an early night, but she couldn't get comfy and so lay awake looking at the ceiling. She was staying in the flat she shared with Mark in Shepherd's Bush. Her mum was staying in the spare room and would be travelling with her to church later that morning. Her father had passed away some years previously so mum had stepped in to give Mel away.

Mel looked out onto the road. The grey wet asphalt seemed to merge into the charcoal sky, and a sense of despondency enveloped her. She sighed,

*Ahh well it could be worse,* she switched on the bedside radio. It was 6am and the news had just started, "*John Major announced today…..*" She laid down and tried to relax and think of anything to take her mind off what was happening in a few hours' time.

There was a faint knock at the door. She sat up and pushed up the pillows behind her.

Her mother nudged the door gently and uttered,

'Morning darling',

Mel could smell the coffee. Her mum handed her a mug and perched on the edge of the bed.

'Thanks, Mum, did you sleep ok?'

'Not a wink, I was too excited, how about you?'

'Me neither, think I dropped off around 1-ish, I was desperate to look all bright-eyed and bushy-tailed on for my wedding day!'

Her mum looked at her quizzically,

'Mel, are you sure you are alright? You didn't seem yourself last night at dinner.'

Mel knew what her mother meant, she and Mark had a heated conversation about the seating arrangements for one of Mark's cousins which meant bumping an old school friend of Mel's to a different table. Mel recalled Mark saying, 'You've got more people coming to our wedding than me, it's only one person I'm asking to move.'

That had been that. Maybe I had got too many people from my side of the family coming, Mel thought to herself, feeling a pang of guilt. She had phoned the hotel where the reception was taking place and the table arrangements had been duly altered.

Sipping a hot coffee, Mel looked at her mum,

'No Mum, I'm fine honestly, just nervous. I want everything to be perfect.'

'Don't you worry it will be, now drink your coffee I'm going to get the oven on.'

'Thanks Mum.'

Mel lay there, mulling over all of the plans for the day. A sudden feeling of unease crept over her, was it anxiety? Was Mark the right man for me? Why was she thinking like this?

They had met at a mutual friend's barbecue in London. Mel had been invited down by some friends, it was at a lovely house situated near the river in Barnes. She remembered being introduced to Mark, who she thought looked rather handsome. Later on, that same day she recalled helping him remove some tomato ketchup from his linen blazer following an altercation with a burger. They had laughed and Mel liked laughing. Somehow the time had flown by and now, three years later she was going to be marrying this man. They had decided to move in together and share the flat that Mark had chosen. Now all that was changing. Mark had discussed with Mel the prospect of moving out of London once they were married, somewhere they could walk and hopefully bring up children. Mel had always preferred the verdant openness of the countryside to rush hour on the Central line.

Today was the last day in the London flat. They were being driven down to West Sussex after the wedding festivities were completed. Together they had fallen in love with a modest detached cottage on the outskirts of Chichester. It allowed Mark to commute by train to London. Mel had been keen to stick with work, but Mark had convinced her that she should find a new role locally and then when the time was right she was close by to raise children.

Mel got out of bed, slipped on her navy blue dressing gown and leather Moroccan slippers and went out into the kitchen where her mum was piling up some croissants in a breadbasket.

'There you are Mel, now do you want more coffee?'

The question hung there, and Mel looked at the rainfall dripping down the large sash windows, she involuntarily shivered. She couldn't shake off this doubt. Why did she have this overwhelming feeling of uncertainty?

## Chapter 3 - Here I Come France

Mel had spent the evening ensconced by the fire with a very large glass of Rioja, clasped in both hands as if trying to find some warmth from within. She was mesmerised by the flames in the fire, as they licked around the logs, she recalled chopping up some months previously. The red wine slipped down and warmed her throat, deliciously deep and comforting.

She hadn't slept well, first of all, she had a panic that she'd forgotten to pack any plug adaptors. But rifling through her bag she had found not one, but three! Secondly while sitting up in bed watching her iPad, a mug of Camomile tea on her bedside table was sent careering over, as the charging cable had snagged and sent it tumbling to the floor.

Therefore, it was well past midnight by the time Mel had fallen asleep, but everything else was sorted and she had spoken to Theresa again that evening. Theresa was all set to pick her up from the airport and had explained that there were only two terminals so getting lost shouldn't be an issue. However, Mel was nervous, she hadn't travelled alone for years, probably not since her boys were born. Mel mitigated her anxiousness with the thought that at either end she would be dropped off and greeted by people she knew and that hundreds of thousands of people travel alone every year.

She woke up around 7am. She had set an alarm but needn't have bothered, the excitement coupled with nervousness was enough to wake her. She wanted plenty of time to get her handbag together and check her passport and purse just one more time. Mel also had a very important thing she wanted to do before leaving and that was saying goodbye to her horse.

Checks all done, she made a cup of tea and began to flick through an old copy of the Sunday Times magazine, Mel had a habit of thumbing a magazine from cover to cover, marking any articles that struck her of interest so she could go back and read them later. An advert for a well-known drink grabbed her attention, firstly because she loved Aperol Spritz and the second because there was a competition to win a week in Nice. She read the competition blurb, *the rich history...wonderful food... sparkling azure...* It sounded delightful and somehow helped ease her nerves.

It had been less than a week since receiving Theresa's letter and here she was about to go to Cote d'Azur. It would be like winning that competition, Mel thought. She began to think about when she had last gone away, was it Italy? No, there must have been something more recent, she considered for a moment. Of course, there had been that trip to Madrid when Mark had been attending a conference. He spent most days in meetings coming back later and being tired when Mel had wanted to go out for dinner. It hadn't been much of a holiday, but as usual, she had gone along to support Mark.

'Why did I go along with it?' Mel said aloud, 'I barely saw any of the city.'

Before she could answer any of her questions, there was a loud knock at the door and a cry of 'Bonjour'. Mel let the catch off and there was Cathy, her beaming smile, instantly taking Mel away from her thoughts.

'Bonjour ça va?' said Mel

'Salut, Bien merci' said Cathy, 'that's it! I don't know much more.'

'Oh don't worry, me neither, do you want a cup of tea before we set off?' Mel asked over her shoulder, as the two of them made their way into the kitchen.

Nestled around the table with their cups of tea, looking out to the clear crisp morning before them. Mel began going over the checklist to make sure Cathy was happy with everything and that she must help herself to anything in the fridge.

'I know, and thank you, now stop worrying everything will be fine.' soothed Cathy.

'Thank you, I'm just nervous that's all, I was trying to remember the last time I travelled alone. The whole thing is just so exciting and scary.'

'Honestly, I think this will do you the world of good, good food, good wine and good weather, it will be fab.'

Cathy stopped speaking, the news on the radio began, it was 8:00am and the two of them needed to get going, Gatwick was an hour away and the flight was at 11:05.

'You ok? Right, got everything?' enquired Cathy

'Yes all set', just as she said that her phone bleeped, she started rummaging in her handbag, 'I've only just put it in here, how has it got right at the bottom?'

'Who is it?' asked Cathy

'Hold on, it's a WhatsApp from Theresa', she opened it. A pang of fear crept over her. *What if Theresa was cancelling? Or something was wrong? Now stop it, Mel, just read the bloody message.* Scolding herself mentally.

The screen blinked into life, and the green logo had a "one" next to it, she tapped.

*Darling can't wait to see you have a safe journey. I'll be waiting in arrivals, the weather is 31 degrees today. Txx*

'Thank goodness' said Mel, 'everything's ok she can't wait to see me!'

'Now let's get you to the airport. You lucky thing, *31 degrees*!'

As they loaded Mel's suitcase and bags into the car, her next-door neighbour was wheeling himself by.

'Off somewhere nice?' Winked David.

'Morning David', Mel crouched down to be at the same level as his wheelchair. 'I am off to Nice, house sitting, how are you?'

'Hi David,' chirped Cathy.

'Hi, Cathy! Mel you lucky thing, I am fine, my arms get stiff pushing the wheels, but the doctor tells me I need to get fresh air, it's good for me. I think this trip will do you the world of good, get away from here and the grey days.'

'Thank you, well I better be off, you look after yourself, do you need a hand?'

'No not today, have a lovely time.' And David wheeled himself to his front door.

'David, don't worry I will be keeping an eye on things whilst she is away,' Cathy thoughtfully added as they climbed into the car.

'Poor thing, must be tough. How old is he?'

'Eighty-eight or Eighty-nine I think, I know, his eyesight isn't great or his hearing for that matter, funny to think he was the one who saw Mark fall and rang me to tell me.' Mel paused. 'He does alright though, seems to keep himself busy with grandchildren and writing.'

They drove through the Sussex countryside, over the South Downs where the view across the valley into Amberley was still relatively clear and the mist clung to the river below, like a large gossamer-thin cobweb. They crisscrossed through the countryside until they joined the M23. The sign they had just passed read *Gatwick 9* . In 9 miles they would be there and Cathy would be gone and Mel would have to go it alone, her hand began to feel clammy, she began rubbing them on her black jeans, at that moment Cathy stretched out her hand and grabbed one of Mel's.

'It will be fine, think of the sun, sea and sand, you've got this Mel.'

Mel squeezed her friend's hand,

'Thank you. I just can't remember the last time I flew alone, it feels like a big step for me.'

Returning her hand to the wheel and indicating to take the exit, Cathy replied,

'You've nothing to worry about, you travelled when you worked in London, nothing has changed really except security is a bit tighter, and we've sorted the 100ml thingy, look here we are, *North Terminal*'.

They arrived at the drop-off area where a constant queue of taxis were depositing their passengers. *I wonder where they're going*, thought Mel. Cathy pulled up in a space, squeezed Mel's hand and got out of the car, Mel walked around the boot, grabbed the case and hauled it out.

'Thank god it's got wheels, it weighs a ton!'

Mel and Cathy hugged, and Mel thought she was going to cry but she composed herself and wished her friend goodbye.

'Cathy, thank you so much, I...' her bottom lip began to quiver.

'Now stop being silly just have a super time. That's an order! See you soon.'

And with a wave, Cathy had hopped back into the car and was gone. Mel made her way towards the ominous glass and grey building clasping her passport as she walked into the terminal carefully following the yellow signs for "Departures".

The process was very smooth and the airport seemed to be relatively quiet, Mel had checked in her luggage and made her way to security. Her ancient Russell and Bromley loafers had beeped but other than that all went to plan. She could not believe the amount of perfume, chocolate and booze as she negotiated the circular and somewhat disorientating duty-free.

She stopped at a big screen, the time now was 9:30, and the board showed her flight "BA1025" to Nice, boarding at 10:35.

Mel meandered around the shops and stopped at Pret, she had practically lived in Pret when she worked in London, she ordered a flat white and a croissant. *Well, I'm practically in France. I might as well start as I mean to go on*, she thought to herself.

Perched on a barstool, she started to watch people. Families struggling with many bags, Business people looking very efficient with small black wheeled cases, and a couple that had caught her eye, they sat together with a small bag between them both reading. She had a Jackie Collins and he had a Tom Clancy. Mel continued to watch while she sipped her coffee.

*They haven't spoken to each other once, and don't look very excited about going away*, mused Mel.

Having navigated the endless escalators and travelators she found herself at the boarding gate. Sitting down she flicked through the copy of a Hello! Magazine, and saw an article about Joan Collins glamorously sunning herself in the South of France. She couldn't quite believe that an hour or so should also be there,

'...*Ding dong* rows 1 to 14 boarding now.' Interrupted the tannoy announcement.

Mel duly walked down the tunnel stopped and considered the massive advertising by a well-known bank, *would have cost a pretty penny* - remembering her days in marketing and wincing at the cost of a colour double-page spread.

Finally seated in row 12, by the window, she gazed onto the shiny wet tarmac and the people loading the plane with all the luggage. Her attention became preoccupied by a well-dressed man, with brown hair and brown eyes, who looked similar to Mark. Her curiosity led her to rifle through the seat holder in front of her, endless sick bags and menus. Managing to find an in-flight magazine, she began to browse the content, more so to go through the motions, rather than read any of the articles, like she did at the hairdressers or waiting for the dentist.

There was something vaguely familiar about the man who looked a bit like Mark. She watched out of the corner of her eye as he made himself comfortable in the aisle seat, but she couldn't put her finger on it. No one came to claim the middle seat, so the man placed his magazine down in it and the plane began to taxi. The formalities of being told how to do a very complicated bow whilst disembarking the plane commenced, Mel gripped tightly to the armrest as the plane took off, the worst bit was the landing but Mel knew there was now a pause before that eventuality.

The man was now removing his jacket under the constraints of his safety belt, giving the impression of a contortionist struggling out of a straitjacket. During this activity, he knocked Mel on the arm.

'I'm sorry, just felt very hot!'

Mel turned, 'James! You probably don't remember me.'

'Oh god, Mel! I thought I recognised you!'

They did what can only be described as a *back pat like air kiss hug*, the confines of air travel meant a tricky 'hello'.

'I've not seen you since your last day at Blue Dot marketing and PR before you moved down to Dorset, you're looking well,' said James.

'You're very kind, so are you, it feels like a lifetime ago, we moved to West Sussex. What takes you to the Cote d'Azur?'

So far as she could ascertain James had bought a house with his boyfriend on the outskirts of Nice which they were in the process of doing up. It was quite difficult to follow what he was saying as the plane was rather noisy and they kept being interrupted by the air stewardess.

'So that's it really how about you?' Enquired James

Mel felt her heart sink, she didn't feel the time was right to go into her life story, but either it was the holiday spirit or the two large gins James had plied her with, she ended up telling James virtually everything.

'Oh god, I'm so very sorry,'

James was interrupted by the cabin crew - '10-minutes to landing'.

'It's ok honestly,'

Mel looked forward as the noise in the cabin got louder, she gulped her last bit of G&T, James lent in and clinked her glass, and smiles broke out across both their faces.

James reached into his bag and pulled out a silver pen and tore off a piece of paper.

'Here is my address and number. Let's grab drinks and lunch, I'm only overseeing the work so I can certainly escape and we have the evenings'.

James seemed genuinely excited to talk to her, Mel considered. She started to feel excited herself, when did she last go out for lunch or drinks with friends?

As they landed on the tarmac in Nice, Mel switched on her phone and it beeped twice. The first one was Cathy, the second was Theresa

*Darling can't wait to see you - wearing a bright orange scarf. Thrilled to have you staying here xx*

Referring to the later message,

*Hope you're ok? you looked very emotional when I said goodbye hugs xx*

'Ladies and gentlemen, welcome to Nice the weather is sunny with highs of 26 degrees.'

*Lovely,* thought Mel, *beats the grey damp of home.*

'Shall I grab your bag?'

'Yes, thanks James, it's the blue one.'

James stretched up his shirt coming untucked from his jeans as he did so. The scrum of passengers desperate to disembark began and James and Mel got separated, over his shoulder he mouthed, 'Text me, bye'.

Mel staggered along the gangway and proceeded to passport control. Already warm, she had had to pause and discard her black jumper and shoved it into a carry-on bag. Passport stared at by a completely emotionless official, and she was through.

Feeling apprehensive and clutching her bag she made her way to baggage reclaim, the carousels were already juddering round and some very sad looking cases began their journey around the conveyor. Cathy had advised her to tie a coloured ribbon around the handle so when her battered Samsonite came round she knew it was hers. She moved to the front of the crowd who were scrambling for position. As if stalking her prey, Mel had fixed on to her suitcase and she grabbed her suitcase. However the weight without it being on wheels hadn't been factored in, she pulled and tugged.

'Allow me,' and a baby blue arm stretched across her.

Before she knew it, James was heaving her case off the conveyor onto its wheels.

'I'm useless!'

'No just need a hand, we all do now and again,' responded James.

They moved with their luggage out to arrivals, the warmth hitting them as the large automatic doors opened.

'I can't thank you enough and lovely to meet you again'

'Likewise, and you've got my number now, please call or text me.'

Mel suddenly realised she was staring at a sea of people at the arrival gate with only an orange scarf to look out for.

'Sorry Mel I have to dash, see you soon.' he kissed her on both cheeks and that was James gone. Mel stared and tried to focus on the crowd in front of her.

'Mel!'

The voice was loud and assertive though warm, a smile crept across Mel's face, as a lady, similar in stature to herself, though slightly rounder, bounded towards her. Wearing a large orange linen scarf coupled with a stone grey linen dress, bright blue espadrilles, and a Longchamp bag in tow, which nearly knocked a small child flying, Theresa came to a halt in front of Mel.

'Silly thing, the child should look where it's going!' 'Mel? It is you, isn't it? I will look very foolish if not!'

All this was in a voice that made every head turn towards them.

'Yes Theresa, it's me.'

She suddenly felt very emotional, the realisation that she was here and had found Theresa proved too much. Mel hugged Theresa trying desperately to hold back the tears, standing back Theresa said,

> 'Bless you now don't you start, otherwise, you'll set me off and the whole Cote d'Azur, come on darling just outside, had to double park.'

Following in what can only be described as, 'in her wake', Mel trailed behind her dodging the taxis and airport officials, to reach a turquoise convertible mini with its hazard's on.

> 'Let me help you, silly car has a wincey boot!'

> 'Thank you, it's a very "Cote d'Azur" colour.'

> 'Yes I know, I love colour and turquoise is my favourite, watch yourself, you in? Good, better get going – before the Gendarmes catch me!'

Within a few minutes they were driving towards Nice, with the roof down and their hair billowing in the wind. It felt amazing and Mel was soaking up the sun and the atmosphere.

> 'I'm really excited to have you here Mel can't believe it's been so long since I saw you!'

> 'No, I know. Oh Whoa!' Mel stopped mid-sentence, as Theresa was performing a very erratic manoeuvre which didn't seem to raise even a *toot* from any of her fellow drivers, Mel gripped the seat tightly.

> 'Oh don't worry it's like this, you have to jostle for position', winked Theresa.

'Yes, yes it has been too long and to get your letter was a bolt out of the blue', before adding, 'in a good way, I've been trying to think of the last time I was away from home.'

'It's ok you've had it tough, it was bad enough for me when Chloe decided to move to Canada.'

Changing the subject somewhat clumsily but sympathetically, Theresa said,

'Here we are, "The Promenade des Anglais". Isn't it lovely?'

Mel had to agree, the shimmering sea, its beautiful colour and swaying palm trees. The traffic was building up and it gave Theresa a chance to point out some of the sights.

'There's the hotel Negresco, great cocktails!'

The legendary hotel, with its iconic pink dome, stood out as a beautiful regency landmark. The white paint dazzled in the lunchtime sun.

'The private beaches are coming up now'

Mel could see the "Plage Beau Rivage" sign,

'Are you allowed to go on them?'

'Yes you are, but you have to pay, don't worry I have plenty of spots that don't cost a penny or should I say Euro!'

There was so much going on and the restaurants, bars and squares were buzzing. They slowed to let people cross the road, some with towels, others on scooters and some jogging, which Mel thought far too energetic in this heat.

'There's a monument to the world wars, that's amazingly been carved out of the headland.' Theresa followed the road round to the left and drove past a sign that announced as "Nice Port".

'Look at the size of those!' exclaimed Mel as the yachts came into view.

'I know, huge! Too big if you ask me, but great fun when you get invited on one'.

They were now moving along the port side. When unexpectedly Theresa turned down what looked like a one-way street, which apparently didn't, apply in France. Then she fumbled for something, pressed a fob and a grey metal, slightly graffitied garage door began to slide upwards. They swung down into the dark recesses pulling into space 49, Theresa turned off the ignition and retracted the convertible roof.

'Here we are, it's a bit dark and damp down here, don't worry we'll be out shortly, just up here.'

Mel dragged her suitcase, Theresa kindly carrying all the other bits. They moved up some tight concrete stairs that took them onto a side street. Mel blinked as the dazzling sunshine hit her face, she fumbled for her sunglasses. They walked a short distance before turning right to stop outside, what Mel considered to be a typically ornate French door, solid-looking with bell buttons and names alongside.

They moved inside and along a cooling marble-floored hallway, to a lift that only looked just big enough for one person.

'Are we going to get in here?' gasped Mel.

'Yes, it's fine, a bit of a squeeze I admit.'

Theresa just managed to press "7", and the door shut, and the lift jerked into life. 'You ok?

'Yes, I'm fine just feeling a bit warm!'

A few minutes later Theresa was opening the door to her apartment.

'Oh wow, it's lovely, so airy and bright,' said Mel as she walked in and gazed around. Peeking around the wall, she could see a roof terrace.

'Thank you, look let me help you,' Theresa wheeled Mel's suitcase along the hall and into a bedroom. 'This is you, hope it's ok, it's got a good view I think'.

The tall bedroom window with white shutters looked out over to the mount on the old port side, Mel sighed, 'It's wonderful.'

'Now you get settled in, the bathrooms just through that door there. I'm going to go and sort some gin and tonics, ok?'

Thinking back to the two delicious gins she had knocked back on the plane, should she have more? Yes, I am on holiday. 'Perfect', came her reply.

Mel washed her hands and set her things right in her bedroom, went looking for Theresa.

'Theresa, Theresa, where are you?'

'Here darling', a hand waved from outside the French doors, Mel followed the wave and onto a terrace that overlooked the port.

'Theresa, it's amazing!'

Theresa sat in one of the four large wicker chairs that were scattered with large blue and white patterned cushions, she was sipping her G&T. Mel stood for a moment looking at the view, the azure blue sea lapped gently against the port walls, nudging the moored fishing boats and super-yachts. Overlooked by the belle époque buildings that lined the old port and looming above was the verdant castle hill with its steep edges, the sun was high in the clear sky, Mel put her hand up to shield her eyes.

'What a view! What is that called?' and she pointed to the green hill that jutted up between the port and the city.

'Oh that's "Castle Hill" and the monument is a World War Memorial to all the citizens of Nice.'

'Cheers', Theresa passed Mel a drink which she suspected would be stronger than the ones from earlier. She took it and sat down.

The sun was high and hot, so in no time at all Mel had to pop inside and change, she chose a light blue linen summer dress and slipped her feet into a pair of Birkenstocks.

'You got everything you need?' Theresa's voice boomed throughout the apartment.

'Yes thanks, actually could I have a glass of water?' Mel shouted back at the host, as she smoothed sun cream over her arms and legs. She plopped a large faded pink summer hat on her head, even though it had become slightly crumpled in the suitcase.

As she walked into the kitchen, Theresa looked concerned

'You look warm, are you ok?'

'Yes, I think it's the sun and the gin, not used to either!'

'Well, we can soon change all that', vowed Theresa, 'right so shall we get some lunch?'

This didn't seem so much a question, but more of a statement, as Theresa had already begun locking the terrace doors and slung a bag over her shoulder. They walked to the port area, where a line of restaurants stood.

'You ok with seafood?'

'Oh yes lovely, not much I don't eat.'

'Good to hear, there! Get that table, yeh the one with the umbrella,' commanded Theresa.

\*

Gino stretched out, his tanned lean body framed by the crisp white bed sheets, his arm slid across to the other side, delicately probing for something or someone. He suddenly sat bolt upright, rubbing his eyes and looking around. There was no one there. He knew it hadn't been a dream, he had gone out with some friends to the village down the road, and he had ended up chatting with a large breasted blonde, apparently visiting from New York, she had wanted to explore the mediterranean. Gino had convinced her, after several glasses of vino rosso, that he was the man to show her the sights, sounds and, he hoped, his sexual prowess. They had stumbled home in the early hours and made love until the sun began to rise.

He sighed, swung his legs out of the bed and sat there, looking out of the french doors as the thin white chiffon curtains flickered in the morning breeze. 'Well Bella, at least I showed you one of those.'

Though he had to admit that recently the bedding of random hookups and one night stands hadn't given him the same turn on as it used to. He certainly enjoyed the chase, the flirting and the body contact, but this bit. Waking up to find they had gone, or in some cases wishing they would go and leave him to his tranquil world. He grabbed the glass of water by his bed, drank it, wiped his stubbled chin and walked naked towards his bathroom, picking up his phone enroute. He stood, relieving himself of a full bladder as he scrolled on his phone and caught up with what had gone on in the world. A couple of texts had dropped in and some emails. He began to read.

*Bello, thanks for a great evening, sorry I had to leave to catch my ferry to Greece. It was fun ;) maybe on my return trip? Bettany x*

So that was her name, Gino had been struggling with recalling that since he had woken up. He washed his hands, towelled them, and picked up his phone again. There was a text from his French carpenter.

*Gino, we are needed at James's Villa - issue with staircase. Can you be there for 3pm?*

*What could be wrong with that uptight Englishman's villa now?* Gino thought to himself. Walking to his bedside table he picked up his Tag Huerer watch, it was just past 1:30pm, how had he slept so heavily? Must have been the Ligurian wine. Replying that he would duly be there, he questioned why the English were always so timely. He needed a swim and a coffee, he pushed the delicate curtain aside, still unclothed he strolled to the edge of a stone kidney shaped pool. The cool blast of the freshwater is what was required to clear his head and focus on what Gino needed.

*

Pascal had woken early, the noise from the Nice port harbour had started around 7am, and not subsided. After he had been for a jog along the Promenade de Anglais he ventured into a local boulangerie and grabbed a croissant and a small espresso. He sat and watched as a scary looking lady did a 300 point turn to get out of an underground parking space, the small convertible MINI seemed incapable in making the manoeuvre at the hands of this person, brightly clothed and gesticulating furiously. He made his way back to the apartment that he was borrowing from a friend who was away on business. A text dropped in from the owner of a property he was helping on, apparently Pascal's boss, Gino, was not replying. Pascal and his boss were needed at the property that afternoon. Pascal sighed, 'Why do I have to chase him?' He resolved mentally that he needed to focus on what Pascal wanted.

## Chapter 4 - Ladies who lunch

Mel squeezed herself into her seat, a typical bistro-style small black metal bucket type chair with spindles for legs. The port side restaurant was busy, and she was grateful for the large parasol, realising how unaccustomed she was to the warm weather.

Before she could open the menu Theresa had gesticulated at a waiter.

'Ahh Madame, enchanté…' The conversation continued, but Mel could only grasp the odd word here and there, but in essence, it was how nice to see you again, and the last bit was about drinks.

Theresa turned back to face Mel,

'I hope you don't mind, but I've ordered some rosé and some water. I love the buzz of this place. I come here quite often, but rarely for a girlie lunch, I miss those.'

'Do you not come here with friends or your daughter?'

'Well Chloe is away so much and I do have friends here but they seem to prefer eating at home or going out in the evening, plus making friends is the one thing I have found hard since moving here. I like a long lunch, it seems more decadent.'

'I have always felt going out for breakfast was a treat', mused Melissa as she thought back to the last time she had gone out for breakfast…

Lunch was a very relaxed affair, the food was delicious and the wine flowed as did the conversation. Then came a couple of questions that rendered Mel speechless.

'So what gets you up in the morning Mel? What makes you tick?' Mel took a very large swig of water and felt her face flush, she hoped that her oversized sunglasses and hat helped mask it. She stared at her wine glass not knowing what to say, what did she want? When had she last been asked?

'Mel, I am sorry that was my work mode, I forget not to *manage* some times!'

Theresa had picked up the awkwardness.

Gulping wine, Mel pulled herself together and looked up,

'It's fine, I just can't remember the last time I thought about it, or what I do want. I haven't been able to focus since Mark's death, sorry.'

She began to feel her bottom lip quiver, she must not cry, you're in Nice, on holiday! The realisation that she did not have an answer to Theresa's questions had floored her.

A "chink" of wine glasses brought her back to her senses, as Theresa refilled their glasses with a reassuring warm smile on her face.

'Don't you worry, you finish that, and we will walk into the old town. There's a fab ice cream place, let me just sort this out, Garcon!' She bellowed.

Mel went to her bag that was hanging on the back of her chair, as she did so her chair shifted and the thin back legs went over the edge of the decking - what happened next was all over in a flash. Luckily the fall was softened, but no less embarrassing, by some large floor cushions. For what seemed like an eternity she was suspended with legs flailing in the air.

Helped by what felt like every person in the restaurant, from waiters, the manager, other diners and Theresa, she was righted once more like a stricken capsized dinghy. She was swiftly guided to the toilets by Theresa who had gathered up all their belongings.

Mel didn't know if it was the embarrassment, the shock, the wine, or all three, but she began to cry. Taking her sunglasses off she leant over the small washbasin. She looked back at her reflection in the small oval bevelled mirror. The image that greeted her horrified her, there was what can only be described as a wave of mascara down both cheeks, and a hideous amount of snot emanating from her nose, and a massive bogey hanging from her left nostril.

'O darling, this won't do,' Theresa soothed. 'Now blow', she held out a crumpled, bottom of a handbag type tissue.

Having adjusted herself and attended to her face, some dignity returned, they made their way back up into the glare of the sun and the other diners. Theresa whisked her out, and arm in arm they walked across the road to the edge of the port.

'I'm so sorry Theresa, what a fool I've made of myself on my...'

Before she could finish Theresa had spun round to face her, scarf, and dress billowing before her,

'…None of that. You have had it tough, I should be the one apologising for not being there. Look, if all this is too much, I can get you home tomorrow.'

Mel stood looking at Theresa, for the second time today she wasn't prepared for such a question and how to answer, though this time she was more sure of her response.

'No!' Came the initial reply, slightly more forcibly than she had expected herself. It didn't seem to faze Theresa. Mel looked at the boats in front of her, across to the castle on the hill and up to the sun, she turned back to face Theresa.

'This is my first break since Mark's death, the first in years, I have done something for myself and by myself, well nearly! I am determined to enjoy every minute, minus the falling backwards and bogies.'

'Mel, you are fabulous, bogies and all! Plus you have great legs, you need to show them off!'

They ambled along the wide avenues, through large squares and meandered into smaller side streets, they chatted all the way, Theresa would occasionally point things out, 'oh that's a great place for lunch, they do a menu de jour for 15 euros - delicious', 'or that's a great leather shop, no not that kind! All sorts of gloves and handbags in amazing colours!'

Suddenly Theresa stopped, 'Here it is.'

They were standing outside a very brightly coloured shop front, displaying all sorts of gelato. A small group of foreign exchange students were hovering outside, but they were no match for Theresa as she marched through. The array of Ice cream available was quite bewildering and more so in a language that Mel was not that familiar with, well not since school.

'Une pistachio et chocolate, pour moi' came Theresa's order.

'That sounds yummy.'

Holding up two fingers, Theresa looked at the lady behind the glass counter, 'Deux, merci.'

Theresa began fumbling in what can only be described as her bin liner sized handbag, and Mel, not wishing to delay the queue any longer, produced a 10 euro note.

'Please let me get this, you got lunch.'

'Are you sure? The bloody purse is in here somewhere, ahh here it is! At the bottom of course!'

Holding her found purse proudly aloft and with an ice cream in the other hand they began strolling back towards the sea. 'That's the flower market, you must see that, but another day as it's best in the mornings.'

They followed a path that led them to the Promenade des Anglais. They stood, almost transfixed by the ultramarine glistening sea and watched a group playing volleyball.

'Far too energetic for me', observed Theresa as she tossed the last piece of the cone into her mouth of what was left of the ice cream.

Mel stared out to sea and contemplated her new temporary situation. She couldn't quite believe her luck and how much she was enjoying being away. A nervous pang crept over her as she thought what it would be like when Theresa left for Canada. She internally reprimanded herself, *now, don't be silly and enjoy the moment.*

They walked back around the headland and past the war memorial back towards Theresa's apartment.

'Right so this long key is the main front door, you have to wiggle it, ahh there we go' Theresa demonstrated.

In the time it took Theresa to unlock the door and proudly show Mel the key, the door promptly shut and locked again.

'Bollocks!' shouted Theresa, a man walking towards them on the pavement now changed his trajectory and gave them a much wider berth than had been originally intended.

Once finally back in the loft-style apartment, Theresa flung her handbag onto the sofa and made her way to the French doors and opened them and began moving the seating around, 'Drink?' she shouted back at Mel.

'I'll have whatever you are having, thanks.'

'Ok, make yourself at home.'

Mel pushed up the parasol, the late afternoon sun was still strong, and much stronger than she was certainly used to at home. A similar thought crossed her mind as she gingerly sipped her white wine spritzer...

'So how did you find your first day in Nice?' questioned Theresa.

'Was lovely, except falling off my chair! It feels like a very friendly and vibrant city, but relaxing at the same time, if you know what I mean?'

'Of course I do, that's why I decided to move here, plus I needed a clean break from 'Matt the prat'. Sorry, that is a long story and one I don't want to bore you with right now,' Theresa said with a wry smile.

'Honestly, I'm all ears if you want to talk about it', Mel raised her glass towards Theresa miming cheers.

'Well ok but I did warn you,' Theresa lent forward

'First and foremost, I ended up with a fabulous daughter, but the rest is not so fabulous…

*Children* thought Mel.

## Chapter 5 - Birth of the boys

To say that the pregnancy had been plain sailing would have been an understatement. It began a couple of months after they had been away at a friend's wedding. Mark had worn his linen suit, a light blue open shirt, he had looked good and been particularly attentive that weekend.

'Darling' came the muffled voice from inside the bathroom.

Mark was busy getting ready for work and was perched on the edge of the yet to be made bed tying up his shoelaces, head bent forward.

Mel tried again, 'darling', this time slightly more assertive but her mouth was dry.

'Mmm yes, what is it?' still looking down, 'There!' as he finished tying his shoelaces. He sat back up and twisted to face Mel.

Mel stood with her navy blue dressing gown wrapped around her, covering her small cotton nighty. The giveaway was that in her right hand the pen-like shaped pregnancy test.

'Oh my god'! Mark stood up and rushed over to her, his arms outstretched ready to hug her,

'I'm pregnant,' Mel's voice began to falter, she began to cry.

Mark squeezed her tightly and caressed her hair.

The anticipation and excitement accelerated when, following a more thorough examination it transpired she was having twins, two boys. There was suddenly so much to do, as well as dealing with bouts of morning sickness and becoming gradually more cumbersome, but Mel managed to keep focused on work until her maternity leave started. Mark had gone from excited to stressed very rapidly, work was very busy and he had just been given a new client. Mel tried to be as supportive as possible. The demands of home life and work-life started to take their toll. First, the sex dropped off, but Mel had been told this can happen during pregnancy, and then the conversation became stilted.

'I thought maybe we might go and stay with my mum this weekend?' Mel had suggested after they had finished their supper one evening.

'Why? You know I have so much on Mel, why don't you go' replied Mark

'Mark I am eight and a half months pregnant, and thought it would be good…'

She was interrupted, 'Yeah I know, I know, I just don't feel up to it, not right now.'

'Ok well mum can come and get me, I just thought a break….'

'I'm not up to it'

Mel pushed away from the table so she could manoeuvre herself out of the chair, but somehow in the process, she managed to knock over her water and simultaneously stepping back to avoid the spill, she stood in the cat food.

'Now look at me, fat, tired and stinking of bloody Whiskers!'

Safe to say that their mood remained frosty. The next morning Mel rang her mum once Mark had left for work and asked if she could come and collect her. She had just said goodbye, when she felt a warm trickling sensation between her legs, she could only liken it to when you wee yourself in a wetsuit. Oh god, her waters had broken!

She immediately redialled her mum and left an urgent message for Mark with his PA, Laura, to call as soon as possible. The next few hours flashed by and before Mel knew it she was being wheeled into hospital.

That was all 21 years ago, Mel and Mark had been blessed with 2 wonderful boys, who had grown up fit and healthy and were now off leading their own lives, with their own adventures to be had. One had studied business at university and now worked in finance, the other had taken a different path and was currently living in Lisbon with his Portuguese girlfriend. Mark had thrown himself into fatherhood, he was devoted to his boys. Both boys had their differences and from time to time, as all children and teenagers do, caused upset and anger, regardless of this Mark had been a very proud father and supportive. In the early years, he would take them to the beach, where they would go swimming and crabbing. He'd taught them tennis, rugby and shared his love of cars with them, they in return thought the world of their father. Mark was always there when times were tough and helped them find their feet when they started heading into the big wide world.

The boys had been distraught at the news of their father's death and rushed home to console her. Mel wondered what their lives would be if Mark was still alive? They would miss him of course, and hopefully remember all the good times they had shared. He was always the one to help out and support them when he could.

The boys had stayed with Mel for a couple of weeks after the funeral and continued to check in daily to see how she was. As the months passed this turned into weekly and gradually lapsed back to ad hoc texts or calls, which is how it should be considered Mel.

Had their lives changed that much? She had always wondered if Mark's death had affected them, she was sure it had, but they had bounced back. She'd never liked to pry, they certainly seemed fine on the surface.

Their lives seemed to have gone back to normal. OK, the first Christmas had been tough and the boys' birthday had been difficult, but ultimately they could continue as before and follow their life paths. *'Mine'* she thought, *'has stalled...'*

## Chapter 6 - Theresa gets a phone call

'So, that's it really! I did warn you it was a long-winded story, or as I call them a "2 gin saga."'

'You have been through it with him, and then you lost your brother too.'

'I wasn't as close to Mark as maybe I should have been, I was 7 years older, and when I was off travelling he was only just starting at grammar school. Matt was just an annoyance and it's taken some time to adjust, but I suppose it makes life interesting! Now, what about you?'

'What about me?' queried Mel.

'How has the last year been, and are you ok, I mean really ok?'

'I'm fine.'

'That's the sort of answer you give a doctor. I want the real deal, losing my brother was hard, especially a younger brother, but he was your husband and that must have been so tough on you.'

'Losing Mark has been hard', Mel mustered her energy and thoughts. 'It's been very weird, to tell the truth, many months since Mark's death and if I am honest my life has stood still.' she paused in case that honesty had not gone down well with Theresa.

'You poor thing, I do understand.'

Mel didn't need any further encouragement.

'The thing is, Mark died and it was a terrible shock, and the accident made it all the worse. Since that day everyone else's lives have gone back to normal, and mine has got bogged down in a rut. I try to keep busy but it feels like I am treading water, and I can't believe I am about to say this, but, what should I do? I can't keep going like this, something needs to change.'

'You don't need to be guarded with me Mel, I have seen it all and life has to go on, it's often the people left behind that it's hardest for. Well, I think you have already started to make changes, you are here for one thing. The sun, the sea and the sand will do you the world of good.'

'When I got your letter, I nearly replied saying "no", I just couldn't see myself coming out here and house sitting. Something in me decided to go for it, but it's been so long since I have done something like this, I feel like I have almost forgotten how, and I do know how silly that sounds.'

Mel pushed her hair back with her hand, and took a deep breath, making the admissions out loud made her situation feel more real than ever before.

*

The next morning, with a slightly fuzzy head, Mel vaguely recalled tucking into the red wine, and there had been laughter, tears and hugs in equal measure. The weather was as lovely as the day before, warm and clear.

'Are all days like this here?'

'Honestly? No, some days we have awful storms and downpours, but it is always pretty mild, how's the head?'

'Well, not going to lie, I have felt better. It was really good to get to know you!'

They sat outside and both had black coffee and two croissants from the Boulangerie across the road. Both agreed they needed caffeine and carbs. Theresa went off to sort out some "boring work", as she referred to it, and Mel decided to go to the "Marche aux Fleurs". Theresa had lent her a very appropriate large wicker bag with an embroidered white flower on it.

'I'll see you later,' came the muffled voice from one of the spare rooms that doubled as Theresa's study. 'Have a lovely time.'

'Thanks see you later, hope work is ok?'

With that Mel let herself out, and shortly emerged onto the street with lined diagonally parked cars. The day was muggy and it felt as if the pavement was giving off heat, like a tarmac coloured radiator. She crossed the road and headed to where she could see the boats they had eaten near yesterday.

Continuing around the angular port area, pausing at the curved headland to look out over the aquamarine water before heading down to her right to watch the throngs of people on the beaches. Following the road round, crossing and headed through the pass they had used the previous day to emerge next to the flower market. It was buzzing and a sheer cornucopia of blooms was on display.

The market was a veritable feast for the senses, the colours and smells of all the different blossoms. She didn't recognise some of the varieties but she did find a gorgeous bunch of Peonies. The vendor was a small man wearing an ancient flat cap with a very tragic looking cigarette stuck to his bottom lip.

'Oui Madame?'

'Oh umm a bunch of these,' and she pointed at the salmon coloured globe like heads.

'Dix Euro,' came the gruff response.

'Ok, yes, merci!' as she handed the seller the note, still mesmerised how the cigarette could stay in that place like it was somehow glued on.

Picking up her bouquet and laying them carefully in her large bag so the heads stuck out the top and hopefully wouldn't get damaged in transit. As she wandered through the market, she scolded herself, *Why couldn't I speak French?* Mel knew she could manage more than 'Merci' and next time she was going to try much harder, just at the critical moment her mind had gone blank.

Meandering through the many streets and gazing into shop windows, she found a new way back to the port area with some help from Google maps on her iPhone. She decided to stop at a cafe that faced straight out towards the port and past the port walls, further to the wide-open sea. The colour of the sea was jewel-like, it sparkled and glistened in the late morning sun. Seated, she had spent the time perfecting her order in French.

'Bonjour Madame.'

'Bonjour, Je voudrais un café au lait, s'il vous plaît.'

Mel felt very smug and happy that she had managed to convey her choice in the local language, and with what she had considered a passable French accent to boot. The reply from the waitress was somewhat deflating all things considered.

'No problem.' and off she pottered, Mel couldn't help looking slightly annoyed, *how had she worked out I was English!*

Mel sat back and looked out over the vista. She was so pleased she had come out here and that for a couple of weeks at least, Theresa would show her the ropes before Mel would be flying solo. The warm biscuit coloured liquid was good and strong, blowing away any of the remaining cobwebs from last night away.

After negotiating the traffic and lots of haphazardly parked vehicles she let herself back into the apartment building, it felt odd but exciting at the same time.

'Hi, I'm back, though not sure my French will be of much use!'

'Just a minute, nearly done with this email.'

Mel opened up the doors to the terrace and started to flick through a magazine that was left on the table, it was full of beautiful people and equally beautiful houses. Then suddenly she paused, there was James! He was extolling the virtues of the French Riviera, with photos of his art deco villa and was discussing how the renovation was coming along.

'Sorry I just had to get that email sorted and sent, you all ok?'

'Yes thanks, you?' she showed the flowers to Theresa

'They are beautiful, sadly I won't be around to enjoy them.'

'Sorry, what do you mean?'

'Bit of a crisis, I had a call from Chloe and she needs me out there sooner to help.'

'O right, is she ok?' Mel tried to sound sincere, but a sudden wave of panic came over her. This meant Theresa wouldn't be able to show her around much and would mean she would do this alone, unguided.

Before Theresa could reply, Mel interjected, slightly more forcibly than she meant but she was panicked.

'What, what about us, and getting to know the area? I can't do this if I don't know things.' she slumped into her chair and looked at Theresa. She stood there in a brightly patterned kaftan and orange espadrilles, Mel suddenly felt she may have overstepped the mark and instantly felt guilty. Theresa rushed over to her and gave her a big hug, slightly too tight for Mel's liking.

'I'm sorry little one, look I can get my cleaning lady in more often or something, I just can't let Chloe down.'

Mel felt embarrassed now, of course, Theresa couldn't let her daughter down and as Mel had found out the previous night, Chloe was the only family Theresa had left since Mark's death.

'Look', Mel said, trying to pull out of the vice-like grip, 'I'll be fine, sorry I just felt alarmed by the prospect of you not being here and the French clearly don't think much of my French!' A wry smile crept over her face.

''What do you mean?'

Mel regaled Theresa with her story,

'Don't worry, I've lived here nearly 10 years and still, I get spoken too in English, but at least you tried. Let's grab some lunch and we make sure you are happy with everything while I am away - the house, car etc.'

'Ok, but please not the same place as yesterday,' winked Mel. 'I want to hear all about Chloe and how it is going out there.'

Mel found herself looking at the same waitress, who an hour ago had dismissed her French, but clearly, Theresa's accent didn't cut the mustard either.

'They make a lovely salad with prawns, big and juicy ones.'

'The coffee is good too!'

'Don't tell me this is the place you came to this morning? We can go somewhere else, I just love the view.'

Theresa broke the news over the salad that she would be leaving the day after tomorrow.

Mel didn't sleep well that night, she had dreamt of a lovely chilled couple of weeks to settle in, and now that was condensed into 2 days. She wouldn't let Theresa down. At 3am that morning decided she could do this and that she, Mel, who hadn't done anything on her own in years, was determined to have a good time and enjoy everything that the next few weeks would throw at her.

Actually, when was Theresa returning now? They had gone through all the items in the house that Mel needed to know, and when Theresa was leaving, Mel made a mental note to ask Theresa in the morning as she finally drifted to sleep, as the sun started to rise over the Cote d'Azur.

## Chapter 7 - Going solo

The storm that raged the night before Theresa left was biblical, thick dark looming clouds covered the moon, and the thunder boomed across the southern Mediterranean. They had watched from the security of the terrace windows, as the lightning struck across the brooding noir sky lighting up their faces and the whole of the city.

Eventually, they called it a night, and with earplugs in, they duly went to bed. Theresa had been packing most of that day and she was due at the airport at midday the following day. Mel slept well, surprisingly so, she felt a sense of calm and cosiness as she snuggled into bed whilst the downpour continued outside.

The morning started with the sun blazing through the gap in the shutters. Mel rubbed her face and blinked as the rays struck her face. Climbing out of bed, she made her way, barefooted, into the kitchen and took a large glass from the cupboard above the sink and began filling it up from the tap. The heavy sleep required water and coffee to revive her. On went the kettle and she unfurled the ground coffee bag and took a spoon to measure out into the cafetiere. A hand then landed on her shoulder, Mel jumped out of her skin! Spinning around, and covering Theresa in coffee grounds.

'I DIDN'T HEAR YOU'

'You don't need to shout!'

'I'M NOT'

'You are, and I now smell like a Barista!'

'WHAT?'

The penny suddenly dropped, Mel hadn't taken out her earplugs, they had been completely forgotten. Pulling the yellow and pink earplugs out, which now resembled a squished rhubarb and custard boiled sweet.

'Theresa, I am so sorry,' as she sheepishly popped the offending earplugs down on the counter.

'It's ok, I'm sorry I startled you.'

'Look at your t-shirt, it's covered.'

'Don't worry, its my old "sleepy tee"'

Once the sand like coffee was dusted away and a change of top, they sat, clutching their steaming dark beverages. Mel certainly felt much more awake now. The dawn of the day, also coincided with the start of Mel, finding her feet, her way around and the thought of going solo drained her energy.

'Right, I must get ready, are you ok?'

'I'm good, feeling a bit daunted by it, that's all.'

That was putting it mildly, what if she falls backwards at a restaurant, what if the market stall sellers don't understand her? Mel was trying to push these worries to the back of her mind, but it had been 20 plus years since she had done anything like this.

The last 2 days had gone in a flash, 'there's the supermarket', 'this is a good bakery', 'she's tricky to reverse', those had been the snippets that Mel was now frantically trying to recall, so she could make a go of this. She had travelled with work, and on holidays, she just had to find that spark to keep her going. Maybe if she channelled a strong person - Catherine, Princess of Wales? Kamala Harris? Angela Merkel?

She couldn't decide who was best for inspiration, maybe the trait of determination was something they all shared, that was what Mel needed to be, determined. This thought was disturbed by the car horn that had just gone off, as she negotiated the scramble to turn off "Voie Pierre Mathis" onto the "Promenade de Anglais" and follow signs for the "Aeroport". Gripping the steering wheel tightly, gingerly pushing forward, her jaw felt clamped down.

'You need to push forward, imagine you are French!' as Theresa lent over and pushed on the horn, 'you just have to join in'.

The goodbye had been rushed, as Theresa had insisted on Mel double parking so that she could 'hop out' and not pay. A flash of pashmina and waft of Coco Chanel and she was gone. Mel didn't have time to wallow as the stern-looking parking attendant was on his way over, slipping back into the driving seat, letting out the clutch, she stalled, second time lucky she jerked out the Aeroport, she wasn't convinced but in her rear-view mirror was that the parking attendant was looking on crossing himself.

Traffic built up, as it seemed to always do, as she approached the city and the lanes narrowed. Starting to feel a bit more comfortable, Mel could look and see some of the points of interest. Managing to get back to the apartment, she made herself a good cup of tea and as she did so her phone bleeped,

*Darling, thank you, see you soon, you will be fine and enjoy it! :) Just text me or call if you aren't sure of anything, I'm 9 hours behind xx. You may need to grab milk.*

Yes, Mel had noticed as she made her tea that the milk was indeed low and then her phone bleeped again, this time a French number she didn't recognise.

*Hi, it's James, this is my French number, are you still up for a drink or something? Building work is taking longer than anticipated - surprise surprise. Bring your relative along too. J x*

A sense of relief enveloped her, sipping her tea and making her way out to the terrace, she pushed up the large parasol and made herself comfy before reaching her phone and replying to the messages.

*I made it back in one piece! Thank you for this opportunity, have a safe flight, text me when you arrive :) Mel xx*

The anxiety settler message was the next she would reply to, James could do it, she could. He is someone I know, in this city, I'll be fine.

*Hi James, great to bump into you on the plane, sounds good to me when are you thinking? Mel x*

The 3rd message was to the person who gave her the confidence in the first place to start this adventure.

*Hi Cathy, how are things, it's very sunny and hot here, how is it there? Hope Rocky is behaving and everything is well at your end? Mel xx*

She laid her phone in front of her and squinted at the bright sun, the sun-dappled on the water in the port and it looked very inviting. Mel decided to change and put a swimming costume underneath her clothes. Checking her phone, the weather was due to peak at 27c, definitely *swimming weather* thought Mel. She wore a light denim coloured summer dress over her bathing attire and slipped her feet into some brown leather wedges. She took the large shopping bag and grabbed some sun cream and a towel.

En route, a copy of "La Monde" was purchased in a Tabac, not to be fully understood, but to at least *glean* what was going on in the world. She was determined to immerse herself in the culture and "la langue de preference."

By the time she had arrived at the beach, the bit Theresa had said was free, Mel was panting to get into the cerulean water. Mel enjoyed her dip, she reprimanded herself for not going more often at home, the caveat being that it was often too cold and wet!

Swim complete, the newspaper was unfurled, Mel could make out some of the news, mainly from the photos, but it was a start. Realising she didn't want to know about the news and the outside world, she put the paper to one side and wiggled to get comfy on her towel as the pebbles pressed into her back. The escapist feeling was a good one. The sense of anonymity that the language barrier afforded her was good, and not knowing anyone was like starting a new job or new school, a clean slate.

Shutting her eyes, enjoying the sun's warmth on her salty skin. The pebbles did mean quite a lot of shifting around to find a suitably comfortable position. After wrestling with her damp towel and moving some of the larger stones, a pleasing setup was established. A short while passed, when her phone beeped and vibrated. Scrabbling from her laying down position to find her phone was unusually tricky, the phone of course was right at the bottom of her voluminous bag.

*Glad all is well, it's drizzling here - you lucky thing have fun! Cathy xx*

She realised that she also had a missed call from a French number, she suspected it was James. Replying with two kisses to Cathy and dialled the number.

'Mel? Hullo, it's James, how are you?'

'Sorry I missed you, I was swimming, couldn't get to my phone, all good here, how are you?'

'No worries, I was thinking... o hold on...' there was some loud banging and some muffled French...' sorry about that'.

'Don't worry, everything is ok?'

'Yes just builders asking lots of questions, it is a bombsite at the moment.'

'I saw you yesterday, in a magazine'

'O yeh the local one? Haha now you know what I have been up to!'

'How is it all going?'

'I was thinking maybe we could catch up over a drink? Are you free tonight? I need a break!'

'Sounds great, where and when, and I'll try and find it!'

'The Negresco? Do you know it?'

'Yes, the domed building with very smartly dressed doormen?'

'That's the one, shall we say 7?'

'Perfect see you then'

'Call me if you get lost, bye'

'Will do, bye James'

With that, she opened google maps on her phone, a 30/40 minute walk or 10-minute taxi, Mel decided she would walk. It looked like it was a relatively formal place, what should she wear? She couldn't remember the last time she'd got properly dressed up, certainly not since the boys, was it for Mark's promotion dinner. That was 25 years ago.

## Chapter 8 - Flashback - Mark's Promotion

Mark had done well, they said so, so it must be true.

Mel was looking at her reflection in the long wall mirror that hung in their bedroom, she tugged at the waist of the knee-length black dress,

'Urgh, when did this happen?'

Squeezing a small amount of her flesh between her fingers.

'Hurry up love, we're going to be late.' barked Mark from downstairs.

'Coming!'

Mel picked up her sparkly silver clutch bag and tottered downstairs in her silver high heels. The boys were glued to the PlayStation in the living room with Cathy sitting watching them with one eye and casting a glance over Home and Garden magazine.

'O Mel you look lovely,' flattered Cathy. The boys swivelled round from the TV, smiled momentarily and went back to their game.

'Balls!'

'What is it?'

Mark was struggling to knot his bow tie.

'Do you want me to try?' asked Mel.

'No, no, I can do it.'

'Right boys, now not too much of this and be good for Cathy.'

'Yes mum'

Kissing them both on the top of their heads she turned to see how Mark was getting on.

'Taxi is here.'

'Ok ready', as Mark adjusted his now straightened neck wear.

'Thanks, Cathy, see you later, I'll text when we are on the way back.'

'No worries, have fun!'

They walked out of the front door to the waiting car, it was to take them to the venue. A grand old country hotel, the evening was all about the company and there would be a raffle, dinner and dancing. It was also when the business would make any big announcements or changes.

'I wonder if they might announce anything about me?'

'You? What do you mean?'

'Well, there have been some hints that I might be made a senior partner.'

'Wow, that would be amazing darling.'

They slipped through the traffic and criss crossed their way to join the dual carriageway and made their way through the Sussex countryside. Mel was looking out the window as the day became night. Mel had given up work shortly after moving from London. Mark had said she should focus on the home and then looking after the boys. It was a thoughtful gesture and one that Mel had taken full advantage of, spending all her time devoted to the children and running the home.

Arriving at the venue, Mark stepped out of the car and started to head up the steps.

'Hey, wait for me!'

'Come on darling, why did you wear those silly shoes?'

Mel stood for a moment with her hand resting on the car door, she looked at Mark, standing there in his black tie looking very handsome. Taking a deep breath, she shut the car door, steadied herself and slipped her arm through Mark's and made their way into the hotel.

The evening was the usual affair of making small talk with people you wouldn't normally interact with. Luckily Mel was put next to Luke, a guy that Mel had known since Mark had joined the business. He was always good fun and topped up Mel's glass, as Mark seemed to be otherwise engaged in a heavy conversation with his fellow directors.

'I hope you won't be offended, but you look really lovely tonight Melissa'.

'Haha is that the white wine talking? And please call me Mel, Melissa makes me sound so old!'

'Honestly, Mark is a lucky guy.'

'I am not sure in the glamour stakes, I feature that highly', as she gazed around the room, at the 20-somethings in tight-fitting dresses and not a sign of fat anywhere on their person.

'More wine?'

'I'm good,' she placed her hand over the top of the glass.

'Ok, shall we dance then?'

'Sure', but as she went to push her chair back, there was a loud screech on the microphone, it felt like the whole room groaned simultaneously.

'Ladies and Gentlemen…'

*Here we go*, thought Mel, and she sat back down, as did Luke.

'Thank you for coming and contributing to a wonderful evening… ' It went on for some time… Mel did top her glass up.

'I have one more duty to perform and then dancing can get underway. As you know we have been looking for a senior partner for the firm since Harold's retirement, and I am pleased to announce that Mark, our current director of operations has agreed, congratulations! Where is Mark? Where are you? Come on up here!'

Mark duly stood up and walked toward the stage.

'Thank you, Thomas, this is a great honour, thank you to all of my colleagues and the board for allowing me this opportunity.' he paused as applause rippled throughout the dining room, he went to turn away, Thomas stepped closer to him and mouthed something into Mark's ear.

'Oh and thank you to my darling wife Mel, thank you.'

Mel clapped with the rest of the crowd and as all eyes fell on her she looked up and forced a smile. She had noted the pause and that Mark had to be reminded. In her haste to cover up what she was feeling, she decided to stand up and go to the toilet. As she did so a rather full glass of white wine got knocked over and deposited its contents all over Luke's trousers.

'Bloody hell, sorry Luke'

'Don't be silly, it's fine, it will dry'

'Look let us get some napkins, look there some at the back'

She followed him to the back of the large room where the tables groaned under the weight of the amassed food, bottles of wine and beer.

'Look, there's some'

'Honestly, it's ok'

She dabbed his shirt and trousers, kneeling slightly to do so, she slipped and head-butted Luke in the groin area.

'O God, ouch'

'Woah'

She steadied herself by grasping for the nearest thing which happened to be Luke's jacket, the resulting image was not flattering and at that moment.

'Mel, Mel, what *ARE* you doing?'

*Bloody typical!* thought Mel, her head was swimming slightly, possibly she had overdone the wine, with Luke's help she was up and a rather red face was staring at her, her face equally flushed.

'Sorry' she mouthed at Luke.

'Mel I asked what was going on?'

'Nothing, I was just trying to help dry Luke off, and…'

'Enough!' Mark interrupted, 'Our taxi is here.'

## Chapter 9 - Drinks with James

Mel had considered a taxi but the allure of walking to her destination on a warm spring evening had proved more inviting. Theresa had suggested using an app to order the taxi, to avoid any language barriers, Mel had decided against it. Walking out into the dry still early evening air, she breathed deeply, consciously so, she was nervous.

After her swim earlier, she had meandered back to the apartment and spent two hours deciding what to wear and what not to wear. She even resorted to Googling the hotel and seeing what the pictures showed of the other guests to give her an indication. The result was some white jeans, which she had purchased in the few days between receiving Theresa's letter and leaving for Nice, coupling this with a pale blue silken blouse and a pair of dusty pink suede pumps. Just as she exited the apartment she grabbed a navy shawl that was hanging in the hallway, one of many of Theresa's billowy numbers. She hoped she didn't mind.

Striding back the way she had come earlier, the sea looked more inviting than ever, the lights of far off ships in the sea had started to twinkle and the promenade was awash with people. The walk had been a touch longer and warmer than she had anticipated. Stopping outside the meeting place for a few minutes to cool down and gather herself. A keen-eyed doorman spotted her loitering.

'Bon Soir. Madame'

'Bonsoir, je suis chaud!'

She was shown inside and escorted to the bar. The walnut woodwork was stunning and the blue chairs looked like something out of the 1920s.

'Mel!'

James was perched at one of the wooden bar stools and beckoned her over with a wave. They hugged and kissed on both cheeks.

'How are you?' asked James

'All good, now I am here, the walk was slightly further than I had expected!'

'A cocktail! That will cool you down.'

'Sounds good to me', as she steadied herself into a seating position.

'Ramond, deux bombes à la mangue, merci.'

'You know them here then?'

'Well, I like to come here as a treat when I can, and bring special people here.' he winked at Mel.

'I can see why, just look at those tapestries, 18th century?'

'17th century I think, I know I just love it here.'

'I can see why, so tell me what we are drinking?'

As she asked the question, two martini shaped glasses were placed in front of them, the stem off to one side so the dish element looked like it was floating.

'They look amazing.'

'Merci, Ramond.'

'Cheers'

'Salut'

'Wow, that's delicious, mango and champagne?'

'Spot on, I mean what's not to like? So come on, you never filled me in on his mysterious letter you got from a relative, where is she by the way?'

Mel explained the letter and that Theresa had now gone to Canada and that Mel was nervously excited to be here and flying solo.

'Great so this means I have you all to myself and can show you my favourite places!'

'Well it's certainly started well, and I have to say I love the look of the house you are renovating, I saw the magazine article.'

'Yes, you mentioned it, well I guess I need to update you now.'

'Please', mumbled Mel as she tucked into her sweet yellow drink.

'Well after you left Blue dot marketing, I became a director, long story short, my dad passed away and I left our family house for something smaller. I put the inheritance from dad into doing up and selling property down here. I met Darren a few years ago, and since then he and I have sold a couple of places and now this Art Deco villa is the latest and biggest project yet.'

'And Darren, what does he do?'

'Well, he's an actor, well he's had some success in a Midsomer Murders, and a Miss Marple I think, and an episode on Holby City where he played a stiff! But now he is focusing on the theatre.'

'Sounds great, can't wait to meet him.'

'Ahh, sadly he had to leave yesterday, but will be back later this month.'

They chatted away, caught up on the last two decades, consoled and celebrated each other.

'Monsieur, another one?'

'No, thank you Ramond, we have to be going, the bill please.'

Mel looked quite crestfallen, she was enjoying herself, more so than in a long time, it can't end now.

'Mel, don't look like that, I've got a dinner reservation.'

'James you cheeky sod, where are we going?'

'Not telling', and he poked his tongue out as he threw a note into the silver tray that had been put in front of him.

'Right off we go.'

'Oh no, that's not fair... blimey is that how much they cost?' as James had started walking away and not stopped for change.

'Yes, but worth it,' he winked. 'Now come on, love your outfit, very summery.'

'Haha it's all thrown together, I was worried about what to wear!'

'The colours suit you, this way.' James guided Mel out of the front door and into the balmy evening air. The Cote d'Azur felt alive and kicking, groups were playing games, lovers strolling by arm in arm, and those of a more energetic disposition, were jogging.

"Le Frog" screamed the restaurant sign. The petit restaurant was on a side street just off the main road, and just up from the flower market. The welcome was warm and Mel enjoyed her 3 or was it 4 courses?

'That was delicious,' as she sipped some coffee.

'I have never guessed you had such a voracious appetite!'

'Look at my middle and my thighs.' Now Mel was several glasses of wine in, and her inhibitions had started to relax, she grabbed a midriff as she spoke.

'Mel, stop that, you're a good looking woman, as we walked in eyes followed you.'

'Yeh, yeh, bet they are all 80 plus, with no teeth!'

'Seriously Mel, you look good.'

James was being sincere and genuine, Mel wanted to focus on the moment but she desperately needed a wee and couldn't concentrate on anything else.

'Sorry, I just need to pop to the ladies.'

She made her way to the back of the restaurant, she looked for eyes as James had mentioned, James was right, people were looking!

'Les toilettes, s'il vous plaît.'

'Here Madame'

What was the point? Thought Mel as she entered the cubicle, locking the door she sat down. She inhaled through her nose and farted, she started to laugh.

'Ohh god shhhh.'

Once vacating the lavatory and making sure no further noises were uttered from any orifice she strolled back into the restaurant.

'James it has been great to catch up', Mel lowered herself back into her chair.

'I couldn't agree more.'

'Right so shall we get the bill?'

'Done'

'What do you mean, done?'

'I paid while you were having a wee.'

'Right next time it's my treat!'

Outside the night air was cool and the stars shone brightly.

'Now are you sure I can't walk you home?'

'I'm fine, honestly. She tapped him on the arm. 'The fresh air will do me good!'

'Text me when you get home.'

'Of course, night night'

They embraced and went their separate ways, James watched Mel slightly weave her back toward the main road and toward her apartment.

*

That morning she woke suddenly with a jolt, the rays of the sun were piercing through the gap in the curtain and hit her right in the face.

'O God', clutching her head she made her way into the kitchen. She located her handbag and bleary-eyed she fumbled finding her phone, she slumped down into the wide armchair in the living room. 5 messages...

*Mel are you home? Jx*

*Mel are you ok? Jx*

*Mel? Have you passed out, going to bed now please text me or call! Jx*

The two other messages were from Cathy and Theresa,

*Hi Mel, how's it all going? Rocky is good as gold. Cathy x*

*Hi darling, Vancouver is warm! Hope you are finding your feet, can't believe it's been 2 weeks already! Forgot to say, please feel free to borrow any clothes or anything! Txx*

Phew well, nothing from the Gendarmes, so can't have done anything too bad, how much had she drunk? She tentatively dialled James' number.

'Hullo Mel, I've been worried.'

'James I am sorry, I must have got in and gone straight to bed.'

'Not too worry, how are you feeling?'

'Umm, I have felt better, you?'

'I am fine, just the loud banging from the builders is doing my head in!'

'Bless you, last night was fun,' as she placed a coffee pod in the machine.

'Look Mel, I am having a 'last night' type bash for all the builders, probably in a couple of weeks. I will see you before, but please say you will come?'

'Umm yeah sure, what day?'

'Well, that depends on how much of the work gets done, but hopefully next Friday.'

Mel didn't exactly have a packed diary.

'Sounds good, sorry for being a bit slow, only just woken up.'

'Haha good on you, well text me when you are fully awake and we can make plans.'

'Ok, bye'

'Bye'

She grabbed her steaming hot coffee, added two sugars and reached for her sunglasses, this was going to be a long day.

## Chapter 10 - Monte Carlo or Bust

One element of the trip that Mel was most concerned about, above all else, was driving. She drove at home of course but somehow being on the wrong side with the gears on the right felt completely alien to her. The constant honking of horns and the manic driving style of the city's residents did nothing to allay those fears. Mel thought it very brave of Theresa to have let her drive her car back from the airport, but for now, until the inevitability of a proper supermarket shop was required, the car would remain safe in the garage.

Until that eventuality, Mel was determined to walk, use the trams, or the train. Walking was easy and she was becoming used to her surroundings and her map app helped. Today was overcast and cooler than the previous, so Mel decided this was a good opportunity to visit the Oceanographic Museum in Monaco. Mel had looked this up and she gathered that back home it would be similar to an Aquarium or Sea-Life centre, but this was Monte Carlo, it looked grand! She had downloaded the app for trains in Europe, but couldn't seem to buy the tickets. Therefore that day she ventured to "Nice Riquier" station to catch a train.

This was a twenty-minute walk according to her app, and Mel had decided the evening before that she would get the train around 10 am to avoid any sort of rush hour. She walked directly north along the "Rue de Arson", she noted the apartment blocks that lined the street and some large electrical and supermarkets.

'Bonjour, un billet pour Monte Carlo return, s'il vous plaît.'

Mel had planned that sentence.

'Oui, madame, première ou deuxième classe?'

*Bollocks*, thought Mel, she hadn't considered a follow-up question, rather than cause a fuss, she simply replied 'deuxieme, merci.'

The very large airline-style ticket was issued, in exchange for Mel's €8. Looking at a timetable she had picked up as she walked to "Platform 2" she noted that the journey should take 20 minutes.

'Perfect'

It was now, 10:05, the next train was due in 7 minutes as the electronic board counted down the waiting time.

As she boarded the train Mel felt it odd as she stepped up into the train rather than back at home the train is the same level as the platform. The views as the train wound its way around the craggy edifices was stunning. The sun had started to break through the clouds and the water dappled in the rays. Mel could see large yachts moored off the bays and pretty looking coastal towns and villages. The train seemed to cling to the promontories and plunged right through some parts using tunnels hewn out the rock. The final tunnel brought her train into "Monaco - Monte Carlo" and the airy, subterranean station carved into the earth. The escalators and lighting gave the station a feel of a below ground airport. The destination was plugged into her phone and she began to follow the guidance. The signs along the route were very small but resulted in seeing very pretty parts of Monaco. She wound her way down through small steep passes, navigating steps that lead further towards the port area. All the ochre-coloured buildings with an array of climbing plants had an instant charm about them, which in turn required photos to be taken which allowed Mel to take all of it in.

Once at sea level, she looked over the port area. Looking up she could see the gray stone fortress of the Royal palace. She could just make out the Jonquil renaissance style building attached.

*I must take a closer look at that later,* considered Mel.

Crossing the road to follow the port round to the left, the path was busy with joggers and e-scooters. She noted a promontory and ignored her electronic device to make a detour. The view was covered the sky rise buildings to the right, with cranes looming adding to the concrete jungle, in the foreground were superyachts, their hulls and metalwork glistening in the morning sun. Pausing to try and take a panoramic photo only ended up looking like a photo that had melted.

Double backing and following her map, she followed the path round past a road tunnel and now was looking out at the open sea, the trail gradually wound round to the right and Mel caught her first glimpse of the museum, a huge Baroque style building clinging to the edge of the stone precipice.

*Wow*, thought Mel, definitely beats the Sealife centre! Finding her way to the front of the museum, it felt more like the National Portrait Gallery in London than an aquarium. When Mel felt a nudge.

'Excuse me, do you know where you get tickets?'

'Huh?'

'Parlez-vous anglais?' tried the grey haired bespectacled lady.

Mel, slightly taken aback, regained focus.

'Sorry, I'm English. I haven't been here before I'm afraid.'

'Oh I see I've lost my husband and he said he was off to get tickets.'

'Well, I was just going to head that way myself.'

'May I follow you? I may find my husband!'

When the husband was eventually located, the issue was that Mel now felt obliged to stick with them. Her inner Britishness meant she couldn't bring herself to say, 'right I'm off now and enjoy your day', no she wandered around with them, Mary and Brian. Mel could gather from their keenness to talk and willingness to engage with Mel, that they were grateful to have another soul to talk to, that wasn't each other.

'Brian come on, she doesn't need to know about your hip replacement.'

He paused momentarily for breath,

'Yes dear', turning back to Mel who had by now glazed over somewhat to Brian's list of ailments,

'As I was saying, it was amazing walking within hours.'

Mel did manage to photographically record the array of marine life in the incredible two-storey or was it three storeys water tanks. A myriad of fish from clownfish, sharks and turtles occupied the water-filled vessels. In a couple of hours, Mel had concocted a small white lie, that she needed to take action to escape Mary and Brian's clutches.

'It has been great... Now mind yourself,' as Brian knocked into an exhibit, 'I have to get back to my friend in Nice, really nice to have met you.'

She had escaped but the lie had been draining on her mind. She felt guilty, but she was only doing it for self-preservation and so the day could be enjoyed. Maybe she felt guilty for Brian, was it something in him that reminded Mel of herself? The delivery of such a fib, a silly social fib but a very necessary one. In her mind, small harmless ones were ok and sometimes needed.

Heading back towards the railway station she walked past the palace, not quite as grand as Buckingham Palace but still a lovely thing to see and experience. Mel was hungry, she hadn't eaten since a croissant first thing that morning. The unwritten rule, it would seem, was that at 2:30 p.m. nowhere she had planned to eat was open. Eventually, she found herself in a very 1980s vibe shopping area where a vegetable galette was devoured, the last slice in the cafe.

She ambled back to the station trying to make sure she absorbed all the sights and people, Mel was determined to make the most of every day. The train was slightly delayed and this gave Mel the chance to grab a coffee to go and marvel at the underground station. Once on-board she made sure she sat facing the direction of travel and at a window seat to fully take in the scenery. She noted a promontory of land joined to the mainland by what looked like a thin road, she Googled where she was on her phone and it was called St Jean Cap-Ferret. She gazed out of the window, mentally planning to visit soon.

Exiting into the dazzling sun at Nice Riquier station, Mel traced her earlier journey back towards the apartment. The heat had meant she had discarded her scarf and hat which were now crumpled in the bottom of the floral beach bag. Mel considered what she had done today. I caught a train by myself.

*I explored somewhere I have never been before and I did it because I wanted to.*

Mel wasn't sure whether the nervous energy had drained her slightly, or the heat or a combination of both. A glass of chilled rosé was in order to celebrate. As she made her way back to the port area, there were some new large yachts, the crew of one were busy washing with long hoses and a huge brush attached to the end of a pole, and a couple of young guys were scrubbing the teak decking. Making her way past she was sure she had heard a wolf whistle, turning to look in the direction of the noise she noticed the two lads on the deck looking after her, they smiled, waved and then went back to their work. Mel wasn't quite sure what to do so she quickened her pace, found a small cafe and placed her order.

Mel was aware that today wolf listening was something to be scolded not encouraged, but for her, the affirmation that someone thought she was worthy of a schoolboy action felt quite flattering. She was sure of that, they didn't mean any harm, but more to the point had they thought her attractive or was it a joke?

'There you go again Mel!' she mumbled under her breath, 'thinking of the worst-case scenario, not the best!'

With a slight spring in her step and a certain sense of achievement and self-confidence, she made her way back to the apartment with the intention to go to the big supermarket tomorrow that Theresa had pointed out.

## Chapter 11 - Loo or Loire?

The car started and the roof was lowered. Mel brimmed with mild- confidence coupled with trepidation, she reversed the convertible out of the tight space and opened the garage door to find herself staring out an advert for a well-known fizzy bottled water. A delivery van had parked across the access to the road. Mel remained in the car revving slightly trying to subtly draw the attention of the driver. A couple of minutes passed and nothing she climbed out and as she did so, a stout tanned man got into the driver side of the lorry and moved off, with a shrug. Mel got back into the car only to see the electric door starting to close and about to shut onto Theresa's beautiful car, without thinking Mel found first gear and kangaroo out of the garage nearly taking out an E- scooterist.

'Pardon!' Mel shouted loudly as the rider continued waving a fist in the air.

Regaining control she let out the clutch and moved off in the direction of the supermarket. The plotted route in the sat nav didn't look too tricky and traffic was flowing. The route took her the way she had walked earlier in the week turning left past the railway station following signs for 'P' duly parked, oversized bag and a couple of other shopping bags in hand she made her way into the shopping complex. The airy and bright supermarket was located within, pulling out her list she began filling up the trolley, luckily Theresa had left a metal size coin on a fob to release the trolley. Getting used to the front wheel steering only was challenging but Mel persevered. Eventually, her trolley was piled high with gorgeous fruit and vegetables, including some meat and fish, plus essentials such as wine, water, and kitchen roll. Mel couldn't for the life of her find a toilet roll pushing around and around, she came across a young guy stacking shelves in the tinned goods aisle.

'Bonjour, un est le loo roll.'

'Eh, loo?'

'Oui'

He stood up from his crouched position and started to walk, Mel obediently followed. They seem to be going to the far end of the supermarket.

'Voila, Loire.' He gestured to the wine section.

'Non, toilette paper umm roll.'

Mel wasn't sure why, but she involuntarily and mimed wiping her bottom- a truly dignified sight in the middle of aisle 23.

A slightly bemused shopper walked around her. The shelf-stacker was very bemused, he now led her to another part of the shop where there were rows and rows of toilet tissue.

'Merci' Mel offered.

'Madam', he raised both eyebrows and shrugged.

Exiting the shop she spotted a cashpoint and thought topping up and cash was a good idea. Notes dispensed, she wedged them into her purse. Since Mark's death money had been one thing she hadn't had to worry about. She'd been careful over the last year and she hadn't been frivolous. This was the first treat she had had in over a year. The insurance paid a lump sum and a weekly amount to cover expenses "survivors' pension", the lump sum wouldn't last forever. Mel knew that in a few years, she would need an income. For now, though she could enjoy this freedom and without monetary burden, before the eventuality of finding gainful employment became a reality.

It crossed her mind, *maybe I could work here? Though my French is very bad!*

Loading the shopping into the boot, retracting the roof, she made for home and a nice cup of tea. She fancied a strong cup of tea, tea wasn't done here and would be something she would miss if she moved abroad.

'What am I thinking?' she uttered out loud. Whilst manoeuvring across sets of traffic lights, 'why would I move for goodness sake? I have the house, the horse and the boys!'

Mel had never considered leaving her country, but the warmth and sun were drawing her in. *It's just that holiday spirit, wouldn't be the same if I lived here, would it?* Considered Mel as she manoeuvred the car back into its space.

\*

Mel began to feel very at home in Theresa's apartment. She had done all the mundane typical household jobs. She'd emptied the bins, cleaned and cooked, it did start to feel like home. Theresa had a cleaning lady every week, Simone, she had a key, but the first time, Mel wondered who was trying to get into the flat!

*Oops sorry, I forgot to say she has a key! I hope you are ok and you are enjoying it? Chloe is fine we are due to open the shop in two weeks with love Tx*

Theresa's text had come after Mel had assumed it was a burglar trying to gain access. Texted her asking how often Simone came, turned out it was every 2 weeks. Mel couldn't quite believe that two weeks have passed already. Was she really making the most of her time?

*Stop it!* scolding herself, whilst dressing one morning, *of course you are, now relax and enjoy it.*

Grabbing her phone she messaged Cathy, once Mel knew everything was ok at home, she hoped her mind would be at ease. Taking her coffee out to the terrace, the day was overcast, muggy and humid. Scrolling to find the weather app, it did show improvement in the weather outlook. Sipping the coffee she leant back in the padded wicker chair, she really was feeling comfortable here, serenity, getting away from normality was doing her the world of good.

Her phone beeped and flashed into life,

*Hi M, all good here. Just mucked out the horses- another damp day here, how is the weather there? Have you met any nice Frenchman?*

Cathy was always trying to match me up thought Mel, ever since Mark died, maybe she thinks I need someone. Mel's shoulders sank further into her comfortable position knowing all was well at home.

*Hi, you! Haha no no Frenchman to speak of, I'm not looking! The weather here is hopefully brightening up later, so I might go for a swim. Thank you for looking after things, can't believe it's been 2 weeks already Mxx*

Laying her phone down, she cast her eyes out over the rooftops down to the port. Even today the vista was appealing. It is lovely here, she thought back to the day she left home. It had been cold, damp and grey. Even when there was a storm this place felt special somehow.

Her phone began to vibrate and shimmy across the table, she leaned over and answered.

'Hi, Cathy, is everything ok?'

'All good, so no romance?'

'Haha, this isn't a kiss me quick Ibiza holiday!'

'I'm only teasing, look sorry to be a pain but I need to get into your garage for some feed for the horse, I need to move your car.'

'Of course, the keys are in the bowl in the hall.'

'You're a star, thanks.'

'You are the star.'

'Now bugger off and enjoy yourself, did you say you were off swimming later?'

'Yes hopefully as St Jean Cap Ferrat."

'Sounds fancy!'

'It looks lovely.'

'Well thanks for rubbing it in, we have rain forecast later!'

'I'll send you a photo of me sunning myself.'

'Meanie! Right speak later'

'Bye Cathy.'

'Bye-bye.'

Mel was lucky to have such a friend and neighbour as Cathy. I hope the car starts, worried Mel.

## Chapter 12 – Flashback – Blown off course

The rain had started, Cathy swung the garage door up and stared at Mel's very sad looking knackered old car covered in dust.

'What a mess!' Cathy exclaimed.

She manoeuvred Mel's car out of the garage, and as she did so the heating blowers came on and a piece of paper from a recess of the dashboard struck Cathy in the face.

'What's this, a crumpled parking ticket.'

She squinted at the faded black printed date and time, "29th of March expires at 11:40 a.m.". She tossed it onto the back seat that seemed to double up as Mel's storage area.

Lugging the bag of feed out of the garage, she hauled it into a wheelbarrow and headed along the street to the field at the back of the row of houses.

'Morning.'

'Morning David, how's the arms.'

'About 12:20?'

'No your arms', Cathy jabbed her own to highlight the topic in question.

'Ah, they are fine, how are you getting on?'

'All good, Mel seems to be getting on ok in France, lucky thing!'

'I'm pleased, she needed to get away from here and put Mark's death behind her.'

'Couldn't agree more, look it's started raining, do you need a hand I can push you in?'

'No no I'm good, what are you going with that?' David pointed at the wheelbarrow.

'Off to the field, feed for the horses.'

'How many courses?'

'NO HORSES.'

'I see, we'll catch up later.'

'Bye David.'

Cathy watched him wheel himself up the path to his front door, and let himself in.

Walking through the now drizzle filled air, Cathy thought about that parking ticket. Funny how it had hit her banging the left cheek. She threw the feed at the horses, she couldn't put a finger on it but the date on the ticket seemed familiar.

"Bleep."

Fumbling inside her jacket, she checked the messages on her phone.

*Hi sorry got to work late don't wait up I'll be back around 11 pm, C xx*

Late again, thought Cathy, Chris seemed to be doing that a lot recently as she went to reply, another message dropped in.

*You'll be pleased to hear it's raining here now, so beach tomorrow! Thank you for looking after Rocky, hope the car started :-) Mel xx*

Deciding that Mel deserved more attention than her husband she responded to her first.

*All good, car started fine, a funny thing happened as the heater came on, a parking ticket hit me in the face! Sorry not sorry about the weather ;) Cxx*

Cathy would reply later to Chris. Now, what should she treat herself to for dinner? Certainly a nice bottle of wine.

## Chapter 13 - Boulangerie and Beach

Mel placed the phone in front of her as she sat looking at the rain outside, poor Cathy, but she hadn't paid for parking in ages, when was the last time?

Suddenly she spotted a cushion outside, 'bloody hell', she opened the terrace doors, ran out and picked it up, and dashed back inside and propped it up against the window, hoping it would dry out. The day's weather didn't improve, so Mel read and later managed to find Netflix on Theresa's overly complicated TV, snuggling down on the sofa, just a few minutes nap, and Mel drifted off to sleep.

Waking up on the sofa was never a nice experience, and one Mel had forgone since her student days. Rather than walk or taxi, you would bunk in with whoever was nearest to where you'd gone out. Stretching and moving her head from side to side, it clicked, pushing herself up from her awkward position she rubbed her eyes and turned to glance at the wall clock that hung in the kitchen area.

"5:20"

*About an hour, perfect. S*he thought to herself.

Moving to the bedroom she looked out of her window and streets in oddly quiet she checked her phone.

'Shit I've been asleep for 12 hours!'

Mel couldn't remember the last time she slept so long and so soundly, right well time for a cup of tea.

Once showered and the teacup drained, she felt refreshed and the sun rose from the direction of Monte Carlo. A perfect day for the beach, a swim and exploring. She decided to pop into the boulangerie to grab some fresh bread rolls. Locating the brown and yellow faded facade that was the bakery. Mel stood patiently in the queue.

'Petit pain, merci'

'Oui, est ce tout?'

'Oui, merci'

Two rolls in hand, she pushed them into her large beach bag alongside her cheese, apple and beach towel, the indispensable items for a successful picnic.

Exiting the dank garage was much less stressful than last time, and the sat nav was set to St Jean Cap Ferrat. The road signs pointed to "Villefranche - Sur - Mer", and then winding around the coastal road, she turned onto the M25, *not quite the same as the one at home*, Mel thought to herself. Pulling into a parking space, double-checking no one else had parking tickets on their windscreens, she locked the car and noted a sign for "Plage de Passable".

'Very passable I think!'

With a view stretching back over the bay towards Nice. By now Mel was peckish so she found a small sandy spot and unfurled her towel, made some rudimentary sandwich rolls and sat looking out to sea, taking in the view. The rippling water lapped the sand, as the sun-dappled through the few trees that surrounded the sandy cove.

It started to get quite warm, and though Mel enjoyed the heat, it was starting to get too much and by one o'clock she had shifted to the only bit of shade she could find. She recalled seeing a map near where she had parked the car and decided that maybe a gentle stroll might be cooler than sunning herself on the beach.

    The map outlined a route that took you right round the promontory and near a lighthouse and past the Grand Hotel Cap Ferret. She made use of the facilities and began the circular walk. The path tracked alongside the sea to the right and wooded land to the left. The flora outcrops provided a welcome respite from the sun, and Mel began to slow down in the parts that were shaded to maximise the effect. Mel passed through a tree tunnel where she had to be sure-footed over the gnarled roots which carpeted this section of the trail, as she emerged into the light there was a large Buddleia bush, the delicate cone-shaped blooms bounced gently in the sea breeze. 'There was a Buddleia by the shed where Mark had died', muttered Mel, as she gracefully stroked one of the flowers, a butterfly landed on it as she did so. 'Red Admiral', admired Mel.

The exquisitely patterned creature slowly flapped its wings as if to dry itself and then it took off to find its next landing spot, Mel watched as it danced through the air and disappeared over the trees. Mel moved on, careful not to trip, she couldn't help thinking that the butterfly landing when it did was symbolic somehow. Pausing as she passed the lighthouse for some water she looked out over the great expanse of water and, she assumed that eventually, you would reach Italy or Northern Africa, she wasn't sure which, Geography not being her strongest point. She continued on coming into a pretty small harbourside town of Cap Ferrat, complete with fishing boats bobbing in the port.

Mel spotted a nice looking bistro and ordered a coffee and some water, it had taken her a couple of hours and she had built up quite a thirst and sweat.

'Madam, something to eat?'

This waiter had already worked out that Mel was English, as in her rush to get cooled off she'd exclaimed,

'It's so warm,' whilst tugging at the top part of the dress she was wearing in an effort to create a breeze down her cleavage.

'Yes, could I have the tuna salad and more water please?'

'Of course.'

Off he went into the recess of the restaurant to reappear shortly with a very cold, condensation forming on the outside, bottle of water. The delicious salad came and the crisp leaves and salty tuna flakes were just what she'd wanted, munching away looking out over the vista, her phone began to sound. Embarrassed by the sudden noise she scrambled to turn it off and discovered it was James, she dial back.

'Hello, how are you?'

'Hi you, I'm good just having a late lunch at St-Jean cap-Ferrat.'

'Lucky thing! I'm stuck inside looking at paint charts.'

Mel couldn't think of anything worse than being stuck indoors and such a lovely day.

James continued. 'So Darren is back in a couple of days' time, arriving from the UK, thought we could grab lunch, go out?'

'Sounds great, when and where?'

'He arrives back tomorrow, so Wednesday?'

'What's today?'

'Haha, real holiday mode for you! Not sure what the day is!'

'Well I am on a holiday, where are you thinking?'

'Thinking may come near you, one of the portside places.'

'Ok, perfect, text me on the day and I will meet you.'

'Lovely, well enjoy St-Jean.'

'I will, bye James.'

'Bye-bye Mel.'

    Mel put her phone down and jabbed a rather large piece of lettuce deftly twisting the fork around, she managed to get the vinaigrette covered serving in one mouthful.

James hadn't really said much about Darren, pondered Mel. She couldn't help thinking that James might be hiding something or maybe he was just keeping his private life, private. Though nothing had been off-limits the other night, come to think of it James had dodged questions or been vague about any reference to Darren, *but that might be my slightly wine-soaked memory*, thought Mel. Well either way she was looking forward to meeting him.

Lunch was rounded off with a nice cup of camomile tea, Mel now made her way back through the town, aiming for the car. There were some little shops, with their wear hanging outside. One she glanced at had some kaftan style linen dresses hung up, alongside some raffia beach bags. She crossed the road and on closer inspection, she decided that this is the sort of place Theresa purchased her clothes.

An Olive green dress with a V-neck caught Mel's attention, right she knew this phrase.

'C'est combien?'

'€35 madame.;

'Sold! I mean Merci, sorry!'

She would wear it for the lunch date with James and Darren, maybe with some brown leather sandals? Mel couldn't remember the last time she'd bought new clothes and thought about an outfit before the event.

Back at the car, she stood back with the door open to let some of the roasting air out, she noticed a couple of cyclists coming along the road, so she manoeuvred herself into the gap of the open car door to let them pass.

'Bella!' shouted one, clad in his red and white lycra outfit.

By the time she had spun around the cyclists had headed off into the distance, Mel got into the driving seat.

'Second time this week I'm enjoying this! But really my hair is a mess,' as she just readjusted her brown curly hair in the rear-view mirror.

She plonked the beach bag on the passenger seat, and began to rifle through, wrenched out her phone and started a new message.

'Now Theresa had mentioned that leather shop, and I need some brown shoes for this dress,' considered Mel as she scrolled on her smartphone.

It turned out there were quite a few Leather goods shops in Nice and in a town called "Ventimiglia" in Italy. This according to her app was only about an hour away, that's if she wanted to avoid motorways and Mel did. She convinced herself it was to see more of the country but in reality, it was to avoid the scary fast roads and tolls. She wasn't comfortable with either of them or why the French couldn't employ a simpler system like car tax in the UK. For the time being, she was quite happy using the smaller roads or the 'scenic routes' as she liked to call them.

## Chapter 14 – Italian Stallion

The car juddered out of St-Jean, and onwards to Italy. Mel followed the Satnav instructions and tried to enjoy the drive. The sun shone, today was going to be a lovely day, thought Mel.

Her hands gripped the steering wheel slightly tighter than was comfortable and sat closer to the steering wheel than she would have done at home. Concentrating hard she moved out along the winding road towards the Italian border. The image Mel had formed in her head was a mixture of Audrey Hepburn and the Italian Job, whizzing along with the wind in her hair and scenery wafting by. The realities started to hit home when some temporary traffic lights on the hill climb en route to Villefranche-Sur-Mer, held her up for at least 10 minutes and the sun was getting gradually warmer and higher until prickly heat on the back of her neck began to irritate, a pit stop was required. She pulled over to raise the roof, which allowed Mel to enjoy the cool blast of air conditioning.

The now refreshing breeze invigorated Mel, the views below were spectacular and the Riviera looked simply stunning. Taken aback by the beauty of Eze and maybe the ever so slight vagueness of the sat nav instructions, she managed to end up on the Grand Corniche rather than the originally planned Moyenne Corniche.

'Bollocks! There is nowhere to turn.'

The Sat Nav chimed in with, 'Route being recalculated!'

The routes looked very similar to Mel, so easing back she pressed the throttle and sped along, beginning to relish the twist and turns as the road cleared. Higher and higher she climbed until the view looked very distant, and as she passed Monaco she spotted the motorway on the other side.

*Glad I took this route, much more relaxing.*

'Bang!' An almighty sound ricocheted through the car.

'What the hell?' Mel tried to turn her head to see what had happened.

Glancing in her rear-view mirror was a truly humorous yet harrowing sight. A pigeon was spinning, feathers going in all directions, it looked like a Greek wedding plate twirling out of control.

A rather smart-looking sports car was right behind her with the roof down and the male driver didn't look impressed by Mel's bird culling methods.

Mel immediately pulled over, shaking.

'God Theresa's car!'

Managing to untangle herself from the seatbelt, she inspected the car, there wasn't any damage as far as she could tell.

'Thank goodness', a relieved Mel said out loud.

As she was checking the bonnet for any bird debris, she noted a scarlet soft-top was pulling up behind her.

'Cosa fai! Quell povero uccello!'

Mel saw him getting out, panic swept over her like a wave, she felt sick and hot.

'I'm sorry, I'm English sorry.'

Walking with purpose the man closed in on her.

'You are trembling.' Consoled the kind man.

*What a lovely accent,* considered Mel

'I know you English like shooting birds, as do we, but driving into them?' He raised his arms, Mel froze.

'Signora! Don't worry, do you have any water?'

She nodded not saying a thing, she could have cried. Reaching into the car and she pulled out her Paddington Bear style water bottle. Taking several sips and catching his gaze, she caught him staring at the bottle. Apologetically Mel offered,

'It's the only one I could find,' gesturing at the bottle.

He winked and pushed his hand through his slicked black hair. His white shirt was open between his pecs, a pair of black chino style shorts and some black driving shoes completed the look. He was tanned and simply gorgeous, thought Mel.

'Can you see any damage?' he lent over the bonnet.

'Nope, nothing I can see.'

She noticed a Pigeon feather on his shoulder, moving closer.

'You, umm, have a feather…'

'Where?'

Mel instinctively picked it off his shoulder, he must have been in his late 30s.

'There you are', and she blew it off her finger into the air

'Thank you.'

'I am so sorry.'

'You saved me from having a feather on me all day! I must thank you properly.'

He pulled on his sunglasses and dazzled with shiny white teeth.

'What do you mean?' questioned Melissa.

'Well Signora, would you have dinner with me?'

'Me and you? Ha!' Mel genuinely thought that at any minute a TV crew would jump out and shout, 'Surprise!' She looked past him, round him, nope, nothing there.

'Well?'

'I am not sure, I mean I don't know if I can, I am new here, visiting. I'm on my way to Ventimiglia to buy shoes.'

'I can take you!' He gestured to his car, Mel couldn't remember which one was which, was it a horse or a bull on a Ferrari? This car had a prancing horse.

'Wow, I don't know what to say.'

'Say yes Signora.'

Bloody hell, this guy was attractive. Mel felt like a teenager, all giddy and a fuzzy sensation in her stomach.

'Where would we put my car?'

'Well, I know a place to eat further down the road, in La Turbie. Could we leave it there until lunch is over?'

'I'm not sure, you see it's not my car and...'

'Not your car?'

'Umm, I'm borrowing it while I'm here.'

'Ahh'

'I suppose I could follow you there?'

'Of course, come on Signora, I'll race you!' he winked, and as he lowered himself into the car shouted, 'Mind the birdies! Haha.'

Nervously laughing as she got back into the Mini, what am I doing? This man might be a murderer? *It's a public place Mel!* Right deep breath.

She heard the powerful engine behind fire up and Mr Italian revved off in front, Mel duly followed behind the horse or was it a bull?

*

Mel drained the last remnants of her Aperol Spritz.

'You enjoy?'

She looked across at her lunch date, he was confident and had tonnes of sex appeal, olive-skinned with a touch of designer stubble.

'Yes, delicious thank you.'

'That's good, how long did you say you were staying in Nice for?'

'At least another 4 weeks, not sure exactly.'

'That gives us time to get to know one another.'

A warm hand rested on Mel's, she felt a sudden flash of excitement. Who was this guy? It must be a hoax? But tingling sensations began to ride up from somewhere deep, she tried to swallow it down

'Sounds good.' She nervously added.

'Very lucky you came out here, all because of a letter.'

## Chapter 15 - Flashback - Theresa writes

'Bloody hell!'

Theresa sat at a table, a very untidy one, but in her mind a methodical desk. Her grey knee-length linen kaftan crumpled as she leant forward twirling her Moroccan slippered feet as she tapped ferociously at her keyboard. After the fourth time of punching searches into google, she was ready to give up. Where the hell is this woman? 'Right, well I do it the old-fashioned way, funny not to be on any social media.' Wrenching the central drawer, a multitude of paperwork and items spilling out, her hand clasped a lined notepad and she began to scribe.

*Now, where did I put the post-it note, the one with my sister-in-law's address on it?*

The myriad of bits of paper, cables, a laptop and a phone hindered the search somewhat. Looking up from the mess she noticed a bright pink post-it stuck to the top of her computer screen, she found it! Theresa sat back pleased with her efforts, she had found someone who may be able to house sit. It was a long shot but being in France, with her daughter in Canada, and being perpetually single, meant she hadn't found a suitable candidate. The only issue was that she hadn't seen Mel since Mark's funeral, heaven knows whether she would accept.

The whole episode of finding someone had driven it home. How few close friends she had in Nice. The main issue had been that separating from Matt, the ex, had divided the friends. Oddly and annoyingly so, most sided with him. Theresa wasn't sure why, it wasn't fair. Having lived a gipsy life, always moving for work, it had been hard to form close friendships and put down roots. She cast her mind back to the day of her brother Mark's funeral. Mel had been very composed, a lady similar in height to her, smartly but conservatively dressed in a quarter length wool coat with big black buttons and knee-length black skirt, matching tights and appropriately coupled with low heeled noir leather shoes.

'Poor Mel.' Theresa mouthed as she gazed down at the letter in front of her.

Theresa recalled they had chatted at the wake. Mel had clutched a small black square handbag so tightly, her knuckles were white, as they exchanged sympathies. No hats had been worn. Mark didn't want hats. *What a stubborn thing he was, he'd always been difficult.* considered Theresa. Not that she or Mark had talked much over the past decade. She had exchanged details with Mel, or more accurately Mel had given Theresa her details and she had copied them down quickly on a crumpled old piece of paper out of her handbag. The piece of paper in question was an old used envelope, she'd written the address on the back;

*Mrs M Baker, Grove Lodge, Acacia Avenue, Chichester, West Sussex, UK, BO19 1AD.*

Theresa recalled now, that she'd struggled to hear if Mel had said B or P.

'Oh well, I'm sure it will get there!'

Licking the envelope she tossed it into her open beach bag. Theresa mulled, 'What if she likes it and stays? I'd like a friend here.'

Theresa hoped Mel would accept, and the airline vouchers and a bit of cash may help sway the deal. Since Chloe had left Theresa longed for girly lunches and chats, she missed those. At least she had her work to get stuck into and distract her, as she wondered what Mel was doing. She suspected Mark hadn't wanted Mel to work when they had the boys. Now two handsome guys, she recalled seeing at the funeral. Mark had never really got used to the idea that Theresa wanted to live abroad.

'Why there?' He would question.

Then Theresa would feel compelled to justify at length her reasons for doing so. Mark and her had rarely seen eye-to-eye, even as children. There was something about Mel, there was a kindred spirit waiting to be unleashed if only Mark would have let her.

'God, I couldn't have married the man, I would have throttled him long ago!'

## Chapter 16 – 'Bonjour' Neighbours

Mel arrived back at the apartment in the late afternoon. The lunch had been as delicious as had the eye candy. Though a doubt was brewing in Mel's mind – why did he want to have lunch with me?

They had swapped numbers and after a very exhilarating drive round the town in his sports car, via a shoe shop, he had kissed her on both cheeks to say goodbye. Mel had flushed like a teenager, 'bye then.'

'Ciao Bella!'

With that, he sped off with a roar, in a cloud of dust and tyre squeal he was gone.

As she entered the apartment a note was wedged in the door frame, there was nothing written on the outside, she unfolded it to read its contents.

*Hi, we are the downstairs neighbours, Albert and Annette…*

*Whoops, have I been too loud?* Worried Mel.

Continuing to read, she walked inside and shut the door with her foot, and threw a tea bag in a mug.

*…and Theresa explained why you are here, we would be pleased to meet you. Number 11 downstairs. A & A x*

Mel read the letter again, *What a nice thing to do*, she thought.

Pushing open the terrace doors, she took her tea and got comfy. She texted Theresa, trying to work out if she would be awake yet due to the time difference.

The sun began to lose its warmth and clouds gathered ominously, *time for a drink I think.*

Mel pulled on the fridge door and selected a chilled bottle of rosé. With the wine poured she settled down in one of the large sofas, curled up and began flicking through one of the numerous magazines laid on the coffee table. She stopped on an article about West Sussex, at that moment her phone flashed into life.

*Hi Mel, all good here, yes I just let the couple downstairs know, in case you need anything. Hope that's ok? T xx*

The letter! She'd forgotten all about it, slipping her feet into some trainers she grabbed her keys and went down the echoey marble stairs and rapped gently on Albert and Annette's door, well she thought it was their door. When a stout, bald man, who reeked of tobacco, opened the door, it wasn't what Mel expected. She proffered a smile and waved the note towards him.

'Ahhh non!'

'O sorry.'

The door slammed in her face, as she turned, a friendly looking face was peering out of the door opposite.

'Mel?'

'Yes'

'I'm Annette, we left a note, I hope that was ok?'

'Of course, I just wasn't sure..'

'Anytime really.'

Annette seemed to be able to anticipate Mel's questions, there was an eagerness about Annette, fidgety almost.

'Does tomorrow early evening work for you?

'That will be lovely, shall we say 5?'

'I will look forward to it.'

Mel smiled and made her way back upstairs. She seemed to sense something odd about her neighbour, and was trying to work out what it was - Furtive? Afraid or Scared? Nope on *edge,* that was it, Annette was on edge.

*

Mel found herself outside the same door the next evening, she had considered whether she should take anything. A bottle of wine perhaps or some flowers? She was only going for a quick drink, so she plumped for a bottle of white wine.

'Sorry I'm late, I lost track of time at the beach.'

'Please don't worry, come on in.'

It was true she had lost track of time but a more accurate summation might be – 'I nodded off in the sun.' Anyway, it had only just gone 5:20.

Annette led them into a dimly lit, square room, with modest but expensive furniture.

'Albert, this is Mel, Theresa's house-sitter.'

'Bonjour, Albert.' Mel said to a slightly wizened but strong man, sat in a high backed chair in the corner of the room by the window.

'Hello Mel, right door this time?' he stood to greet her, by shaking her hand. Mel wasn't sure if Albert was trying to be funny or if as she had begun to realise, that irony was sometimes lost in translation.

'Yes, silly me! Here is some wine,' which she handed to Albert.

'Merci, Annette could you get some glasses and the wine in the fridge door?'

*Oh not my wine?* Mel thought to herself.

'Yes Albert,' Annette scuttled off to the kitchen.

After discussing the usual topics that pass as 'chit-chat,' they moved on to discussing their situations. It turned out that Albert had been born in France but left as a baby shortly before the outbreak of the second world war and then they had met at a dinner dance in Brighton in the late 60s. She had a career in publishing and though her family were based in East Sussex, Albert had wanted to retire back in France.

'How funny I live in West Sussex!'

'What a small world. I miss it.' sighed Annette. She looked pained but turned away from Albert.

'Nonsense! The weather here is better, the food, the sea…'

'Yes but it's not home.' Interrupted Annette.

They stared at each other, Mel thought this was an opportune moment to make her escape. 'Well, look I must get back upstairs to sort out my dinner.'

Mel pushed herself out of the incredibly soft sofa, 'thank you for the drink.'

'Of course, well thank you for coming and for the wine, I'll show you out.' and Annette scuttled out of the room.

'Bye Albert, thank you.'

'Bye Mel, see you soon.'

As Mel turned to face Annette in the front doorway, she grabbed Mel by the arm.

'Please! I mean would you mind coming back?'

'Of course, are you ok?'

Annette released her grip, 'Yes I'm fine, I just miss company and Sussex of course.'

'Why don't you come up to me? Just us girls one night.'

Annette was, Mel had surmised, in her mid to late 60s and didn't quite qualify as a "girl", but Mel wanted to lighten the mood.

'May I really?'

'Anytime' Mel beamed a smile at Annette.

'Annette? What's for dinner?' The muffled voice from Albert came from the living room.

'I better go.'

'Go, see you soon.'

Mel grimaced, as the thought of cooking someone else's dinner, day in and day out, filled her with dread. She turned to mount the stairs as Annette and Albert's door clicked shut, she distinctly heard Albert's voice...

'You can get that one for €3 in Carrefour!'

*Cheeky git*, Mel thought. It was a bargain and surely it's the thought that counts.

Pity is what she'd felt for Annette, Albert had, well it had seemed he had, all the power. Because of that, he could create pain not a physical one but an emotional one.

    She continued to sip some wine as she cooked and after supper she relaxed on the sofa. Suddenly she heard thunder and rushed to close windows and blinds, she recalled the petrichor smell, the earthy waft that always reminded Mel of holidays abroad, which conjured up memories of sunnier climes. However, in the dash, she hit her shin against the side of the bed and unequivocally decided where she would stay for the remainder of the evening, in bed. Safely wrapped up in her duvet, away from the storm outside and away from bits of protruding furniture.

\*

A slight fuzziness in the head enveloped her as she rose, pushing her hair back gingerly over her head, she made her way to the main living area, picking up her sunglasses from the kitchen table and put them on, and began rummaging behind cushions. *Where the bloody hell had I put it, bloody phone.*

The phone was nestled under a magazine and the wrapper of a bar of chocolate. A cork, which gave Mel a stab of guilt, rolled onto the floor. Feeling a sense of shame she jabbed at the phone screen, 3 attempts to enter the pin, and she eventually accessed her messages.

First read,

*Hi M, how are you getting on, I think Leo needs company, can I move Rocky into his field? Raining again, Cathy xx*

Hitting reply, Mel responded.

*Of course, no worries umm think I overdid the vino last night. Headache. Sunny here, again ;) M xx*

Another message showed,

*Hi Mel, hope you are ok? Don't forget we said lunch today, if you are up for it we can come near you, there are some nice places around the port, James x*

*Shit!* Mel slumped back into the sofa, she had to get herself together, and presentable, a lot of coffee and rest hopefully would rectify the issue. *Or maybe a swim,* she squinted through her glare-reducing sunglasses at the clock on the wall - 7:35am, *right so back to bed, then coffee, then swim, then lunch.*

She considered all those options when she was back laying on her bed, coffee then swimming, then food, then makeup, lots of makeup.

## Chapter 17 - Is happiness an illusion?

*Hi James, yes can't wait, where shall we meet? Mel xx*, the text was sent, Mel now needed to shift the after-effects of too much red wine.

A short restless nap later. Mel secured herself a massive mug of black coffee, with 2 sugars, and was starting to feel a bit more human again. However, her tummy was rumbling and therefore she had to brave the outside world. What she really wanted was a bacon sandwich, but that might be tricky. Nevertheless she made her way into the bright sunshine, everything dulled by the sepia tint of her eyewear.

The bakery she now frequented was open and mercifully there was no queue and managed to order a Jambon-beurre baguette, ready to go. She thought it was funny how she only knew what to say or what it was because they sold them in Pret at home.

With her provisions for one, she made her way to the end of the road, where she could perch on a bench and munch away whilst gazing over the sea and beyond. This is where the ferries from Corsica and Sardinia docked, today however the view was clear of ferries and the azure blue stretched for miles, a few small boats further out to sea zoomed back and forth, though Mel suspected these weren't as small as they seemed, Mark would have called them 'Gin Palaces'. Though some probably were the size of palaces.

The baguette was just what Mel needed, it was delicious, slightly chewy with thick smoked ham and lashings of butter. This reassuring dose of carbs had put a spring into her step as she confidently strode off to the beach for what she hoped would be the final instalment in 'operation revive'.

It was around midday when her phone flashed, and another message from James dropped in, *are you ok with mussels?*

Mel loved mussels, all seafood in fact, but she didn't eat as much as she would have liked, Mark was never keen, and somehow the habit of eating meat stuck.

*Yummy, where and what time?*

Mel could have eaten more baguette, she was ravenous, but showing self-restraint waited until lunch.

*L'Escale, 1 pm?*

*Perfect, see you then.*

Mel now had just under an hour to get ready, she had to iron her new olive green dress and luckily the lunch with Mr Italian hadn't completely swept her away and she had managed to get some flat, somewhat Grecian, chocolate brown leather strap sandals.

Ready, with a more than usual helping of makeup, she felt ready to face the day, big sunglasses on and the smallest of Theresa's wicker bags, she was off. The lunch spot was less than a 5-minute walk away and Mel figured they might be late, leaving just after 1pm. She arrived calm and cool, at 1:15pm. She was slightly startled to discover it was only just down from the bistro where she had fallen over backwards at, luckily without any mishaps this time she darted up onto the elevated section of Escale and there was James, looking very handsome in a pale pink shirt, sleeves rolled up, and stone coloured shorts. He seemed to be having a heated discussion with the guy sitting next to him.

'Just be nice and we can discuss it…

'James!' exclaimed Mel as she neared the table.

Turning around 'Mel, there you are, how are you?'

He stood and they hugged and kissed, 'this is Darren,' James indicated to the guy sitting next to him, he wore light blue jeans, torn, a white t-shirt with some black print over it and very large dark sunglasses.

'Hi Mel, James has told me all about you.'

'O God, not everything!' she winked and shook Darren's hand as he hadn't got up plus the angle was all wrong for a welcoming hug.

'This looks lovely, have you guys been here before?'

'James and I, come when we can don't we?'

'I love the moules mariniere!'

'You could try something different this time?' questioned Darren.

'No, I know what I like,' retorted James.

Sensing the mood was slightly frosty, Mel made herself comfy and placed her bag in the chair next to her and faced her lunch dates.

'So, what wine do we fancy?' picking up the menu in front of her and realising there was no English at all on it, which was right of course, but meant she was clueless as to what the wines actually were and what the seafood came with.

'What about a Picpoul? It's dry and good with fish', James lent over and pointed to it on Mel's menu.

Wine order was duly placed and the conversation soon became less stilted and whatever had happened as Mel arrived had been forgotten or at least stored up for another time. Mel gasped as huge metal bowls came out to other diners with steaming hot piles of mussels almost overflowing.

'Wow they look amazing, I am so hungry! exclaimed Mel.

'Have you eaten today? Asked Darren

'No, just a coffee', Mel felt it was the wrong time to discuss her hangover and the massive baguette she'd had to overcome her sorry state.

They ordered, well James ordered for Mel, and more wine was poured. Miraculously Mel started to feel much better, the headache and nausea all vanished.

'So Darren, tell me about your acting sounds very exciting.'

'I guess it is, last week I was at an audition....'

Mel soon regretted asking, the tale of rejection and then who he had worked with and what it entailed, had, in the beginning, been very interesting. As the story went on, Mel lost interest, Darren didn't seem to pause for breath.

Luckily the saving grace was that the food arrived and allowed others to interject.

'Doesn't that look good?' James looked at Mel, and Mel at him. He looked tired Mel thought, and then she considered her own visage, which no doubt looked over made up to hide the hangover, and tired also.

'Yeh, good bread and chips!' Mel salivated.

They dug in, the chatter died down whilst all three moved in on their respective mountain of mussels.

'Could you pass the butter?' James nudged Darren.

'You sure you should have butter?'

'The butter.'

Mel felt awkward for James and for herself for that matter. Darren seems on edge and James wasn't the happy go lucky and buoyant person she had encountered on the plane or had drinks with.

'I'll have more butter too, when you are done,' Mel hoped her interjection would have the effect she wanted, to reassure James and to piss off Darren. James placed an order for more wine, and Darren, with arms folded, decided he wasn't going to drink anymore. 'It's not good for the skin, and as an actor, I have to be mindful.'

Mel was annoyed, why was this guy stunting her friend's fun and conversation. 'Remind me, Darren, what was your last job? I have to admit I don't watch much TV and I don't watch Soaps'.

'Well umm…'

She wasn't sure but had James tried to hide a small smirk and stifle a snort, the sort you make when you agree with someone, but can't show the full emotion for fear of upsetting someone.

Darren was clearly caught off guard, and Mel wanted to put him in his place, who did he think he was? 'Well I am sure you were wonderful, I just prefer the theatre'. Mel was on a roll, she wasn't sure where this spirit had come from but in a diva type way she was enjoying it, relishing it even.

'James would you mind topping me up?' Mel held her glass out and just as Mel went to draw it away, her fingers, slippery from the mussel eating. The glass fell from her grasp and white wine sploshed all over Darren.

'What the hell! How did you manage that?!'

'I am so sorry Darren, here is a napkin.'

She tried to help but the napkin was snatched and Darren went very red and quiet.

'I am really sorry!'

'Yeh, no worries, look I may have to get changed, James shall we get the bill and go?'

'Do you really need to get changed?'

'Yeh, I smell like a pub!'

'Ok well you go ahead and I will sort things out here'

'No James you can't get this too', Mel interrupted.

'What? You paid for that too?'

'Yes Darren I did, I wanted to, is that ok?'

Darren now looked very uncomfortable, he pushed his chair back and tried to cover any damp areas with his jacket. He made his way out onto the street, James and Mel looked on.

'James I am really sorry, I didn't mean…'

'Garcon, another!' shouted James

'Another?' queried Mel

'Mel, the other night I had so much fun, I laughed more than I do with anyone else and it got me thinking about Darren.'

'Can I be honest?'

'Of course.'

'Well I had a heavy one last night, overdid the red, I had a huge baguette before coming here, I'm tired and I am now back on the wine. It seems to have made me more feisty than I have been in a while. I could sense you weren't happy, why didn't you say?'

'Mel, I guess I hadn't seen you in ages and I felt guilty, everything you have been through and…'

'Vin, Monsieur '

'Merci, just leave it there.'

Pouring wine for Mel, then himself, he re-adjusted his seat, leant back and put his right leg over the other.

'I am not happy Mel.'

He looked down, took a deep breath.

'James, it's ok, I am here now to talk to. I know we haven't seen each other in ages and a lot has happened, but somehow I feel I can talk to you, which is why I just let it all out on the plane, and the other night I had loads of fun. I have been bottled up for years, and now I am finding my feet again, and I need to talk to someone, and unfortunately for you, you got both barrels, so to speak!'

'Mel I feel the same, but I was worried about Darren. I wanted you to meet him first before I started to rant.'

'Ok,' She swigged her wine, 'James I have a confession.'

'You're a lesbian?'

'Well, I haven't honestly thought about a woman in that way, but now you mention it', she winked at James and pulled her sunglasses off, 'James I purposefully dropped that wine.'

Mel sat back in her chair, quite smug, but had that overstepped the mark? What if James got up and left? Slowly leaning back up she looked at him. He pulled his sunglasses off and looked back at her, mouth open.

'You mean to tell me that was all a ploy? You didn't like him?'

'It was and I am sorry, I just could tell, plus I saw that smirk on your face when he was spouting off about acting,' she wagged her finger at him playfully.

'Mel you dark horse, you come out here all demure, I think there's a hidden tiger in there, the likes of which I haven't seen since we worked together!'

'Hardly, I just know when someone isn't happy, sadly I haven't used that ability on myself.'

'What do you mean?'

Sighing she leant her elbows on the table, 'I haven't been truly happy in years, and then he died'

'Mark?'

'Yes Mark, and I thought I had hit rock bottom, moping around, then Theresa's letter and here I am, really enjoying myself and finding who I am, but even now I feel guilty for it.'

Mel looked down at the table and watched a small fly scuttle across the table. She looked up at James, he was beaming.

'Well maybe, just maybe, we have found in each other our soulmates. Let's drink to that.' He raised his glass to chime with hers.

'Now what are you going to do with Darren?'

'Do?'

'Well it's obvious, you resent him.'

'I guess I do, I mean I work hard and have invested and that's why I am here today, but he floats around, and between you and I Mel, I am bankrolling it and I am thinking of pulling the plug.'

'Jesus, how much are you in for?'

'Thousands.'

'I feel guilty now about letting you pay for the other night', she grinned. 'Well you can't go on like this James, don't do what I did and settle for something that isn't right, that isn't you and isn't making you happy.'

'Thing is, we share the house I am doing up, the biggest one yet, I need it to work, but I know Darren will want it to fund yet another course, another trip to a producer, another screen test, it is endless, like a black hole for money, and as we are being honest, I would rather fund you and the rebirth of Mel, than that.'

'Haha, the 'rebirth of Mel' sounds like an awful film, would Darren star in it?' Winking and filling their glasses up, she waved at the waiter, and mimed and mouthed 'bill', she was starting to gesticulate more, a sign of a good time.

'What are you doing?'

'My treat, on one condition

'Name it'

'You come with me and see where I am staying now, and have a drink on the terrace.'

'How can I refuse?'

They made their way back to Mel's temporary abode,

'Wow Mel that view is amazing, Theresa struck gold with this.'

'I know it's amazing, I just have to pinch myself every day that I am actually here doing this. I am starting to wish I had a place in the sun, the weather at home and the memories…' she broke off as she remembered that wet foggy morning, over a year ago now. One that changed everything, but in some ways it hadn't changed anything.

James took her hand, 'Come on let's get out onto the terrace, and you did promise me a drink.'

They sat ensconced in the comfy chairs, the sun was dimming now and the afternoon warmth was very snooze-inducing. Chatting away and sipping wine, the conversation returned to the main issue at hand.

'James when we first met you asked me what I wanted out of life, and I couldn't fathom what it was, now I ask the same of you.'

He took a sip of wine. 'I am happy with my work, builders are a pain, but without sounding crude I have made some money now. I can live anywhere, down here or back in London.'

'Ok, so what about Darren?'

'I really don't know, there are glimmers of it being great. When we laugh, and the sex is good, but something is missing.'

'A spark, a connection?'

'Christ, how did you know?'

'I have seen it, I have seen it in others and I am beginning to realise I have seen it closer to home, in myself.'

She gulped down some wine, as the momentous admission hit home. Deciding to move on from that topic, she steered it back to James.

'You are lucky doing the renovating, we were about to finish renovating our house, a small outbuilding, I was looking forward to having a studio and holiday cottage, I wanted a place to be creative, an outlet I guess.

'Mel I didn't realise…'

'It's ok, I feel it coming back, the creativity returning. This trip, meeting Theresa and of course you. I see how much I have missed over the past years and I need to regain my confidence.'

'Well you could help me, and I could help you?'

'How do you mean?'

'Well I have this house we are doing up, be great to have your thoughts, and in return, we can work on that confidence, the hidden tiger, I think we saw a glimmer at lunch!'

James was right, she needed a focus. For too long she had wafted around since Mark's death. The horse and the house only provided a small distraction, of course, there were the boys but they were grown up and living their own lives and that's what Mel needed to do, live her own life.

An hour or so later, James's phone bleeped,

'It's Darren, look I better go Mel, thank you.'

'Of course, well you know where I am now, please pop in soon.'

'You bet I will, look, can we chat about Darren and this renovating idea some more?'

'Would love to, now remind me when are we having the builders thingy?'

'The builders' dinner? Yeah well, it's supposed to be Saturday, are you ok to come?'

'Of course, will Darren want me there though?'

'I'm not sure he will be here, I think he has another screen test in London, no doubt I'll be paying for the airfare!'

'Now look, don't rush anything with him, and make sure *you* are sure.'

Mel realised that she had been quite forceful in her opinions and felt she should peddle back. She didn't want James to make a rash decision and then he blamed her. They said their goodbyes and Mel picked up a magazine, got comfy and promptly nodded off. The mixture of lunchtime drinking and warmth was an ideal combination for an afternoon siesta.

She stirred suddenly some while later when a rather tiresome wasp was buzzing in her vicinity, jumping up she tried to swat it with a rolled-up magazine, but Mel's reaction speed was no match for that of a lightning fast insect. The night was drawing in, and she pulled down the parasol. She heaved the heavy chairs under the cover of an awning, it made her hands hurt, now she knew how David must feel in his wheelchair.

# Chapter 18 - Flashback - David's police interview

'So, you called Mrs Baker when you saw it happen?'

'Well yes, but you see I wasn't in the same room as the phone, my wheelchair you see slows me down.'

'I understand, so you think you saw Mr Baker fall off the roof of his outbuilding at what time?'

'Around 11:30 ish, I think'

'Ok and then you made a call on your landline to Mrs Baker, why not the police?'

'Well you see I wasn't sure, it was a misty wet day, and he may have been fine, my eyes aren't what they used to be'

'Ok I understand,' the police officer gathered up her things.

'No more questions?' enquired David.

'Not at this stage Mr Williams'

'Not on whose page?'

'NOT AT THIS STAGE'

Lisa hated raising her voice to any elderly people, but deafness required her to be forceful.

'Thank you, Mr Williams, I will see myself out.'

'Ok thank you, officer, it's so sad, I feel awful I couldn't get outside to check, this damn wheelchair, and Mrs Baker was only in town…' he paused to draw breath.

'It's ok Mr Williams, I mean David, it's just a tragic accident.'

*

Lisa got into the patrol car and called the superintendent,

'Hi Chief it's Lisa'

'How did it go?'

'Not much in the way of a witness Sir, the next-door neighbour is wheelchair-bound, deaf and eyes aren't great by all accounts.'

'Well sounds like a simple case, 'Accidental death'.'

'Yes Sir, I hope the widow is ok.'

'She's just left the station with a friend apparently, maybe pop in Lisa and check on her?'

'Yes Sir, should have all the paperwork sorted by this afternoon, as you say 'accidental death', I suppose no need to do phone checks or wait for coronary reports?'

'No resources I'm afraid, anyway, I need you to get onto Marsh lane, a particularly nasty road traffic accident this morning, need your expertise.'

'Course Sir, I'll see Mrs Baker and then get straight on it.'

David watched as the police officer had made her call on the pavement outside, he peered from his living room window, he held back the curtain to get a clearer view. He squinted but the state of his windows and another grey day did not help. *Poor Melissa*, he thought, I must order flowers, he wheeled himself to the telephone table in the hallway, squeezing through the doorway.

'Everything takes so long in this damn wheelchair.'

\*

Mel and Cathy had just got out of the car when they saw the police car near the house.

'I am not sure I can face any more questions,' said Mel.

'I am sure they are just checking if everyone is ok, do you want me to stay?'

'No Cathy honestly, you get home, Is it ok if I call you later?'

'Of course, I am just so sorry.'

As Mel exited the car a sturdy looking police officer came toward her, full uniform and her long auburn hair poking out from under her helmet.

'Mrs Baker?'

'Yes,'

'I am Officer Hodge.'

'Hello Officer, how can I help? I answered all the questions just now in the station.'

'No more questions, I just wanted to check on you, see how you were and if you need anything.'

'That's very kind', Mel began to well up again, 'I'm alright, I just want to get inside and sort things out and tell my boys what's happened.'

'Of course, I understand, please don't blame yourself.'

'I just feel like a fool, popping out for groceries, and this happens…' her voice broke and she fumbled for a tissue.

'There is nothing more we need, a tragic accident, I am so very sorry, please do get in touch if you need anything.'

Regaining some composure, 'Thank you, officer'.

    Mel watched as the officer climbed into her patrol car and drove out of sight further down the avenue. Mel turned to face the house, it suddenly felt imposing, large and dark. She made her way inside and saw the shopping that she had dumped onto the floor, tins and vegetables had rolled out. She picked them up, one by one. Sitting at the kitchen table, she pushed all the swatches and paints charts off onto the floor and sat, on her own, in the dark, head in her hands.

'What the hell now?' she muttered to herself.

## Chapter 19 - Have a butchers

The day had been cooler, a sea breeze had muted the temperature and Mel had decided, as it was Friday, she wanted to treat herself to a steak dinner. This was going to be tricky, but doing some research she found that there were a few butchers in walking distance and with a shopping bag in hand she was determined to get something to roast.

'A nice piece of beef, maybe a sirloin', she considered her options as she made her way up to the Place de Garibaldi. A large square with imposing buildings on all sides, with porticos so restaurants and cafes could serve outside even if the weather was poor. Deciding that there was no great rush to get to the butchers, she found a cafe she liked the look of and ordered a 'Cafe au lait'. Watching the people milling around fascinated Mel, tourists with their cameras following someone with a large furled umbrella and a clipboard, locals were chatting and talking over the day with friends, there were young people on scooters and bikes. She felt she was becoming more attuned to the way of life and the people.

*Funny how pigeons are everywhere.* A nasty reminder of her run-in with one the other day.

She hadn't heard from Mr Italian, Gino. She assumed that maybe a middle-aged English woman wasn't his usual fayre, and a lovely beach body ready the Mediterranean was more his style. Maybe she should text him? What harm would it do?

She found his number, saved under 'Italian pecs', clearly at the time she couldn't remember his name and decided this short but graphic description would, in the future, be memorable. What should she say? She didn't want to come across as weird, stalkerish or silly.

'Mel just write the goddamn text', She muttered to herself.

*Hi Mr Italian, it's the birdy killer, how are you? Thanks again for lunch.*

She pressed send.

Draining her coffee she meandered through the square and into the old part of Nice. The wide boulevards and new tram lines disappeared and the windy narrow streets became maze-like, all sorts of shops could be found here. This is where the ice cream shop and one of the brightly coloured leather shops had been that Theresa had shown her. She hoped she could find them again…she now had ice cream on the brain.

She then realised that the route on her app was showing her the way if she was driving not by foot.

'Bloody thing'.

So she turned and followed the updated guidance, which took her through the twisting, narrow streets which no car could possibly make. The streets were lined with baroque style buildings of all colours, rusty brown, dusty pink and pale yellow. The awnings of the shops brought a sense of darkness and intimacy with throngs of people doing their shopping and pottering.

'Madame?'

'Yes, what is it?'

A petite dark-haired lady in an apron stood with a round tray, with what looked like browned flatbread torn into pieces.

'Socca.'

'Smells amazing'.'

Mel took a small piece and a paper napkin, 'merci'.

The thick pancake-like bread had a slightly earthy flavour, nutty with a moist interior and crispy browned edges. There were hints of olive oil and herbs. *God this is moreish*. Mel stood to eat it and looked into the window of the Socca vendor. A massive flat skillet was heated and batter poured in and fried until ready then cut into triangles or folded. A takeaway snack sprinkled with salt and pepper. The temptation was too great, a large folded piece of Socca wrapped in a white tissue was soon in Mel's hands.

'You like Madame?'

'Yes delicious, what is it made from?'

'Ahhh pois chiches', the cook turned to the lady with the tray, said something quickly and she shouted, 'Chickpea'.

'Merci, so same as houmous.'

'Oui Madame, savourez!'

Mel munched away, trying to juggle a phone and the Socca. The 'Boucherie' wasn't far away now. She could see the scarlet and gold awning ahead with a large crowd outside. According to her app that was it. What did she want? Beef? Pork? She remembered the other day that a restaurant had a Cote De Beouf on the menu, she hadn't had one for ages as generally they were sold to be shared. Assuming that 'Côte de boeuf' was 'Côte de boeuf' in both languages, that would be easy, except for her it would be for her, 'pour moi'.

The crowd was about three deep and there was lots of shouting and pointing and general gesticulating, she jostled in and moved with the crowd. The speed at which people were served was incredibly fast-paced, and interestingly the meat was wrapped and put in an overhead conveyor which dropped it down to the cashier sitting at the left-hand side of the store. After about 15 minutes or so, Mel was at the front, Socca bread had been demolished and her empty shopping bag was ready for a big chunk of red meat.

'Oui Madame?'

'O umm, Côte De Boeuf, pour moi.'

The butcher with hands like shovels slapped down a massive rib of beef and started to move the knife along, waiting for Mel to utter when to stop.

'Non, pour moi, une personne.' That was as much as Mel could muster,

'Ahh, 'ere?'

'Oui, merci'

'Trente et Trois'

'Oui Monsieur?'

The butcher had moved on to the next customer before Mel had cottoned on that she needed to remember that number. It was wrapped and shoved overhead, Mel pushed her way through the crowd to the cash desk.

'Madame'

'O ah Trent a trois.'

'Onze euro, s'il vous plaît'

Mel produced a twenty euro note, bundled the plastic-wrapped joint in her bag and took her change. The whole experience had been amazing but draining at the same time. As she emerged back into the daylight, blinked and popped her sunglasses on. She made her way out of the old part and spotted a small Carrefour, darting in for some frites to have with her steak and some green beans, plus a bottle of rosé. This meal was going to be good and sitting out on the terrace to eat it with that view, she couldn't wait. However, on her way home, she did get diverted by a small little wine bar, looked rather cosy and smartly dressed waiters, how could she say no to a little glass of Cote de Provence?

'Bella'!

Mel had to stop herself from spewing wine everywhere, turning in her seat, there was Mr Italian, Gino.

'What on earth?'

'No birdies here for you to kill.'

Wiping her mouth with the back of her left hand, she stood up to greet the unexpected visitor,

'What, I mean, why are you here?'

'I travel all over signora, what are you doing here?'

He was now close to her, she could smell the musky aftershave scent, and today Gino was in tight slim fit black jeans, loafers and a pale blue shirt.

'Gino, umm hi, sorry I am just surprised to see you, sorry.'

'That's the problem with you English, always *sorry*. I am here picking up some shopping and stumbled across the Cote d'Azur's best birdie killer.'

'Gino, not so loud, people are staring, I will get in trouble.'

'Not with me around, I will look after you,' Gino now assumed to take the seat opposite Mel's.

'Gino…'

'Mel!'

Another voice, an English voice, bellowed across the crowded outdoor bar. She couldn't quite believe it, in a city she had never been in, there were two people she knew in the same bar!

'James! hi, how are you?'

'I'm good, am I interrupting?' he gestured to Gino, he'd already stood up to greet Mel's friend.

'James!' They embraced, Mel looked dumbfounded.

'Sorry, what? Don't tell me you know one another?'

James spoke first,

'Yes, of course, we do.'

'Of course?' Mel couldn't quite get over that nearly a thousand miles away from home, in a city of hundreds of thousands of people, she would end up in this, an awkward to say the least, situation.

'Ci, Bella, I run a building company and I am helping James to make the house of his dreams.'

'Well I hope so Gino, more to the point Mel, how do you two know each other?'

'Sit down James, Gino could you get some drinks?' Mel smiled and gazed on, as her Italian stud beckoned the waiter over, his arm muscles strained inside his fitted shirt, god he was attractive.

'Mel?'

'Oh sorry James, yes well, you know I said I wanted to drive to Italy...'

## Chapter 20 - How do you like your steak?

The piece of meat sizzled in the frying pan, as James poured out some chilled wine.

'How awkward was that? Wasn't sure if he would get the hint.'

Mr Italian had proceeded to ply James and Mel with another drink and insisted that he paid. Which Mel didn't mind, but dropping hints about having to eat etc., were not working. Eventually, he went to the toilet, and James and Mel colluded.

'O Bella, so you have to go?'

'Yes, I promised James I would cook for him tonight for a proper catch-up.'

Mel was firm, unusually, but she wasn't sure what she was getting into with Mr Italian. She had wanted this holiday to be a clean slate, to hit "reset" and go home feeling revitalised. Not convinced by Gino's advances, she consulted James, whilst preparing dinner.

'Mel, honestly please don't feel like you have to cook for me, it's very kind of you....'

'James you saved me! Plus this hunk of meat is really too big for just one.'

'Are you talking about Gino?!' James had a wry smile.

She prodded the meat with some tongs, 'James! Focus, I want to hear about Darren, what's all this about him leaving today?'

The upshot was that Darren had to dash back for an audition and wouldn't be back for a week or more.

'I guess there wasn't time to talk?'

'No, I just helped him pack and organise the flights, please say you'll still be there tomorrow?'

'Tomorrow?'

'Mel... don't tell me you have forgotten already?!'

'Sorry yeh', as fat spat out the pan and onto her top. 'Damn, look, James, can you just flip this steak, whilst I change?'

James sensibly took the apron that was hanging up on the back of the door by the kitchen and proceeded to do as instructed.

'Sorry James, o thanks, yes so tomorrow, builder's dinner.'

'Well more a bbq type meal, you are coming then?'

'Yes of course,' she stopped and picked up her empty wine glass, then refilling them both. 'Will umm Mr Italian be there?'

'Haha I wondered if that might crop up, well he has been invited, and he does own the firm after all.'

'What do you think of him?'

'Are you interested?'

'No! Well, I don't know, this isn't what coming out here was going to be about, I just wanted to relax and enjoy my time here, then head home when Theresa is back.'

'Well surely this is part of *enjoying* yourself,' James uttered with a cheeky grin on his face.

'James, I am a middle-aged woman, I am very much out of practice!'

'Well Gino clearly likes you, plus stop putting yourself down, are those chips burning?'

'O God', opening the oven, some very charred looking frites sat smoking on the tray, 'umm well some are ok, right you carve and I will try and resurrect these sad-looking creatures.'

They sat at the round dining table, James had lit the candle in the middle and more wine had been poured, a rather nice St Emilion, Mel was going to try and remember it for the next time she went shopping.

'So, what can I bring tomorrow?'

'Just yourself, honestly, but I was wondering if you might come earlier than the others, help me set up etc.'

'Of course, what time?'

'6:30ish? I have my cleaning lady's daughter helping to serve drinks and food, but I need your cooking expertise,' he waggled a very burnt frite in Mel's direction.

'How dare you', she winked at James, 'Look the frites aren't great, but the cote de boeuf is yummy!'

'Yes, it's delicious, I'm impressed you went to a Boucherie and ordered it yourself, you often get jostled and pushed in those places sometimes if you hold up the queue.'

They chatted away for hours, it was well past midnight by the time James left, and when he had gone, the flat somehow felt very empty. Like something was missing. She cleared up and loaded the dishwasher, as she did so her phone made that familiar text alert sound.

*Hi Mel, how are things? It's 3 in the afternoon here, and I have been on the go since 7 am. I am knackered but the shop is taking shape. Chloe is very stressed and I'm doing my motherly duties to calm the situation, there is a delay in the fitting out. Might mean I have to stay on longer, would that be ok? Completely understand if not, right back to chasing builders! Much love Theresa xx'*

Mel sat down with a large glass of water and considered what impact this might have on things. Mel didn't mind staying, she was enjoying it, but it would be good to know how much longer, and what about Cathy and Rocky?

*Hi T, all good here, just finished dinner with that friend of mine James. Been really good to catch up, he has a business proposition for me, he wants me to join his house renovating business to focus on the interiors. Very exciting stuff. Glad it's going ok out there, hope Chloe is ok? Do you know roughly how much longer, I just need to let Cathy know back home and check she is ok? Love Mel xx*

It was too late to text Cathy, she would wait until morning. She could see a shaft of moonlight coming through the terrace doors, she went outside and inhaled deeply, the air was cool and its freshness brought on a reflective zeal in Mel, she dashed back inside and moments later reappeared with a notepad and pen.

*'Ideas for Interiors',* was the heading she noted down.

She listed things that she would need to read up on and research, places she could visit to get some inspiration and how she could help James. An hour or so later, she had a list, a 'to-do' list you might say. Sitting back and stretching she yawned, shut the book and proceeded to lose the pen, the outside light cast large shadows and it was impossible to find it. Reluctantly she decided she would wait until morning to resume the search.

   Somehow overnight in the damp filled morning, the pen had leaked across the tiles, well at least she could see where it was, but it wasn't her idea of fun, scrubbing away to try and get rid of the evidence. There she was in her baggy old 'Cats the musical' t-shirt and loose grey shorts when she heard a faint knock and 'Bonjour'. Simone, the cleaner was here, getting up quickly resulted in Mel banging her head on the table, after Simone had checked that there was no bleeding, Mel was sent to get changed. Mel re-emerged to see that the staining had been removed and no trace of blue ink could be seen.

'Merci Simone, ça va?'

'Bon, Merci, et toi?'

'Oui, bon.'

Simone scuttled off, Mel got the impression that she clearly didn't like silly interruptions to her work.

Mel dialled Cathy,

'Hi Cathy, how are you?'

'Hi, I am good thanks, ouch stop doing that....'

'You sure you're ok?'

'Yes, sorry Spaghetti is trying to get feed out of my hand and the bag!'

'Haha'

'He's a pain, naughty boy!'

'How's Rocky?'

'Good as gold, more to the point, how are you getting on?'

'Well', Mel could hear shuffling and banging at the other end of the line, so she decided to keep it quick and to the point. 'Theresa texted and is having some issues in Canada, she's asked me to stay on a bit longer.'

'O dear, is she ok?'

'Yes, though not everything's fine, you just know how builders can be, the main problem is she needs someone to house sit.'

'I hope you said yes!'

'Well, I wasn't sure, to be honest, I don't like leaving you with the horse and the house.'

'Look Mel, it's no problem, the house is fine, and Rocky is quite happy sharing a field with Spaghetti, honestly I'm enjoying doing it.'

'Ok you are a star, now there is some cash in my kitchen drawer, please use it to get some feed and bits you need.'

'Ok if you insist.'

'How is Chris?'

'He is fine, I think.'

'How do you mean?'

'Well, he has been working late and we are like ships in the night.'

'You sure you are ok? I will be back soon, please call if you need to.'

'Stop worrying about me, go and enjoy yourself...stop that, ouch...sorry, I forgot to ask, how are you getting on with James?'

'Really good, going there for dinner actually and he has a workable idea for us to get involved together on.'

'Mel that's so exciting, please keep me updated, I knew this trip would be good for you.'

'You are such a good friend Cathy, I don't know what I would do without you.'

'You can bring me back some sunshine and a good brie! Now off you go, I need to muck out.'

'Ok speak soon.'

'Text meee'

'I will, bye'

She heard the muffled sound of the horses neighing and panting, and then the line went dead. Mel googled the address James had given her the night before, which confirmed what he had already told her, that it was about a half an hour walk. It was now 11am. She decided to take something as a gift, but what? Wine and flowers felt boring and not fun, maybe a wander around the town would inspire her, so she flung the wicker bag over her shoulder, 'I'm heading out Simone, might see you later.'

'Oui Madame,' came the reply.

Mel found a bustling and busy Saturday in Nice, it seemed every square had a market, various bric-a-brac stalls, antiques and books.

*What do I get a guy who has everything?* Mel pondered as she browsed, suddenly she saw an Art Deco style poster 'La Plage de Monte Carlo', with two very suitably attired people swimming in the foreground and a stylised view of the Riviera in the background.

'Perfect!'

And after drifting past a food market and picking up a very large string of garlic bulbs, Mel felt that the clichéd bottle of wine and flowers were no match for these.

  Later that afternoon Mel googled the walk, which proved quite straightforward. She followed the route dutifully, through the Place de Garibaldi, crossing into the college area and into the residential northern side of Nice. The roads began to wind and the thrum of the city began to die down, eventually turning into a slightly inclined avenue, there was number 44, a Belle Époque style three storey villa, pale cream with light aquamarine wooden shutters. It looked beautiful, a typical Mediterranean house - the sort you see online and in books or at least expect to see.

Mel pressed the silver button below the speaker, the gates juddered and opened. 'Mel! Lovely to see you.'

James welcomed Mel with open arms, whilst wearing a very appropriate blue and white striped apron, and as they embraced, she pulled out her gifts, 'O Mel they are fab, thank you'.

'Well, I didn't want to be boring! Oh God is that the time? Sorry, it must have taken longer than I thought, 20 minutes-ish longer.'

The wide entrance hall gave way to a large open plan living room, with a kitchen and island at one end, and comfy chairs and a sofa the other encircling a modern log burner. As Mel proceeded through the room, she emerged through large brick arches, out onto a big terrace that overlooked a kidney-shaped pool below and the city of Nice was in the background, twinkling away.

'This is lovely, really amazing. What was it like when you bought it?'

'O god a wreck! Honestly, some rooms had no floors.'

At one end of the terrace was an inbuilt brick bbq, and next to that was a table groaning with an assortment of alcoholic beverages.

'Right, what can I do?' As Mel said this, she hoped that neither the bbq nor serving drinks would be required as she was not adept at either.

'Would you mind helping with the salads? Ahh, Juliette.'

Juliette was a willowy, petite, smartly dressed young lady. She had a crisp white shirt, black pencil skirt and black tights, with a sensible pair of black pumps. She was evidently the 'help' James had mentioned, as Mel watched her, she began laying out glasses and cutlery.

As the building crew that had been working for James filtered in, their masculine scents filled the air and there was lots of chatter and pointing at different elements of the building work. The various sized men seemed to gravitate to the booze and then the bbq, Mel considered it was clearly the *hunter gatherer* instinct, man and fire. Most spoke very good English, Mel felt awkward that her knowledge of their language was, to say at best, limited. One guest who of course could speak excellent English was, no other than, Mr Italian, Gino. His booming voice could be heard across the Riviera, 'Bella, where are the birdies?' 'Bella any new kills?'

Another guest enquired, 'Excusez-moi, vous êtes la serveuse?'

'Haha, non Pascal, this is Mel, a dear friend of mine, she isn't here to serve you!'

'Well, that brings my ego crashing down.' Mel looked on as she noted James deftly turning great chunks of meat over the flames.

'That's Pascal, he doesn't mean anything, in fact, he looked terribly embarrassed.'

She was grateful when James had finished his barbequing duties and was able to join in the party more, he threw off his apron and strode over to Mel. 'Are you ok? Sorry about Gino. He is very excitable. Now come on then, which one do you like?' James motioned towards the motley gathering.

'Huh?'

James leaned across Mel to reach for a bottle of wine, he filled up Mel's 'Which one takes your fancy?'

'I don't know! They are all attractive in their own ways.'

'Come on, which one or ones?'

'Well, he is nice'.

'That's Mario, nice guy, bit lazy.'

'He is nice, but seems very quiet compared to the rest, he's got the thickest arms I have ever seen!'

'That's Pierre, he's the stone mason'

'What about you?'

'Me? Mel I am spoken for!' winked James, 'but if you were to push, I think I like Marcel, he's the one over there, strong brute, I have never seen anyone lift so much as he, plus he is tall, I like tall guys.' James' eyes gazed on after Marcel.

'Darren is shorter than you!..' Mel stopped, realising that such an observation was very insensitive, but the wine was kicking in and her tongue was loose.

'I know, tell me about it, well we need to talk about Darren, but in the meantime let's have some fun.'

'This is Mel have you met?' James took Mel by the hand and guided her into a crowd.

Later that evening, the conversation had reached fever pitch and the music had been cranked up, Mel observed Juliette. She flirted naturally with the guys, it wasn't smutty or lurid, but amorous. Mel didn't know why, or indeed had no justification for, a pang of jealousy that crept over her. Was it because she wanted to have the art of seduction played out to her, or was it because she was not a twenty-something with rock hard breasts?

'Madame?' Juliette went to top up Mel's glass.

'Thank you, Juliette.'

Mel would have usually offered that Juliette should call her 'Mel', but at that moment Mel felt less than charitable toward Juliette. The moon was clear as the inky blue took over the night's sky, the gin-clear sky allowed the nocturnal rays to shimmer on the pool surface, the cicadas began to click away in the background, as the 80's music James had selected drifted off into the night. Mel danced with James and with others as the party continued, the warm evening meant frequent pauses to quench thirst.

'May I?'

'Yes, you may.'

A tall stocky guy, in an open collar grandad style shirt and black jeans, proffered to fill up Mel's glass, she recognised him as the guy from earlier who had mistaken her for a waitress.

'I don't think we have been introduced, as you can see, I am not the staff', Mel had a wry smile across her red lips.

'I am so embarrassed, please I am sorry, I am Pascal, and I am a carpenter for James.'

'Well, you have done an amazing job, the house is incredible'. Just then Pascal reached across Mel and grazed her arm, she felt an almost electric buzz shoot through her, something she hadn't felt for years.

'Are you ok?'

'Yes sorry…'

'Bella, I keep telling you, stop saying sorry' Gino raised up his hands, as he put his arm around her, 'What about a dance?'

Mel turned but Pascal had disappeared, slunk off to be with a group that was discussing, well Mel thought they were, the craftsmanship of the pool. She wasn't getting the same giddy excitement with Gino, though she had to admit that it was very flattering, she couldn't remember the last time she'd felt that shiver of excitement course through her body from the touch of a man, was it really over 20 years ago?

'Gino, I am just having a drink, maybe afterwards, I will dance.' Forgetting all social etiquette, she grabbed a bottle of rosé and filled her glass up to the very top and chugged down quite a bit.

'You ok?' Asked James who was now at her side.

'Yes sorry, where are my manners?'

James pulled Mel into a recess of one of the arches, 'now Mel, be honest, are you ok?'

'Yes, I am fine, just I am so out of practice, I feel like I am going to make a fool of myself. Maybe I already have?'

'Now that's rubbish, you look fab, you are here to let your hair down, both of those guys are cute and clearly have eyes for an English rose.' he nudged her with his elbow. 'Now let's go mingle and have fun.'

She grabbed him by the arm as he turned away, 'I need to know what is happening with you and Darren, I am worried about you.'

'Look it's under control, I just have to wait until the time is right Mel, but between you and me, *it's over*. There is a rumour that he has gotten very close to one of his co-stars. I have to get things sorted, financially I mean. In fact, I am doing that on Monday.' He raised up his glass, 'To you Mel.'

'No James to you and this fantastic house.'

'Wait until we work on our projects together.'

Mel stood and watched James bound back into the social whirl, she swayed slightly steadied herself and took a deep breath - *This is your time Mel, this trip could change everything.*

SPLOSH!

The noise echoed throughout the house, Mel turned to look down at the pool, where the sound had come up from, the lights in the pool made the water dance, a big plume of water shot into the air.

'Who was it?'

'Come on Bella!'

She might have guessed, what would she do about Mr Italian? He was gorgeous to look at, what Cathy might have referred to as 'eye candy', but was he really what Mel needed on this trip. 'Bella, no birdies in here, come.' His bronzed chiselled torso, his tight body and matinee idol features were certainly eye candy, more than Mel had seen for a very long time.

'Well?' James was now by her side, 'he wants you Mel, supposedly he is loaded, maybe just a few lunches and dinners, have fun!'

'James stop it, plus I have nothing to swim in or get dry and I really should be getting back, I need a taxi…'

'Don't be silly, stay here, now let's go.'

She watched as James pulled off his shirt, jeans and plunged boxers only, into the pool. Mel had to admit the evening was a warm one and the pool looked very inviting, soon a few others had joined in, even Pascal had jumped in, his body was not as lean as Mr Italian, but broad and heavyset, with rugby player legs and a hairy chest. His huge hands seem to be able to swamp anyone else when it comes to splashing water at each other. It did look like fun, and James did say *'mingle and have fun.'*

Mel thanked her lucky stars that she had put on a matching pair of underwear on, back home it was whatever selection was on top of her drawer. Mel took the plunge, quite literally in fact, down to her white crop top style bra and matching white pants, she jumped into the pool. As she resurfaced, the refreshing water flowed over her, she used both hands to wipe her hair back, but something was wrong, the noise and clatter had died down, opening her eyes she could sense all was not right. Suddenly there was a commotion and James was in front of her, he tugged at her bra strap.

James spun around in the water, and clapped, 'right where is that beach ball?'

## Chapter 21 - Which one was Pascal?

In the late morning debrief the next day, it had turned out that in her dash to the pool, her left breast had exposed itself, nip and all.

'James what am I like? I told you I would make a fool of myself!'

'Don't be silly it was an accident, and quite honestly, I had to do something to stop the boys from staring! I don't think any complained. Now drink your coffee, do you want a croissant?'

Mel looked down at the noir liquid in her cup.

'Look if it's any consolation, Marcel managed to lose his underwear apparently, he got in the pool naked, no one noticed and when he came to leave, he couldn't find them until I saw them dangling from one of my olive trees on the terrace this morning!'

'Haha, well hopefully that and the booze might erase people's memory of "tit gate". At least it might keep Gino off my back for a bit, or maybe it will make him worse?'

'Well, he's not the only one who's keen you know.'

'What do you mean?'

'Pascal, the one you liked, also likes you.'

'How do you know? What did he say?' Rubbing her head, the hangover was real, 'Remind me, which one was Pascal?'

'Built like a brick shit house and hands like shovels, he didn't say much, but he left you a note, and asked me to give it to you this morning.' James handed Mel a scrappy bit of paper folded.

*Hello Mel, I am sorry for thinking you were a waitress. I would love the opportunity to see you again. Pascal.*

'Christ, are all men like buses, wait for years and two come along at once? What do you think I should do?'

'Honestly? Play the game, when did you last have two guys chasing after you? You said you wanted to enjoy your time here, and it's not forever, you'll go home soon.'

'I don't want to think about that right now. I need another coffee please, then I am going to go for a swim in the sea, do you want to come?'

'Yes, love too.'

James and Mel, went via the apartment, so she could change into suitable attire, and as she entered the sea she tried to subtly tap both her breasts just to make sure they were both safe.

'I saw that!'

'Well, could you pretend you didn't? I am not showing the whole of the Cote d'Azur my baps.'

They splashed and bathed in the celeste coloured salty waters. The beach had started to get quite busy by the time they clambered over the pebbles to their beach bags and towels.

'Shall we head back to mine and continue the debrief?' Mel offered.

'I am dying for a cup of tea, let's go.'

Some clouds had started to appear, although the warm heavy heat remained. In the breeze on the roof terrace, they could relax and ponder each other's futures. From further discussion, it was clear James was terribly unhappy with Darren, and that until he could separate his monetary affairs from Darren's, even though they weren't married, the new house had been bought in both names, James was stuck, he needed a clean break. It turned out that Darren had just got a part in an obscure daytime soap, and was relishing the newfound fame, which also brought in temptations of the flesh with over-excited fans.

'I am sure that the new soap he has a part in wouldn't like negative publicity?' Mel had her old marketing and PR hat on.

'How do you mean?'

'If you could get evidence of his behaviour, I am sure an anonymous letter to the producers would bring an untimely end to his career.' A smirk crossed Mel's mouth as she thought about Darren and how self-absorbed he had been at lunch.

'Mel, how can we do it?'

'Well, you could say you had been contacted by a newspaper back home, and they are threatening to run the story, "New soap star caught with trousers down etc."'

'But we don't have anything, why would he believe me?'

'Well, you could say you have been phoned by the editor of "Smash Spy magazine", who says they can get proof. You are so disappointed and for the sake of both parties, you will deny the story to avoid any bad publicity at this crucial time in *his* career. But after learning this, the only course of action is to end the relationship as you need to spend time abroad with a new business partner.'

'Blimey Mel, you are good at this, what do I need to do?'

'Let me think, one thing on our side is that Darren's ego is bigger than his brain, he won't want to risk losing the soap job.'

Occasionally in the past, she had concocted a good story, with a believable rationale behind it, she just hoped that by calling Darren's bluff and making it all about him the plan would work. Only time will tell.

'I am going to do it now!'

'What? Wait, James... '

Before Mel could stop her friend, he was speaking to Darren. Mel watched on and occasionally mouthed, 'What's happening?' 'What is he saying'?

As James spoke, he scrawled on the back of an envelope.

*D not happy with me either, please deny, doesn't want to ruin career, have told him I want house.*

'OK well, I think it's best then that I set up a meeting with Clive, the solicitor tomorrow, to confirm in writing? Yes. OK. Well I hope all goes well, no hard feelings. Yep, thank you. Yep, Good luck. Bye Darren.'

'Well?'

James stood for a moment, the phone held out in front of him, clasped in the palm of his hand, he was just staring at the screen.

'Turns out he wasn't happy either and that he is very grateful for everything, and please could I deny the rumours, plus the house is mine, he has agreed that London is where he wants to be not down here.'

James turned to Mel, 'I don't know what to say, how did you come up with that?'

'I don't know, reading too many magazines and too much time on my hands.'

'I think we should celebrate!'

'James no, I haven't recovered from last night, let's celebrate when the papers for the house are sorted, yeh?'

'Ok, wow I feel like a weight has been lifted, what do I do now?'

'Let him sweat a bit, he will most likely be worried until he knows you have denied the rumours, and if he starts to play up then you can threaten to say the rumours are true, which they are, so you haven't lied.' A smug smile now covered Mel's face, she tried to shield it under her sunglasses and beach hat, but to be honest she wanted to yell from the rooftop. I did *it, I helped my friend!*

'Right ok, please can we turn to you now, it's much more exciting, two guys after you!'

Mel sat back, sipped her tea. She was out of practice with men. What would she say or do if either suitor made advances, was she ready for that sort of thing? Should she even contemplate getting involved in such activities?

'What are you worried about?'

'I am worried James, I haven't been with any other guy since I was in my twenties, then I got married. I have only known one guy in that way. It's the sex that worries me, plus do you realise how much work I need to do on myself before any such fumbling could happen?'

'Mel, you are worrying when there is nothing to worry about, these guys just want to take you for lunch or dinner, yes, they may get amorous but only if you want it too. Also, I know a great spa where we can get ourselves sorted', James winked.

'You and me?'

'Course, I want to get out there too!'

That was settled, James was going to sort out the house and legal matters on Monday, they were both going to hit the spa on Tuesday. Mel just hoped the beautician was well versed in dealing with a middle-aged lady, whose nether regions looked more like a woodland thicket.

'So, who are you going to text first?'

'I don't have Pascal's number…'

'I do', said James cheekily.

Two messages were duly sent, 'Well let's see what they have to say, I am very surprised by both men, why me?'

'Mel, we have talked about this, now I am going to love you and leave you. I have to be bright for my chat with the lawyers tomorrow.'

'Ok, now you got everything?'

'Yes,' he kissed her on the cheek. 'Be kind to yourself.'

'I will see you soon, keep me posted on what happens tomorrow.'

As she closed the front door, her phone flashed and bleeped.

*Bella, how are you? Last night was fun, no? Dinner with me next week? xxx*

Mel wasn't sure if she had the energy to get into a texting session with Gino. The lunch the other week had been lovely, and he was stunning to drool over. She replied.

*Hi Gino, yes it was great fun, how is your head? Sounds good. M x*

Mel was not about to go overboard with the kisses at the end of the message nor was she about to add emojis. A bath is what she needed now, a long soak, get the saltiness off and a good night's sleep was what was required. Her phone flashed again.

*Hello Mel, I am glad you got my note, I must say sorry for my rudeness last night, please will you let me take you out for lunch? Pascal x*

All she could think of was the size of his hands, like dinner plates, no wonder he was good at what he did. With those hands and arms he could lift anything, Mel now had a mental image of Pascal picking her up and... a bath, she must run a bath and reply later.

Warm and foaming, the bubbles overran the sides of the bath. Mel soaked as she considered her choices. Two very different guys, two potentially different outcomes, but one issue - she would be gone within the month. Well, what was there to lose? She made a mental note to chat through with James the next time she saw him. Wrapping herself in a bathrobe, her feet pitter-pattered on the tile flooring as she whipped up her notebook and pen from her bedside table and sat in the living room, and continued her notes on business ideas. She didn't want to let James down, she wanted to show him she had proposals and 20 years hadn't dulled her killer instinct for colours and fabrics. Suddenly jumping up, she moved over to the bookshelves. Theresa had an array of interior books and even some old paint charts. Mel was excited, this is what was lacking, a focus. Now she had to make it work.

*

A good night's sleep had helped, Mel felt good, better than good, she felt the best she had felt in a long time. A lot was going on, new avenues to explore work-wise and potential holiday romances, but she was in control. This was truly a time for rediscovery, all because of a chance letter. Energised to start working. She'd read all about women who had gone back to work and started again, but Mel had not been ready or that anything offered was not right. This time it felt different, she would be working with someone fabulous and in an industry she knew.

## Chapter 22 - Flashback - 9 to 5

'How is the presentation coming along?' - The words of Bluedot Marketing & PR Chief Executive sent panic into Mel, this was the first big client she had to prepare for alone, and was attending the meeting with her junior colleague.

'Ummm it's going well Faust, just last-minute additions'.

'Ok sounds good, now you have to go get them, and don't work late tonight, get rest and be raring to go tomorrow.'

Mel didn't know why she panicked, Faust was a genuine and kind man, his father was German and his mother Danish.

'Thank you, we won't.' Mel gestured to a bespectacled and lanky junior designer, James. He sat opposite her, gazing up at Faust, nodding like one of those dogs that sit in the back of people's cars.

The pitch was ready, the mood boards were done, they just needed to print out the presentation notes and they were done.

The client was in the hotel industry and needed to combine tradition whilst keeping up to date with the latest trends. 'Don't forget the fax machines,' injected the Procurement Manager at the first briefing meeting. Subsequent meetings had been productive, and Mel had enjoyed the buzz, speed, and intensity of the work.

Though initially things had felt daunting, 'Go on, do this one Mel.' She had, and now she was leading the business into new directions, with carte blanche to go for it, and to take her graduate with her.

He had proved himself on smaller projects and now it was time for both of them to go for a large contract, one that could propel their careers and credibility. With that in mind, she and James had put in the hours and worked hard on the pitch, concept, and planning.

'How you feeling?' inquired James as they fought for seats on the 8:14am train from Waterloo. Doors slammed shut, the whistle sounded, and the train juddered as it built up pace, as they stowed their massive carry bags in the overhead space.

'I am ok, just a bit nervous. I feel like we have covered all the bases, how about you?'

'Yeh good, just like you, a bit nervous... 'James paused as a gentleman in a wide pinstripe suit pulled out a brick-sized mobile phone. 'Do you think they will catch on?'

'Not sure, they are very big, maybe if they were smaller, plus you'd never get any peace and quiet!'

'How long did it say to Guildford?'

'About half an hour, means we are there in plenty of time.'

\*

The next few hours had flown by and before they knew it, they were back standing at Guildford station, the train was late, but the mood between the two was high, full of nervous energy.

'We did it, James!' Mel clung to a lukewarm polystyrene cup of coffee.

'You did it Mel, they loved your ideas.'

'Hold this will you? I am going to find a payphone and give Faust a call'

As she shoved the coins in the slot, her hands were shaking as she dialled the number.

'Hi Sharon, it's Mel, can you put me through to Faust?'

There was a brief pause, before she heard the receiver picked up,

'Hi Mel, sorry but I am about to…'

'We did it, we got the contract!'

'What? You star, you did it, Mel. Well done.'

'Thank you, I am just so pleased, James too.'

'Right well you two have the afternoon off, get lunch, somewhere decent - company treat, then tomorrow we can get heads together for a proper celebratory catch up.'

'Faust, I am not sure…'

'Mel, go! Congratulations, and thank James for me. See you tomorrow'.

'Thank you, bye Faust.'

She replaced the receiver.

'Mel this is our train!' James shouted across the platform.

James was holding the door open, Mel ran, she leapt on board. He slammed the door behind them, puffing and panting as they slumped down into dusty, worn seats, the train clattering along. James and Mel were just gibbering with excitement. 'James, do you like Mussels?'

\*

She opened the door with her latch key, pushed the door with her hip, and threw her keys onto the hallway table.

'That you?' Mark questioned from the kitchen, she could hear the radio on. The lunch had been quite a long one, over-excitement was to blame.

'Yes love, you ok?'

'All ok thanks, you?'

'Darling guess what?'

She handed him a cold bottle of Champagne, as she kissed him on the cheek.

'What's all this?'

'Well, you know that big client we were presenting to?'

'Yes, you didn't?'

'I did!'

'That's amazing, well done you, shall I crack this open?'

'Yes, that's what it is for! Also, dinner, what do you fancy? Takeaway? My treat.'

'Here, sip this.'

Mel took the glass of the sparkling liquid, but what was that? Something in the bottom of the glass - a ring!

Mel was elated, but oddly she felt deflated at the same time, the one triumph she had felt was worth celebrating was now gazumped by a marriage proposal, and a rather clumsy one at that, what if she hadn't come home with the fizz?

*

The career Mel had foreseen had never come to fruition, the wedding and the pregnancy had put a stop to that dead in its tracks. James had gone on to do great things with the company, Faust had been at the wedding. 'If you ever want to come back…'

Mel devoted her time to the boys and marriage because that was the right thing to do, surely? How could she be so selfish as to stop all that because of one success at work? Mel was offered other roles but turned them down because her life had changed, she was a mother and a wife. All girls dream to be that? Don't they?

## Chapter 23 - Problem solver extraordinaire

It was in the afternoon when there had been a knock at the door. *Who could that be*? Pondered Mel as she walked down the hallway to the front door.

'Annette! Lovely to see you.'

Annette somehow looked younger, more vibrant than before. Removing herself from the confines of the apartment, out into the light had done wonders, the initial age that Mel had put on her, now seemed way off. Taking a closer look as Annette stepped in through the doorway, she realised that she couldn't be more than 55.

'I hope you don't mind, but Albert has gone out to meet some friends for a drink and I hoped you might be in.'

'Of course,' quickly trying to tidy up the papers and books that were scattered across the coffee table and on the floor.

'Sorry about this, I was trying to get some bits together for a project.'

'Looks interesting, tell me more.'

As it was only just gone 3, and Mel feeling like she could give her liver rest, offered tea.

'Lovely thanks, wow what a view.'

'I know, everyone says that. Do you take sugar?'

'No thanks, just a bit of milk.'

Annette was now standing in the doorway between the outside and inside, 'Please go out, I won't be a moment, make yourself comfortable' proffered Mel.

'Here you go, hope it's ok?' Mel handed Annette her tea.

'Yes lovely, so you are house sitting?'

The conversation seemed to follow a similar vein to the one they'd had the other day, until Mel asked her where home was normally.

'I miss it terribly. I thought I could get used to it here. I do like it, but I miss home.'

'Do you not get back?'

'Well not really, Albert isn't keen and to be honest, I haven't had the courage, that sounds silly, doesn't it?'

'No not at all, I will let you into a secret, I nearly didn't come here, I didn't think I had the courage or will, to do it.'

'Really? What changed your mind?'

Sensing that the time wasn't right to go into all the details and bore poor Annette with her life story, Mel simply said, 'My life was not all I thought it should be and this offered a change.'

Annette sat there in silence, she looked down into her cup of tea, then her blue eyes drifted out to the view. Mel was aware that this lady wasn't happy, a deeper emotion lay just under the surface, was it sorrow? Looking on, it hit home how much this woman's life was just like Mel's but 10 years ahead, and if Mark had survived would this have been Mel's life? Or would he have been a changed man, wanting to live life to the full and not waste a second?

'Would you like to go back?'

'I would,' Annette turned to face Mel, 'I really would, just for a few weeks.

'I don't see why you can't, why don't you stay at my house?'

'What?' Said Annette as she choked on her tea.

'Why not, I am here, or even if I was back home, you could come to stay, it's just me, and a horse.'

'I don't know what to say?'

'Say yes! That's what I did and now look, I am here and having a great time, you will be the same I am sure.'

'What about Albert, he doesn't like being left alone?'

'Leave him to me.' As Mel uttered the words she began to panic, what would she say to Albert, how would she convince him?

At that moment, Mel's phone flashed and vibrated, 'Sorry do you mind, just in case it is Theresa, the lady I am house sitting for.' To be honest Mel just wanted a quick respite to think about a solution for Annette.

*Bella! How nice to get your message, does Wednesday work for you? I can pick you up? Gino x*

She looked up at Annette, 'sorry about this.'

'Please don't worry, is it your friend?'

'Well, a friend of sorts, he's a guy I met at a party.'

'How lovely, what's his name?'

'Gino, a tanned stunner, and I'm not sure why he wants to take me for dinner?'

'Mel, look I know we hardly know one another, but when I met you the other week. I could tell you were a warm-hearted, lovely person. A lady with a lot of love to give and you are if you don't me saying, a very attractive woman.'

Mel considered what Annette had said. Annette had said it with such warmth, no maliciousness, no jealousy. She had, wrongly, assumed that when women compliment each other it is usually tinged with a hint of spite.

'Annette that's a lovely thing to hear, well to tell you the truth, I have another guy who also wants to take me out,' and as that sounded conceited, Mel added, 'but that is to apologise for mistaking me for a waitress.'

'Men are mad! You've just told me to go for it, well I am offering you the same advice, go for it Mel.'

As she replied, she considered the problem surrounding Annette's trip to the UK, 'What if we said we had a mutual friend, who was recovering from an illness and needed someone to help her, and as I am out here, she thought of you?'

'That could work, I like this, who shall we say I am going to look after?'

They discussed the details of the ailment the mutual friend had, and when and for how long Annette had known them.

'Do you think Albert will be ok with it?'

'I don't know, he is just a bit of a stick in the mud, he is good hearted though, I think it's the age thing, he is 70, and I am 54. It didn't matter so much early on, but now I want to do things, see people, and explore and he's just happy to sit at home most days. As you were saying, I just would like the opportunity to do something for myself.'

'Well maybe we don't have to lie, just be honest with him. Tell him how you feel and what you need, it's only fair that you enjoy your life too.'

As she spoke, Mel could sense the similarities between Annette and Albert and her and Mark, both going in different directions in life, and possibly impacting the longevity of the relationship. As the sun started to lose its heat, Mel took down the parasol, 'I like to feel a bit of warmth on my skin at this time of the day.'

'Would you like another?'

'No thank you, I will pop back if that's ok? I want to tell Albert what I want to do.'

'Ok well, take my number, let me know how it goes, I am sure it will be fine.'

'Thank you again', she took Mel's hand and kissed her on the cheek. 'You are lovely inside and out, remember that.'

The latch clicked shut, Mel hoped that Albert would see reason and not stop Annette going. Mel poured herself a cool white wine spritzer and sat out on the terrace and replied to Pascal's message from earlier in the day.

*Sounds lovely, no need to apologise! Sorry for the delay in replying, where and when? M x*

The sun was low now, rather than the bright yellow, it was beginning to have a hazy orange hue about it, as it sank below the castle hill.

Two further texts dropped in as Mel absorbed the early evening sun.

*I will pick you up at 8, on Wednesday evening. Gino xxx*

*Hi Mel, does Wednesday lunchtime sound ok, a picnic? Pascal x*

*Blimey!* thought Mel, *2 dates in one day, what will James think of this!* She wasn't sure whether to tell Theresa or Cathy, it didn't feel right somehow when one was trying to help out her daughter and the other was looking after her house and horse! She quickly typed out a text to James.

*Hi, keep me posted on how you get on tomorrow with house/Darren, shall we get together tomorrow evening? Mel x*

She had almost forgotten about the James saga, she hoped that it did go ok for him, he deserved it too.

She needed to tell Cathy about Annette, but she would wait until morning. In pursuit of trying to solve people's problems, she was mentally drained, and tomorrow could well be another long day. She slept soundly that night, her last thought had been that of Annette, and how she wished she could be a fly on the wall in the downstairs flat.

## Chapter 24 - Houses and More

'So that is all he said?'

'Yeh and he would rather just make a clean break and doesn't even care about the house. Clive, my solicitor, has sent over papers today and by this afternoon, if Darren signs them, then the house is all mine!'

'I feel like you need a comical villainous laugh at the end of that.'

'Huh huh ha ha.' James hysterically mimics her suggestion.

'James, that's awful! Right, so I have also started to pull together business ideas.'

'Great ok, well if you come to mine, that sounds good - *mine*, and bring some overnight stuff, we can plot and plan over some bubbles.'

'Sounds great, 6ish ok for you?'

'Perfect see you then, this is going to be exciting!'

'I hope so, what can I bring?'

'Nothing, now pack your bag.'

Mel couldn't believe it, the plan had worked, and Darren had scuttled back into his dark little hole from where he came, and James and she were free to pursue this business idea. She stopped and said out loud to herself. 'What are you doing, you idiot, you are going home in a few weeks, this can't work!' She could feel her bottom lip quiver. 'I want it to work though'.

She decided that she needed to talk it over with Cathy and see what she would say and how she reacted. She dialled the number, but there was no answer, she looked at the time. Mid-afternoon, a Pilates session was probably keeping her away from telling her closest friend what was going on. Just at that moment, her phone jumped into life, it was Cathy.

'Cathy, hi it's Mel'

'Hi yes, I know, are you ok? You don't sound alright, what's happened?'

'No, no, I am fine, sorry, I just, well there are a few things I need to talk to you about.'

'Just promise me you are ok and safe.'

'Yes, I am fine, I am in the apartment and safe.'

'Ok well, what's up? You've got me worried now!'

'I just wanted to tell you what's been happening, that's all and I need your opinion.'

'Sounds exciting, I am all ears…'

Mel recalled everything that had happened, in as succinct way as possible, Cathy had been very quiet and just the occasional 'Uhm' or 'ok'.

'Wow sounds like you have loads going on, look I think you should just enjoy the boys, when was the last time you let your hair down and went on a date, even if you did flash them your boob!'

'Please don't remind me, and please don't tell a soul'.

'Course not, now look about the business, why can't you just see how it goes, you can split your time between here and France, even with Brexit I am sure you can. I can do some digging for you to check, I can ask Chris?'

'Thank you, I can do some too and I will ask James. What do I do about Rocky? I can't leave him with you for half the year!'

'Well, oh hold on,' the phone went muffled, 'you there?'

'Yes, I am here, you ok?'

'Sorry, I was just trying to hang up some washing and the phone fell in the wash basket, now where were we, yes Rocky, well I am happy to look after him, but do you remember that niece of mine, the one in Oxfordshire? Well, she has always wanted a horse, nothing fast or scary, just one for children to sit on and ride. I could ask?'

Mel considered for a moment, was she being selfish? At least he would go to a nice home, and in all honesty, she hadn't ridden him in ages.

'Ok well see what they say, but honestly, I will be coming back to sort stuff out and we can go over it all then, in more detail.'

'OK so you are ok, let me send you some money for feed and stuff, I insist.'

'Ok, do you have my bank details?'

'Yup, so quickly, you think looking into this business idea is a good one?'

'Yes, next question.' Cathy was joking, Mel could tell.

'Alright, I think I know what you will say to my next one…'

'Yes, and double yes, stop worrying Mel. It will be fun and if it stops being enjoyable, just say no thanks, or say you have got to go back to England.'

'Thanks Cathy, I want to know about you now?'

'About me?'

'Yes, how's home, Chris?'

'Well, Chris and I have been a bit, umm…'

'You can tell me, Cathy.'

'Well distant, hardly seeing one another. He keeps having to work late and then at weekends we just seem to do different things. Did this happen to you?'

Mel had to think quickly, she couldn't very well tell Cathy that the last 20 years of marriage was a drudgery.

'Every now again, I think what you should do is plan a nice evening meal, cook something you both love, good wine.'

'You are right.'

'I know I am, but are you ok?'

'I am, I am just longing for the weather to get better, I miss the sun on my face.'

'Well, if I do start this business, you better be coming out to see me!'

'Of course, just let me know when!'

'Deal.'

'OK well let me know how it goes with Chris.'

'Will do! You two timer'. She could hear her laughing

'Stop it you!'

'Bye, Mel

'Bye Cathy'

Cathy dropped the phone that was sandwiched between her chin and ear and caught it in her hand, turning to her lunch date - 'You won't believe it, she's got two men on the simmer and got her bap out at a bbq!'

# Part 2

The walk to James's was now much easier since Mel knew where she was headed. She had felt much more confident since talking to Cathy. It was good to have her as a sounding board and a dear friend, especially in times of trouble.

The evenings were getting lighter, as the longest day approached as did the amount of sunlight and heat. By the time she had reached the villa with its imposing wooden driveway gates and high wall, she was rather warm, resembling a sweaty pomegranate, so she dabbed her face with a tissue. The gates drew open and walking up the brick steps to the front door, she was greeted by James, glass in hand already. Though his initial expression wasn't what Mel was expecting.

'Umm you ok, you have ummm....'

'bloody hell, is it a bug?'

He was looking at her face with a deep expression of concern, 'James tell me!'

'Umm, you have tissue remnants all over your face. Come in, let's get you sorted.'

Looking in the hallway mirror, she saw a truly bizarre sight, a mixture between damp tissue that had blended nicely with damp foundation, the impression of peeling skin or a "Doctor who" villain.

'Here drink this.'

James handed her a champagne flute brimming with icy cool bubbles which she swigged while wiping her face with a cloth James had provided. 'God look at me'.

'Don't be silly, you can't help it.'

'Jesus what if this had happened before my dates!'

'So, I am not on a date?' winked James.

'O darling you are of course, but you bat for the other team!'

'Haha right! Are you all done looking like a star trek extra, we need to get to business and gossip.'

They made their way out onto the sun-speckled terrace, there were two large grey wooden chairs with huge, enormous yellow cushions on them. Between was a matching table with an ice bucket and a bowl of olives on it. Mel also noted a flip chart board to one side.

'This looks lovely, but this slightly concerns me.' She said while gesticulating toward the office equipment.

'I can see behind that wry smile of yours, now have an olive and tell me what's going on with the boys!'

'Well…'

James was suitably updated and was able to give his appraisal of the situation. 'Well, I think you should go with the flow, enjoy it.'

'Right ok, so that's me, what about you, tell me about Darren.'

'There isn't much to tell,' James got up out of his seat, 'two secs'. On his return, he had his laptop with him, 'look at that.' Mel squinted and nodded as she read some long-winded legalised document.

'So that's it? Just one bit of paper and it's all sorted?'

'Basically yeh, he just wants to focus on his acting.' James mimed as if he was doing a very flamboyant bow. Laughing together, Mel dug out her notebook and some magazines from her bag and plonked them onto her lap.

'What are those?'

'These are my notes and some ideas I have had for places where we can research and get inspiration.'

They talked through the ideas and James showed Mel some design he had for the next project, 'It's a villa that needs doing up, it's just outside of the city on the way to Avignon, set up in the hills. You will love it!'

'Ok, and what is the investment we are looking at?'

'You are being all businessy today! Well, it's coming on the market soon, I have a guy that looks out for things for me, he thinks around €400,000, but we may be able to work it down a tad.'

Mel's feet began to wriggle slightly, twisting and turning. She did have some money, but that was a big chunk and what if it didn't work out?

'Ok so is that €400,000 each?'

'No no, it's €200,000 each if you want to be 50/50.'

'I don't know, I haven't done anything like buying a house, let alone one in a different country, I would need to check what cash I have left since Mark died…'

She broke off, unable to think about Mark, with everything going on she had barely considered Mark, usually, she would have thought about him most days.

James topped up her glass, 'look let's leave this for now, the groundwork is done. We can hopefully view the place in a week or so, and then we can go from there, plus I want to get you on the website and sort the paperwork out to bring you on as a partner.'

'James I am sorry, I am excited, just my head is spinning as to what I should do.'

'I know it's a lot to take in, let's pick it up another day. My only bit of advice would be to go with your gut instinct.'

## Chapter 25 - Double Trouble

Mel tried to use her gut instinct when it came to her suitors, she knew that the Italian stallion, Gino, was very much the playboy. Pascal on the other hand had a rugged charm about him, the tall broad-set Frenchman appealed at first sight, but then Gino had interrupted at James' party. Did he do it by accident or on purpose? Unsure of which, Mel decided there was only one way to find out.

She had a lot to think about, what to do about the business idea with James, €200,000 was a lot of money, but she trusted James, she had confided in him, and he had reciprocated. Strolling downstairs in a borrowed pair of jogging shorts and a vest, she had completely forgotten to pack those essentials. 'Morning, sleep ok?' James was just pouring a steaming hot cup of coffee from the cafetiere, 'Yes great thanks, you?'

'All good, just excited about these,' he pointed at Mel's pad and notes. 'Really? I wasn't sure if I might be a bit rusty!'

'No, I think they are really good, I want you to meet some of the people I use for projects, builders, designers, and carpenters', he winked, 'but I am sure you will get to know my carpenter very well.'

'James, stop it! It's only a picnic.'

'Picnic? That is romantic, I wonder where?'

Tomorrow lunchtime Mel would find out, she would also find out more about Pascal. James had offered to ring her halfway through to check she was ok. 'I am sure I will be fine, plus you have known him for how long?' 5 years apparently, Mel felt that was a good length of time to know someone pretty well.

Mel had woken to a couple of text messages that morning, one being Theresa checking Mel was ok to stay on for a bit longer as she had asked, the other was Cathy telling her that Rocky would have a home if she did want to sell him. Mel hadn't even considered selling, she was going to give him away, but the thought of some extra cash would be useful, especially if she needed to invest in this house with James. Responding to Theresa first,

*Hi darling, very well thanks how are you and how is Chloe? All good to stay on, there are some things I would like to ask you when you have a moment. M xx*

Then she jabbed at her phone,

*Hi Cathy, That's good news, what do you think price-wise? I hope all is ok? Lots going on here, I need to update you. Are you free later this week for a chat? Mel xx*

Later that day, whilst Mel was picking through her clothing selection, and appraising each piece for its suitability for a picnic and another hanging ready for her evening date, Theresa called.

'Hi Mel, how are you?'

'Yeh all good, how are you?'

'Not too bad, just a nightmare trying to get things done. Workmen seem to work on their own time frames!'

'I can imagine, how is Chloe?'

'She is good, stressed, but slowly we are getting there, how are you getting on, still enjoying Nice?'

'Yes, I am, actually that's one of the things I wanted to run by you.'

'Of course, you are ok though aren't you?'

'Well you know that friend of mine James, he has a business proposal, well idea, for me and him to work together and join forces on the next property.'

'Fab sounds great, just make sure you get it sorted legally, I can help with that if you need.'

'I may do, though James seems to be in control and I do trust him.'

'Go for it I say, but what has this got to do with Nice?'

'Well, James and his business are mainly based here, and I wondered how difficult it would be for me too…'

'You mean you want to live here? That's amazing, I would love you to be nearby!'

Mel knew that Theresa may get over-excited and take over somewhat, maybe she should have thought this through a bit more before announcing her intentions to Theresa.

'Yes, that would be fun, do you think it would be doable for me?'

'God yes, simple, I can help you with visas etc.'

'There is something else… I have *two* dates!' As she said it out loud, Mel's excitement turned to worry, she was mid folding a jumper and stopped and waited for Theresa's reply. Would she be annoyed, how dare this woman run off with two men after my brother dies…?

'O my god! That's so exciting, you need to fill me in!'

Mel sat down on the bed, fingering a silk scarf, as she told Theresa some of the details, she didn't go into boob-gate or the amount of wine consumed, Theresa had an air of a schoolmistress that could easily be used to scold for misbehaviour.

'You dark horse, so when are these dates?'

'Tomorrow, one at lunchtime the other in the evening'

'Well, I hope the lunchtime one doesn't overrun.'

Mel went quiet, she hadn't thought of that, she had assumed possibly very incorrectly, that it would be over quite quickly.

'I am sure it won't. It's just a picnic and I'm sure he is just being polite, to offer an apology, have a bite to eat and probably never hear from him again.'

'Mel! Stop that! He wouldn't have left you the note, he wouldn't have texted. He wants to see you, just enjoy it, and go with your gut instinct.'

'That's odd!'

'What's odd?'

'James used the exact same expression, *go with your gut.*'

'Proves it must be true, any problems with the apartment or car?'

'Yes all good thanks,' suddenly worried that Theresa may think she may use the flat or car for dating purposes, and like a frightened teenager said. 'I won't bring them back here, and I am being picked up.'

'Mel, if you didn't, I would be cross.'

'I just don't want you thinking…'

'I don't, do you think I have not?'

'Haha, I am just very out of practice, So what do you think I should wear?'

'Well, something floaty and cool for the picnic, maybe jeans and a shirt or summer dress for the dinner. Have a look in my wardrobe. Look darling I have to dash, but keep me posted, super excited you might move here! I have to go and tell Chloe the good news.' Mel was imagining what Theresa would wear, a bright linen smock type dress, bright shoes and an even brighter scarf.

'Ok give her my love,' not that Mel had ever met Chloe, but seemed like the right thing to say, 'Bye Theresa'

'Bye darling and have fun!'

Mel looked at the clothes she had laid out, they weren't very exciting. She got up and parted the wardrobe doors in Theresa's bedroom. A cacophony of colours, *maybe it's time I play dress-up.*

'James that isn't helpful!'

James had made a very louche remark about the length of the skirt Mel was now showcasing, whilst Mel tried on various outfits in a rudimentary, kitchen based fashion show.

'You asked! I think the skirt is a great colour for you. Gino will love it', James smirked.

'Hmm I am not sure, what about this?' Mel held up a flamenco style black dress with delicate floral detailing.

'Yes yes, yes.'

'Great, so this for the evening, the striped t-shirt and denim shorts for a picnic?'

'Perfect, right so we are having a drink? Champagne.'

'Did you get the papers back?'

'Yes, all done!'

'No, THAT is important, and worth celebrating.' they high fived, though in cringe-able fashion they missed each other's hands.

'We are so crap at that.'

## Chapter 26 - Pascal's Picnic

*I BLAME YOU!*

The text had been sent, Mel held her head in her hands, elbows planted on the kitchen table. A tumbler of water to one side and a mug of strong black coffee to the other, and in front of her were two tablets. The evening had started in a small wine bar near the port area, where some champagne was ordered to celebrate, fast forward to 1am and Mel had collapsed on the bed and woken up feeling very sorry for herself, to say the least. Her head throbbed, the area above the eyes were particularly sore, and nausea kept creeping over her.

*Bloody hell! I need to be perky,* ruminated Mel.

Her phone lit up,

*I am sorry! But you insisted on the magnum. Coffee, paracetamol and eat something!*

It vibrated again. Bleary-eyed she tried to focus, it was an unknown number.

*Hi Mel, it's Annette from downstairs, are you free today?*

That was the last thing she needed, looking like shite for her dates and trying to sort out Annette's situation. She didn't know if she should ever drink again, the burn was real. Pushing her chair away, she decided to have some cereal, healthier than another Jambon Beurre, and wouldn't spoil any food that was coming up later in the day. Bowl and box were placed on the counter and pausing to pour the cereal in the bowl, somehow, slight nausea coming over her, she tore the bag open, and managed to tip most of the contents on the floor. 'Bollocks!' In a voice loud enough to be heard two streets away, at the same moment, an unsuspecting Simone entered the apartment.

Mel was now kneeling on the floor, and from behind the sight was suspect, her baggy t-shirt was tucked into her knickers and all Simone could see was Mel kneeling, shouting. As she braced herself she swung round the corner, 'Madame?'

'Christ!'

'Are you ok?'

'Yes, yes, sorry I knocked over the cereal'. Mel climbed up using the kitchen cupboard and work surface to steady her ascent to a standing position. Sunglasses slid down her face and landed up on the end of her nose.

'Let me.' soothed Simone.

Upon entering the bathroom, Mel was horrified. Her sunglasses still hanging off her face, t-shirt tucked in her knickers and lipstick smudged across the right side of her face. In two hours she was being picked up, what the fuck would he, they, think?

\*

Mel had given Pascal the address via text, and he was bang on time. Mel was still trying to pack her beach bag, which currently mainly consisted of brimmed water bottles and a large brimmed hat. The headache was not subsiding, the nausea was, thanks to a cold shower and gallons of water.

The apartment buzzer sounded.

'Hello.'

'Bonjour Mel, it is Pascal.'

'Great, give me two minutes and I will be down.'

'Ok'

She dashed to the window that overlooked the road and craned her neck to see him, there he was, dressed in a black polo top, and light stone coloured shorts, he did look very masculine and rugged. Mel felt that swell of butterflies deep within her core. She hoped that it was the nervous excitement, not another bout of sickness.

Presently a rather jumpy and apprehensive Mel got into his car. A large and comfortable estate car, which even by Mel's standards felt quite old.

'How are you?'

'I am well, how about you Pascal?'

'I am fine, all the better for seeing you. I am very sorry about the other night…'

Mel began to feel herself blushing and to hide the fact she rifled through her bag to disguise this obvious show of emotion replied, 'Please don't be sorry, and umm where are we going?'

'Cap d'Ail, you have been?'

'No, I don't think so, sounds lovely.' Mel was nervous, she clutched the handles of her bag tightly. Sitting very upright and stiff.

'Are you sure you're, ok?'

'Yes, I am fine, sorry, just a bit nervous, this car is nice.'

'Haha, why are you nervous? Are you a nervous passenger? I have a lovely picnic in the back, and some chilled rosé, that is what you were drinking at James".

Mel had to swallow down a bilious feeling at the mention of alcohol which didn't do much for her hangover.

'Mmm lovely, may I open the window?

'Of course, and yes the car is also used for my work.'

'No, it's nice, very comfy', cool air coming from the window helped Mel regain some form of calmness as they sped along the Moyenne Corniche. Mel felt awkward, what should she ask about, she didn't know what to do or say. She felt like a fool, what was she doing here, with him?

'We got interrupted the other night, you haven't told me why you are here.'

'Yes, oh yes, Gino.' An image of those tanned limbs and chiselled body and face came into her mind, Mel tried to dismiss them and concentrate on Pascal's questions.

'Well, it's all by chance really, my sister-in-law needed a house sitter and here I am.'

Pascal suddenly looked worried, gripping the steering wheel he rubbed his hands in a screw-like fashion, considering the next question carefully.

'Your husband is back at home?'

'O no, he is umm he passed away.'

'I am very sorry to hear that, have I made a mistake again?'

'No, you haven't, it was years ago, and I am enjoying my trip.'

Mel wasn't sure why she had said *years*, it had only just been over a year, but somehow saying only a year meant it was all too close for comfort and Pascal clearly was worried about the other night, she didn't want to cause any embarrassment.

'What about you, how long have you worked for James?'

Conversation flowed as they passed through the villages of Villefranche and Eze, the signs showing Monaco. 'Ahh I was here the other day, I took the train to Monte Carlo.'

'You know I have never done that, I always drive, did you enjoy it?'

'Yes I did, might sound silly to you but back home I don't do things like that or this.'

'Is that is why you are nervous?'

He dropped into a lower gear as he turned off and entered a very twisty section of road, this wasn't ideal, Mel leaned her head out the window and forced herself to take a deep lung full of air.

'I am not really selling myself, am I?'

'You mean you aren't for sale?' Pascal looked at Mel and winked.

'No, I am not!' She playfully hit him on the arm, a strong muscular arm, straining within the confines of his short sleeves.

Taking another deep breath, 'Well I am not used to it that's all, I can't remember the last time I was asked out for a picnic or travelled on my own.' She looked out of the window, she didn't want to see his expression in case it jarred. Suddenly a whoosh of excitement came over her as a warm hand was placed on her leg,

'It's ok, I don't either. Here we are.' He swung the nimbly into a parking space, 'I'm afraid it's a small walk to the beach.'

'That's ok,' Mel stood looking at the craggy, verdant topped cliffs and the small horseshoe bay surrounded by white villas and small ochre-coloured apartment blocks. As they approached the bay Mel could see small low lying white buildings with terracotta tiled roofs serving food, drinks and ice creams. Further along the cove, the buff sand and pebbles gave way to large rocky outcrops, which trees clung to like limpets, providing some shade.

'Can I help?' Mel realised that Pascal was carrying a couple of large bags, 'No I am all good, where would you like to sit? I have an umbrella for shade.'

They had passed some sunbeds and the restaurants, and the beach became quieter. 'How about here.'

'Excellent'

They laid down large beach towels, and a white and blue parasol was planted into the sand to provide some shade from the early afternoon sun.

'Madame?'

As Mel was just getting comfy, and looking in her bag for some water, Pascal was holding a chilled bottle of rosé, 'Yes, maybe a small one to start with.' Mel took a large swig of water, 'Just a bit hot.'

Lying was going to have to be part of the act today, she was hanging, headache and tired, but for Pascal, who had put such effort into this, she was determined to enjoy it for his sake and hers.

'What would you like to eat,' He began to empty the contents of a cool bag, it was endless. Gorgeous baguette, an array of cheese, cold meats and dips. 'Wow, Pascal, this looks yummy.'

'Yummy?'

'Sorry, delicious.'

'I like this word, yummy.'

He smiled, for someone so well built he was very delicate, especially as he plated up a selection for Mel, 'What is that?'

'Remoulade, I think you called it Celeriac?'

'Looks, yummy.' she returned his smile as she took the plate from his hand, the hands that Mel couldn't take her eyes off, the plate looked like dolly cutlery compared.

She built a sandwich, stuffed with some ham, remoulade and salad. She could sense him watching her, and she was getting that inner excited feeling again, that, or she was just bloody starving and needed to eat. Taking a massive mouthful, she tried to munch down, just as an uninvited wasp landed on her hand.

'Arggg'. Yelled Mel, she tried to bat it away, but a mouth full and hand full wasn't much help, she flung her arms and hands wildly, eventually, she paused to check the location of the insect, it had gone. Relaxing back into her seated position she noticed that a large proportion of her baguette filling was now missing. Looking towards Pascal, who had remained calm throughout this juncture. She didn't know whether to laugh or cry, Pascal was now wearing most of the contents of Mel's lunch. In her endeavour to swot away said bug, she had clung so tightly to her sandwich that it had been propelled at Pascal.

'Oh my God, I am so sorry.'

Wiping a piece of remoulade from his chin, 'it's ok, are you ok?'

'Yes, sorry I hate wasps, oh god look at your top, here let me help.'

Putting down the now sorry-looking food, and dabbing at Pascal's top, and his face, he grabbed her wrist. 'There is only one thing for this.'

Mel was sure he was smiling beneath his aviator sunglasses.

'A swim will clean it all away.'

The ultramarine briny sea glistened in the sun, an inviting prospect for Mel, who was feeling terrible, decided a swim was possibly the only cure.

'Pascal, I am truly…'

'Please do not worry, swim with me.'

Mel felt giddy again, Pascal pulled his top off, revealing a wide chest covered in deep dark hair, curling round pink nipples. A physic that any rugby player or American football player would be proud of, he stood up, casting a shadow over Mel as he did so, 'ready?' He held out his hand for Mel to take, 'Just a minute, you go on.'

Mel wanted to take her time getting ready, no more flashes or embarrassing moments, she had worn a bikini underneath her outfit. She wriggled under the parasol, checked nothing was hanging out or tucked in and stepped onto the warm sand.

There was her lunch date, not that they had ever called it a date, he stood with water up to his navel, pushing his hair back with both hands, he cried 'Come on, it's lovely or yummy!'

The refreshing blast of the cool sea and the swim was just what she needed. They swam around each other, which turned into a splashing fight, until Pascal went under the water to bob up just next to Mel, he towered over her, he must have been well over six foot.

'Right, you are going in'. He scooped her up in both arms and bounced her up and down as she lay in his arms, each time threatening to drop her.

Their flesh rubbed together, Mel felt all tingly and girlish as Pascal flexed his strength. 'Don't drop me!' she yelled.

'Ok well don't throw food at your date.'

*Date,* the word hung there, Mel was in a daze. He had called it a date, she wanted it to be a date, she thought. It just felt odd, alien in fact, for a 40 something to be on a 'date'. 'Pascal put me down, or I will...'

'Will what?'

'I will throw my wine at you next time!'

'I will look forward to it.' He put her back on her feet and both of them stood, waist-deep in the water, looking at one another. Mel took off her sunglasses, 'So there will be another date?'

'If that is what you would like.'

Mel did, she did like.

\*

The car pulled up outside the apartment block, 'I had a lovely time, I am sorry about the food throwing.'

'I am not sorry, but you will go on another date with me, I will promise to pack a change of clothes.'

'Haha, ok deal, will you text or call…' as she was about to finish her sentence, Pascal moved in closer and kissed her on the lips, she could feel his stubble rubbing against her soft skin. She inhaled deeply, the strong masculine scent and salty odour from the sea was intoxicating.

'Au revoir, baguette thrower'. Pascal lent back and opened his door, he came round and opened Mel's, 'Well as I was going to say, text or call me.'

'I will do not worry, now enjoy your chilled out night.'

Mel had quickly lied, on the journey back a simple question of, 'What are you doing tonight?' Now it had become a small white lie. She had loved her day with Pascal, she didn't want to spoil it by saying she was going on a date with his boss! Plus, it was now 6pm and cancelling Gino would look bad. She kept saying to herself in her head, *I didn't know today was going to be a proper date*.

Somehow this helped reassure her that her little fib was acceptable. Secretly she hoped today would be one of many.

## Chapter 27 - Supper with Gino

Her head was still reeling from her kiss with Pascal, she now had to dash upstairs and get showered and changed for Gino's arrival. As she exited his car and fumbled for the door key, she stopped, a huge cardboard box had been left outside. 'What on earth?' On closer inspection, she could make out the word 'Fleurs'. She bundled everything through the door and walked into the sparkling clean apartment, Simone was certainly efficient, and Mel pondered momentarily about getting a cleaner for back home.

Kicking off her flip flops in the hallway, she slipped them under a small rectangular table. She grabbed a pair of scissors and cut across the sellotape to open the box. A huge bunch of baby blue hydrangeas poked out from the dark recess. A small white envelope was attached to the brown paper wrapping.

*Bella! See you at 7 pm. G xxx*

'What 7? He said 8', she took out her phone, and went to text Gino, too late. There was a text waiting.

*Bella change of plans see you at 7. G x*

*Ok I might be late M x*

Looking at her watch, it was now 6:15pm, she had 45 minutes. She threw herself into a shower and washed off the salty and sandy remnants from her date with Pascal.

Luckily, she had already selected her outfit, with James' help. Her flamenco style dress teamed with a small black clutch bag and some black wedges she had borrowed from Theresa's extensive clothing and shoe collection. The flowers that adorned the dress were, oddly enough, also baby blue, so she found a nice large light blue scarf to take in case she should get chilly. What Gino had planned was a mystery, just telling her that he would pick her up. Drying her hair was taking ages, she looked at her watch, 6:56pm. Just as she switched off the dryer, the buzzer rang out.

'Hello Gino, I am running late.'

'Do not worry Bella, I shall come up.'

'Umm yeah ok', Mel buzzed him in, suddenly realising the flowers were still dumped in the hallway, she ran to the kitchen, found a massive jug, and plonked the flowers in it and placed them on the kitchen table. A rap at the door, *bugger,* thought Mel.

'Bella!'

'Gino, come in'

He embraced her and kissed her on both cheeks, 'Bella, How are you?'

'Good I just need to finish getting ready.'

'Why, you look beautiful as you are.'

'Gino stop', he was now whirling her round by her hand.

'Gino! Now sit there, I will be 5 minutes.'

'Ci Bella'

Mel dashed back into her bedroom, slipped her feet into the black wedges and quickly filled her handbag, keys, phone, and money. Recalling some of her embarrassing accidents thus far on her trip, she checked her face and body carefully, the dress hugged her in all the right places. She had some new underwear she had bought before travelling, it fitted around her buttocks really well, and she took time to admire her tight looking rear. The dress had a plunging neckline showcasing her round and firm breasts, the addition of a delicate small silver necklace would hopefully distract Gino from ogling, but Mel really didn't know what to expect. She felt good, she thought she looked good and she couldn't deny that being bought flowers, on what was definitely a date, was incredibly romantic and a turn on.

'Bella, I didn't know you could look even more beautiful, but you do.'

'Thank you, Gino,' he stood up and came in close, Mel offered her cheek as he kissed her. A waft of tobacco warmth and sandalwood aroma was a deliciously attractive combination, Mel didn't realise but she had instinctively closed her eyes as he put his arm around her and kissed her again on the lips.

'Gino!' She stepped back.

'Sorry, you just look stunning.'

'So, Gino, where are we headed?' Rummaging in her bag purposefully to make sure she had everything but also to avert his gaze.

'Let's go, I will show you.'

They journeyed out into the still night air.

'Mel?'

'Yes Gino,' worried that he was suddenly being formal and not calling her 'Bella' raised a slight panic.

'You really do look stunning tonight, I know you don't believe me.'

'Gino, it is just I haven't been told this for a long time, and it's all such a surprise.'

'Why?'

'It's a very boring story.'

'I would like to hear It.' He looked at her sincerely, for the first time he looked vulnerable, open and with a hint of seriousness. 'But hold that thought, we are here.'

Here turned out to be a very small pizzeria, lots of small dark wooden tables with hard-backed wooden chairs with raffia style seats.

'Here?'

'Yes, you don't like it? We can go somewhere else.'

'No sorry I wasn't expecting it to be one street away, that's all.'

They were greeted warmly, and 'bonjours' and 'ciaos' were shouted from behind the bar, and from inside the kitchen, they clearly knew Gino. Mel smiled politely and stood by Gino until they were guided to sit down.

'I hope you like Pizza, these guys are the best.'

'Yummy, I mean, sounds good to me.'

'Yummy? What is yummy?'

*Here we go again!* Thought Mel, she duly explained the meaning. Gino was very flattering, and the wine flowed.

'Gino this is lovely,' she looked at him over the floral display and candle that slightly obstructed the view of her olive-skinned Italian date.

'Tell me more, Bella, what do you do?'

'Well at the moment, nothing, but I may have a new project on the horizon, how about you?'

'As you know I run a building business and my family have agriculture ventures, tell me about your new venture and what is a beautiful single lady doing out here all alone?'

Mel snapped, 'How do you know I am single?'

Gino looked totally deflated, he looked sheepish and solemn.

'O Gino,' and Mel instinctively reached across to touch his arm, he watched and looked down as Mel's hand rested on the top of his.

'I am single, I am a widow.'

'I am so sorry,' his big brown eyes looked into hers, they locked, and Mel couldn't deny that it sent an excited shiver down her spine. To Mel's relief, the pizzas arrived and so the awkward discussion around Mark's death would hopefully be delayed, albeit she knew temporarily. She hadn't had to explain the death to anyone other than close relatives and neighbours, so telling a stranger was a new experience, to say the least. Looking down at her pizza, there was something not quite right, it was heart-shaped.

'Gino, did you do this?'

'No Bella, it happens here.'

An enormous pepper mill was offered dispensing a smattering of black specks that would give a spicy warmth. Mel had to admit that the low lighting, the red wine and the pizza felt very romantic, a hint of Lady and the Tramp, though Mel wasn't sure she qualified for a 'lady' and Gino didn't come across as a 'tramp'. He oozed sex appeal, Mel couldn't deny that, but why had he asked her, he must have the whole Riviera after him.

'This is delicious, what a great place.' Mel glugged down some smooth velvety vin rouge, 'I suspect you bring all the ladies here?'

'Bella! No, you are the first actually, we never finished your story.'

'My story?'

'Your husband, Mark, I think you said, does it upset you?'

'It does, but...' taking another massive bite of pizza, 'He umm, he had an accident and died, ages ago now.'

'Poor you, what happened?'

'I think we should save that for another day, what about you?'

'Ok, I understand, sorry. I got married at 25. Friends of my parents had a daughter and the families always thought that we were going to marry, we did, but after five years it wasn't working. We had no children. That is my only regret, I would have loved a child. We are still friends, though she has married again and is very happy.'

'What about you, what did you do?'

'I put all my effort into the business and buried my head in work. Is that bad?'

'No, we all do, I buried my life it seems, when Mark died.'

'How do you mean?'

'I have two boys, they are in their twenties and have their own lives, but mine sort of stood still. That is until I got this invite to house sit, I feel like I'm finding my feet again, working out what I want. Making new memories.' She gazed absentmindedly down at her wine, spinning the red liquid round.

'I see, well, let's get on with making a few new memories.' he raised up his glass and they chinked, smiled. The plates were cleared, and wine was refilled, the music burbled gently in the background, 'Tu vuo' fa' l'americano!' blurted out Mel.

'Ci, you know your music!'

'Not really, I just liked this one and remembered it.'

'So, tell me what do you do for work?'

'Currently, I don't work, but I brought the two boys up and then Mark...but I have worked for a creative marketing and design agency, you?' Mel didn't know why but she felt she had to justify it all?

'Bringing up two boys must be like two jobs! I helped at my father's estate, we grow olives and vines, you must come and try.'

Mel felt it was refreshing for someone, a man especially, to understand the time and effort to bring up children.

'I would love to, but you run the building business too?'

'Yes, I help my father, my mother has passed away and my two older brothers are absorbed in other work and their family. My father is now very old, and I am trying to modernise the place. I would like to start a small hotel or guest house amongst the vines and farms. The building business, well I fell into it, and now it has grown, but I generally leave it to run itself.'

'And you buy Lamborghinis', winked Mel.

'I am glad you aren't perfect.'

'Sorry?'

'You are beautiful, charming and fun, but cars are not your strong point, it's a Ferrari.'

'I always get the horse and the bull mixed up, I mean I am so used to them.' winked Mel.

'You are?'

'No of course not, my life is very mundane compared to yours, I have a small cottage with one horse and a knackered old car.'

'A cottage? I love these, they are very English.'

'Well, it wasn't always so lovely, we made it home and now I live there with my horse Rocky. It has a flagged stone floor in the kitchen and Clematis that grows over the front door.' Mel suddenly felt emotional.

'You miss home?' A warm, slightly sweaty palm was planted on top of Mel's hand, 'I do a bit, but I do like it here.'

'Would you like something more?'

'It was delicious, but I am full, thank you.'

'Can I tempt you out for a drink?'

'I think that you can Gino, you certainly can.'

    Gino stood up, his well-cut pale pink shirt accentuated his sculpted physique, and a tight upper body gave way to strong lean legs that were hugged by expensive-looking black jeans. He wore suede driving shoes, pale stone with a darker grey tassel. He knew how to dress.

'Are you ready?'

Mel had been transfixed by the stud in front of her, 'Sorry, umm yes all ready.'

'After you Bella.'

As Mel went to move, she was tugged backwards, spinning round she crashed into Gino, he stopped her from going arse over tit, he held her tightly.

'Your scarf…'

'Thank you.' She could feel his breath on her blushed left cheek as they stood entwined for what seemed a lifetime.

'Excuse a moi', a waiter was eagerly trying to pass as he juggled five pizzas and a jug of Aperol Spritz. Trying to get on with his job. Gino handed her handbag, 'You, ok?'

'Yes, I am fine.'

She smoothed down her dress and made her way out in the warm evening. No need for the scarf that had impeded her progress, *how do things like that only happen to me?* Mel thought as they walked. Gino held out an arm as Mel negotiated a rather dodgy drain, 'thank you', as she slipped her arm through his. Somehow this felt very comfortable already. Maybe she had misjudged Gino.

Gino seemed as unsteady on his feet as Mel, they weaved their way to a place adorned with feathers and glitter. Once inside the music was pumping and they could hardly hear what one another was saying.

'Mar… I mean Gino, what are we drinking,' Mel fumbled in her handbag for some notes, a clammy hand pressed into hers. 'No Bella!'

He ordered two more glasses of red wine. Mel was feeling tired, all this drinking and late nights, she hadn't done since her university days. They stood at the bar, gaudy coloured and loud, Mel's eyes focused. 'Gino, that's a drag queen', trying to squint in the dark, 'this is a gay place!' As if right on cue…

'Mel!'

'What the hell?'

Mel whirled round and there was James, shirt unbuttoned and holding a very suspect drink, very bright blue.

'What are you doing here?'

Mel nudged Gino, 'did you hear me?'

'I didn't know.' Gino suddenly looked awkward and not at ease.

'Gino! How are you? Are you looking after Mel? You better be!'

James was fully aware of what was going on, he had been fully briefed. 'Dance?'

James danced closely with Mel, shouting in her ear.

'So, which one?'

'I am not sure, after one date, hard to tell.'

'He doesn't look happy.'

'Well, he chose it! I think he was hoping to get to know me.'

'And has he?' James swilled his martini glass at her. 'James! Be careful!'

'Yes boss, now go to him.'

'You having a good time…' as James bumped into a tall dark man, 'Yes I am fine.' He smirked.

'Gino, sorry, James and I…'

'Yes well, I think maybe I will walk you home.'

'Ok?'

'Yeh, just I can't get to know you here, Bella, it's too loud.' They left their drinks at the bar, though Mel, who secretly loved a gay bar, the best places by far for a night out, was a bit disappointed.

It was a still, calm, clear night as they approached the harbour. Mel could smell something, it was that Socca bread again. She looked longingly at the chickpea flatbread, watching the batter poured onto a huge skillet and flipped when crispy. 'I thought you were full?'

'Well yes, yes I am, it just smells yummy.'

'Ahh yummy I see.'

'Monsieur?'

Before Mel could blink, she had a crispy, folded mass of earthy scented bread in a cone-shaped vessel and the moonlight shone brightly, as they promenaded alongside the port.

'Have you had a nice night?' asked Gino

'Yes, it's been lovely, thank you.'

She leant into him, resting her head on his shoulder as they meandered.

'Do you remember an advert about coffee, two people who become involved over the need for coffee?'

'An English advert?'

'Sorry, yes, it doesn't matter, here we are.'

'Well, here *you* are, I need a taxi.'

'Do you want to come up and order one?'

Mel was holding her Socca tightly, she had no desire to let it go. However, the journey in the lift proved too much. The proximity, the musk, the tension. As the door opened, Mel and Gino were kissing, a deep passionate kiss, his arms around her waist pulling her in tightly. Mel was lost in the moment, she hadn't kissed anyone like that in a very long time.

'Bella, we are here.' Gino pulled back as the doors to the lift were now wide open.

'So, we are.' Sadly, the majority of the Socca now laid upon the lift floor, but Mel was hurriedly trying to find her keys without looking nervous or tired.

'Allow me.' His warm hands took the key and twisted.

'Thank you, would you like coffee?' as Mel kicked off her shoes and shrugged off her scarf, she was trembling.

'Yes lovely, thanks, don't go too far away.' He followed her into the kitchen and spun her around for another kiss, he planted his lips on hers, she could feel his warmth, his warm body pressed against hers, she pulled away. 'Now Gino, I can't make coffee with that going on.' She was sleepy and half cut.

'Bella, I really like you.'

'I umm like you too, I just think it's our first date and I am, I am nervous.'

'It's ok, I understand, sorry if I was too much.'

'No, no, you weren't, I just feel very tired and I would prefer to take things slowly, this is all new to me.'

'OK.' He kissed on the forehead, which Mel felt was a tad patronising, 'I go, but say we will do this again?'

'Yes, yes of course, do you need a taxi?'

'I will order one now.'

## Chapter 28 – Flashback - Mark's Funeral

Mel was pacing the kitchen in her three-quarter length blaccoat.

'Mum are you ok?'

'Yes, I just want this bit to be over, all those eyes on me and for the first time in years, doing it alone.'

'Mum you're not alone.'

Her boys had been amazing, they had supported her and helped with the funeral arrangements. Mark has wanted a simple ceremony and to be buried locally. Mark had been very conscious and provided money for this eventuality.

'Now who is in what car?'

'Mum it's ok, it's all sorted.'

As Mel got into the waiting car, she looked back at the house. She saw Cathy helping David into her car, Chris was there holding Cathy's bag. All three looked back at Mel at the same moment.

'Chris just help David, will you?' Ordered Cathy to her husband.

'Of course.'

Cathy ran over to Mel, 'I am not going to ask if you're ok, as that would be silly of me, but I am here for you.' she squeezed Mel's gloved hand tightly. Cathy had been there the day Mark had fallen, she had helped organise flowers and put the notice in the paper. She had been Mel's rock since both of Mel's parents had passed away some years before, she was the closest friend she had, and she trusted Cathy.

'I don't know what to say.'

'You don't have to say anything. I'll be right behind you.'

Mel sat back into the car, with her boys, Andrew and Daniel, and sedately they moved down the avenue toward the main road into the city. Some people took off their hats as they drove by, others stared, gormless expressions on their faces. Mel felt distant and on edge. She was trying to hold it together for the boys and the congregation. 'Shit.'

'Mum what?' Asked Daniel

'How many do you think will turn up?'

'Not sure, I know Dad's work will be sending quite a few, and there is his side of the family of course and friends from local things he did.'

'Why mum?' followed up Andrew.

'I don't know, I just am not sure I can walk down that aisle, with everyone staring and feeling sorry for me.'

The boys looked at one another, their mother somehow looked smaller and fragile, her eyes had dark circles around them. She had lost not only her husband but her usual bouncy energy. 'Mum, you don't have to do anything, we can send you back in the car, and we can do it.'

Mel sat looking out of the window as they pulled up at the church, Daniel got out first and greeted some well-wishers who were standing outside. 'Mum, I know you can do this.' Andrew held out his hand. She took it and between them, the boys manoeuvred Mel through the congregation, as they walked down through the vast cavernous 18th-century church. She noted there was standing room only. 'Where is Cathy?' she gasped as she sat down in her pew.

'I am here.' A comforting hand rested on her left shoulder, Mel turned and managed a strained smile, and Cathy smiled back, mouthing 'It will be alright'. The readings were lovely, Andrew and Daniel did a poem, and Gary from Mark's work read a psalm. Mel struggled to watch proceedings, fumbling and looking down at the order of service, and miming the hymns - she didn't feel like singing.

    The burial had been a sombre affair, the wind had got up, and everyone was holding on to coats and skirts as the coffin was lowered into the dank darkness of the earth. The boys had been very brave, they helped Mel to throw some soil and each, in turn, did the same. Andrew began to cry. Mel reached instantly into her bag, 'Here, it's ok?' she muttered as she passed a tissue.

Mel had decided that anyone who wanted to could come back to the house for a drink afterwards, somehow this made her feel like a party was about to start. Some girls from a catering company circulated offering guest food and drinks, the house was full, and before long some people spilled out onto the patio for a smoke. Mel watched as Andrew and Daniel took a cigarette from a member of the wake, 'Mel don't you think…'

Mel interrupted Cathy, 'No not today, leave them.'

Mel started to feel very tired, and the endless words of sympathy, many of them from people she didn't know were becoming a blur. Cathy stayed by her side most of the time. 'This is Mark's sister, Theresa.' said Cathy interrupting Mel's reverie.

'Ahh yes, how good of you to come.'

'Not at all, I am so sorry about it all, really I am.'

'It was a shock, but life must go on. How long are you staying? You're based abroad aren't you?'

'Yes, I am, Nice in France. Only a few days. I haven't seen you in years, would be great to catch up. Maybe you'd like to come to visit sometime?'

'Yes, that would be lovely, I am sorry, but I must just get some air.'

'Yes of course, are you ok?'

'Mel?'

Mel swayed slightly. Cathy steadied her. 'I think you should lie down, it's all been too much.' The muted gasps from the crowd nearby made Mel only feel worse.

Mel pushed herself up and away from Cathy, 'I am fine honestly, I just want some air and a drink.'

'Theresa, my address is….' Mel dispensed the contact details. 'Please, would you mind?'

'Of course, again I am so terribly sorry, my brother was never one for making life easy.'

'No.' Mel frowned as she considered what Theresa had meant by that remark, making her way out the back door into the garden, 'Here.'

Cathy offered a glass of water, 'No!' Mel shouted.

'Mum are you ok?' Daniel handed the lit cigarette to his brother to hold it.

'I am fine, Cathy I am so sorry, please I am so sorry. I don't know what came over me.'

'It's ok, it's been a long day.' Cathy sympathised.

'A large gin and tonic please,' asked Mel.

Daniel went in to fetch the drink for his mother, a few lungfuls of air and the G&T revived her. She could overhear some guys in a group, maybe Mark's work lot she thought.

'That's where it happened,' a tall gentleman in glasses pointed toward the old pottery cottage. 'Christ and he fell,' muttered another. Cathy scowled at them and then looked at Mel.

'It's ok, I have to get used to it, don't worry, that is where he died. In my own bloody garden.'

 Mel looked down toward the old wreck of an outbuilding, she had grand plans for it. Now that was unlikely to happen, she couldn't do it alone and the boys had their lives to lead. Sipping her drink, she got up, 'Maybe I will have that lie-down.'

## Chapter 29 - A "doer-upper"

After Gino had left, Mel had rolled into bed, and fell asleep. A long deep sleep, the wine and two dates had taken their toll. It was well past 9am when she woke up the next morning. Unusually for Mel, she had slept right on through the blazing sun that was entering the flat. She was hot and thirsty, water, she needed water.

Two massive glasses of water, and with the kettle on, she felt better. Throwing all the windows open, she noticed the clouds seemed to be enveloping the sun, so far, she had been lucky, every day had been sunny, or at least bright and warm. Her bedding needed washing, so she threw the sheets, pillowcases and a towel in the washing machine. Once she'd worked out what setting to put it on, it gurgled and sprung into life.

Finding her phone, which had been thrown down on the sofa, she peered at the screen, two texts and one missed call. Before she checked, she needed tea. As she took her first sip of her brew, she exclaimed. 'Annette!'

With everything going on, she had completely forgotten about her, quickly she tapped out a reply to her.

*Hi Annette, so sorry for the delayed reply, please come up this morning. Does 10ish suit?*

With a mug in hand, Mel read her other messages.

*Hi, how are you? It's grey here, though brightening up later this week :) When did you want a chat? C xx*

Poor Cathy stuck in the gloom at home, Mel duly replied.

*Hey! I am good, glad things are looking up weather-wise, are you free now? xx*

The other message was from Pascal, asking if she would like to have dinner with him on Friday, and the missed call was James. Just as she went to reply her phone vibrated and a melodic tune began to play, it was Cathy.

'Hullo, stranger!'

'Hello Cathy, you ok?'

'All good thanks, the sun is out which makes everything feel better! How is France?'

'Well…'

Mel updated Cathy on her dates, and what was happening with the business idea with James. Mel couldn't help thinking Cathy had gone very quiet, and simple 'mhmms' and 'ok' was all she was getting.

'That's it really, you sure you're alright? You don't sound yourself.'

'Honestly, I am fine, just a bit you know, *flat*.'

'Cathy look, when I am back, we can arrange a trip out here, you and me? I can show you the sights!'

'Yeh sounds good.'

Mel wasn't convinced.

'Cathy, what is up?'

'I am, I don't know, look Mel, I want you to have a nice time and I don't want to be a Debbie downer.'

'You won't be, please tell me.'

'Well, I think maybe, that well, I think Chris might be having an affair.'

The word 'affair' just hung in the silence. What a turn up for the books that would be, Cathy had seemed so happy and bubbly before.

'Mel you there?'

'Yes, I am here, are you, I mean, do you know for certain?'

'No, I may have got my wires crossed.'

'Look just wait, I will sort it out for you, would you be up for coming here?'

'What about the horses?'

'Can you ask that lady who is organising the gymkhanas?'

'I guess I could, and if you were to sell yours, I could get mine in easily.'

'Ok well sell, how much do you think?'

'They said they would go to 4 thousand.'

'Ok, let's sell, I will sort out airline tickets if you want.'

'Sounds good, let me get the sale sorted.'

'Ok, keep me posted, and try to keep your head up.'

'I will do, now you go enjoy yourself and let me know how you want the money.'

'Oh wow ok, you have my bank details?'

'Yeh, I do, ok I will transfer once I get it sorted.'

'Perfect thank you, oh one other thing, the lady downstairs would like to visit Sussex, she lives here now but misses home.'

'You thinking she would stay with you?'

'Yes, well at mine, and I would pay for anything that needs doing.'

'Sure, no worries. When will you know?'

'I am seeing her later today.'

'Sounds good, keep me updated.'

'Bye Cathy'

'Bye bye Mel, don't worry about me.'

The call ended, Cathy looked up at her horse, his huge brown eyes stared back at her, he was a handsome beast. 'Well, she fell for that Spaghetti, that's three grand for me, and four for her. Plus, I wanted a holiday, now I have some spending money!'

## Part 2

James answered excitedly,

'Hi, you! I have some news!'

'Hi to you too, what's the news?'

'Well, that house, we can go see it, the doer-upper.'

'So soon? Ok, when are you thinking?'

'Does a couple of hours give you enough time?'

'Yeh, I guess so.'

'Mel, you sound less than excited!'

'Sorry was a long day yesterday.'

'Yeh, your double dates! How was it?'

Mel started to feel like she was repeating herself, so she shared the key points agreeing to go over it all in more detail later. He would pick her up at 11am.

There was a knock at the door.

'Hello Annette, come in.'

'Look I won't stay long.'

'Tea? It's proper English tea, I brought some with me.' Mel proudly held the tin aloft.

'I won't, thanks though. I spoke to Albert.'

'Yes, and when can you go?'

'He doesn't want me to go, he wants me to stay or at least go with someone when I do.'

'Right, that's a shame, why don't you come with me?'

'Could I drive to yours?'

'Course you can, I just don't know when I am going back just yet, dates keep changing.'

Mel poured the boiling water into her mug and stirred. How are you really feeling about it, Annette?'

' Well, a bit depressed if I'm honest about not being able to go.'

'Can I help?

'You already have, but I did have one favour.'

'Sure.'

'Would I be able to pop up and do this again?'

'Yes of course.'

Annette's face beamed with a broad smile as she rose to leave. Mel guided her to the front door and as they embraced, Mel whispered in her ear, 'I'm here, come see me soon. Look after yourself.'

No sooner had she closed the door that the buzzer sounded, and Mel let James in. She could still see Annette as she took the last few steps back down the marble staircase to the flat below. Mel went inside and scooped up her bag and phone.

'Ready' she announced.

'So you are, how are you?'

'I'm good, nervously excited.'

'Just you wait!'

The drive in James' Range Rover took about 45 minutes, they passed the Negresco, and then on past the airport and followed the motorway round past Antibes, and then headed northwards as signs started to shout 'Cannes.' They exited the motorway and continued through glorious verdant countryside, whizzing past woodland and endless fields of vines. Suddenly the landscapes began to change and become more remote and craggy. 'That's where we are going.' James pointed. Following his finger Mel could just make out in the distance what looked like a small village perched around a green mound. Cypress trees lined the route as the hamlet came into view, then James swung off the main road and up an unadopted track, the 4x4 covering the ground easily, before going between two pillars with blue metal gates that were barely clinging on to stone markers. They followed a hedge trimmed driveway that sloped downwards and ended in the most breath-taking view, of the Cote d'Azur, with Cannes straight ahead and Antibes to the left.

'That is why Mel, that view.'

'James, it's amazing, truly.'

James parked the car, 'Right, you ready to start together?'

'You bet.'

James leapt out of the car, Mel on the other hand slithered out, the height wasn't such of an issue for someone over six foot, but, Mel had to dangle off the seat and graciously hop down to terre ferme. The car door shut with a reassuring 'whump'. As a smartly dressed man in a blue suit walked toward them. He was about James' height, older, maybe fifty Mel deduced, with charcoal grey hair, defined features, a heavy-set nose and wore a goatee and moustache. Smoke lingered around him, as he took a last drag on his cigarette before flicking it into the undergrowth.

Mel watched, and considered, *at some point we will have to pick that up.*

The man greeted James first. 'Bonjour, welcome James.'

'Salut Olivier.'

They shook hands and did, as what can only be described, as a 'man embrace', which is a shoulder into the opposite shoulder of the other, whilst still holding hands and patting the back. Mel just stood looking on.

'Olivier this is Mel, a dear friend and hopefully soon to become, business partner.'

'Enchanté Madame.' He stretched out a hand, which bore an enormous watch on the wrist. Mel wondered how he managed to lift his hand up with such a large timepiece. His eyes felt like they were boring into Melissa's inner core, she felt a tingle, an electric tingle.

'Lovely to meet you Olivier, what a view!'

As they walked inside, Olivier leading the way, James whispered 'He's kinda a hunky daddy, don't you think?'

Talking from the corner of her mouth, so as not to be overheard 'Stop it, I admit he is a looker.'

'What was that?' Olivier turned to face them as he leant against the range in the kitchen.

'What a lovely cooker.' Mel quickly stepped inside the kitchen and ran her hand along the oven rail, 'looks like an old Aga.'

Mel playfully scowled at James as they made their way into the living room, or as Olivier put it, the 'Salon.'

He showed them all over the house, James asked lots of questions, some in French which were lost on Mel, but every now and again James would look at her and smile or give her a thumbs up. There was one question she did understand, in both English and in French.

'C'est combien? How much do they ask Olivier?'

'The vendor wants €440, but I am sure you can haggle your way down, you always do.'

'I need to discuss it with my business partner, now Olivier. Thank you, I will be in touch, no one else has seen it yet, have they?'

'No, you are the first. Au revoir Mel.'

'Auvoir Olivier.' Mel glanced back as she was climbing into the car. The house stood there, light stonework, faded yellow wooden slatted shutters, one hanging off at a jaunty angle. The garden sloped down to a manicured hedge and more tall Cypress trees. She was picturing herself sitting out on the terrace overlooking that view.

The car edged its way out of the gravel drive and onto the winding road back toward the coast.

'Well, what did you think?'

'I love it, I am just scared.'

'Scared?'

'*Business partner* ' *sounds* very formal, and I don't know if I have the head for all this.'

'Mel, you do, and I am here to guide you through the bits you're unsure of and you have to teach me about what you know, the colours, fabrics etc.'

'So, lunch?'

'Yes, I am starving!'

James put his foot down and they glided back to Nice.

'Would you like to come up?'

'Is that what you said to all the boys?'

'Cheeky bugger, I need your help with them!'

'Right well here we are, is there a visitor space in your underground garage?'

When they were back in the apartment, with cups of tea in their hands, James started.

'So, what are you going to do about Pascal and Gino?'

'James, I don't know, they are both very different, and I am not really sure what I want.'

'Ok what if you were based here more, would that help?'

'You mean to go into the business side of things with you and move here?'

James nodded approvingly 'Yes'.

'When Mark died, he had made provisions money-wise, and insurance etc. paid out. I have to be honest I have hardly touched it. I have enough to live off for a few years,' Mel paused, she had never been very good with figures and money. Was she telling James too much? No, he was an old friend and she wanted to help him and be involved.

'I know this is tough, but you have to put yourself first, what do you want to do Mel?'

'That's the question I keep asking myself. I think for so long I've lived through others, first Mark, then the boys, and now I'm on my own.' She began to well up.

'Now you know that's not true, you have me, Theresa, your friends back home, who's the lady looking after your house, Cathy, and the boys of course!'

'You're right! So, what are we talking money wise? He said €440,000? Didn't he?'

'If we do this right, I think we could make 60-100k on this, yeh so €200,000ish each.'

'What about costs to decorate and update the house?'

'I will ask Gino to take a look and quote.'

'Would you mind if I sleep on it?'

'Of course, no rush. Please don't think you are alone Mel.'

## Chapter 30 - Business or Pleasure?

James and Mel had agreed to meet at the 'doer-upper' a few days later, Mel had managed to control the advances of Gino and Pascal while she tried to keep a clear head and work out what she wanted to do.

That hazy afternoon, Mel had ventured out on her own, she felt that somehow driving there and finding her own way, would give her time to think and build up the confidence to give this a go. Once off the main highway, she lowered the roof and whizzed along the country roads, eventually winding up to the house. She pulled in, between the curved walls and pillars. 'That view would never get boring. I would love it.' She breathed.

There were three men standing waiting, leaning over Gino's Ferrari. She was 15 minutes-ish late. Wearing a monochrome midi skirt and a white blouse, she wanted to look good, and couldn't deny she was enjoying the male attention.

'That firms up the suspension... ahh Bella!'

They twisted to watch as Mel closed the roof. She grabbed her bag from the back seat and swung her legs out of the car. Crunching across the gravel to meet the gathering.

Gino was first, he reached out and grabbed her by the top of her arms and kissed her on both cheeks, 'You look lovely. You haven't decided on our next date?'

'Hello Gino, I know,' she gestured toward the villa, 'this has been on my mind. Don't confuse business with pleasure.' Shrugging as she turned, 'Let's catch up soon.'

She hugged and kissed James, he whispered 'Smoking hot' in Mel's ear, and she then held out a hand for Olivier, to her surprise he took her hand and kissed it, 'Lovely to see you again.'

'So, boys, shall we get on?'

'After you.' Gino mimicked a bowing courtier.

Seeing the house for a second time, and with her work hat on, she could focus on ideas for colours and the potential the property had. Standing out on the terrace, she looked down at the sad looking, greening swimming pool, and down towards the coast. 'So, business partner, what do you think?' James lent on the regency style balustrade as he spoke.

'I love it here James, I really do, what has Gino said?'

'Other than he is mad about you? He thinks most of the work is light structural and could do it for around €30,000 euros. He hasn't quoted for all the painting, and that doesn't include furniture.'

Mel was transfixed by the view, the light wispy clouds were high up in the sky, she watched as a plane flew high overhead leaving a vapour trail.

'James, let's do this.'

'Sorry, what?'

'I am taking the plunge, what have I got to lose!'

They embraced, as Gino and Olivier joined the celebration.

'What's going on here?'

'Well Olivier, we are interested, and we would like to put in an offer, what do you think?' He looked at Mel.

'I think €380,000 seems fair.'

Olivier addressed Mel, 'Very well Madame.'

Three of them walked back to their respective cars, Gino ran up behind Mel, 'Bella!'

Mel continued to get into the car, 'Yes Gino?'

'Will you, will you let me take you for lunch?'

'Not today, Gino, why don't you call me tomorrow?'

'Ci Bella!'

He shut the door for her and strutted back to his soft-top like a peacock, he leapt in and then the engine started with a roar, skidding out of the gravel drive he waved and shouted, 'Bye bye Birdie killer.'

Winding her window down, and lowering the roof, she waited for James to wind his window down also so they could chat, 'Well he is keen I give him that!'

'What did you say?'

'I just played it cool, I am not sure Gino is for me.'

'What about Pascal?'

'I need to message him, are you going back to Nice?'

'Yes, shall we have a bite to eat?'

They rendezvoused outside, at the Old Port in Nice, near where Mel had fallen backwards some days before. While Mel was waiting for James to park, she texted Pascal.

*I am really sorry for the delay, I have been doing some business here with James and time has flown by. Are you still on for dinner tomorrow? Mel xx*

She felt bad, the last text he had sent was days ago and she had just been swept up in the whole business planning with James and trying to sort out her finances in the evenings.

Clapping his hands together, 'Right what do you fancy?'

'Not sure, I am starved.'

'What about here?'

'Haha sorry, not that one.' Mel grimaced, 'that's where I fell backwards.'

'Haha of course, ok here is nice.'

'Perfect.'

## Chapter 31 - Ménage à Trois

The hazy slate blue sky with ripples of fuzzy salmon pink clouds adorned the view from the terrace, as Mel gathered up her things and started her bedtime routine. As she got ready for her nocturnal activity, or lack of, her phone pinged in quick succession. She had a mouthful of toothpaste foam and a toothbrush, scanning the messages.

*How are you? Any news on the business front? Would be fabulous if you were to come visit Nice more! Theresa. xx*

Must be lunchtime there, thought Mel.

The other,

*Hey not too worry, yes dinner tomorrow is good, shall we meet at yours? Pascal x*

Mel was about to reply to both, then her phone began to vibrate and flash, a call from James was coming in.

'Hi Mel.'

'Hullo ethering ok?' Mel had a mouthful still. Mel was also worried, had something happened?

'Yes I'm fine, you ok? Sounds like you are eating.'

'Hold on a minute.' She spat out her cleansing white mixture

'What was that?'

'I'm brushing my teeth!'

'God, Mel it's 9:15 pm!'

'I know, I am tired, I need my beauty sleep!'

'Haha, no you don't, silly. Yes I am fine, sorry for the last-minute favour but Gino needs to measure some more bits with a couple of his guys at the villa, I'm super busy tomorrow, are you able, I mean would you mind?'

'Of course, what time?'

'10:30am ok?'

'Sure, you are ok?'

'Sorry to ask but I have some stuff to sort and finalise here before I can focus on the next project. I have also got some paperwork we need to have a look at later in the week.'

'Sounds very serious, ok Mr business partner.'

'Why don't you drop by the day after tomorrow?'

'Right-o will do.'

After the pleasantries of the good night were finished, she ended the call and placed her phone on the bedside table. Mel settled into bed and slept heavily.

    The next morning the day was bright, with a clear sky and the gentle breeze. Mel dashed off in the convertible towards the villa, she felt much happier driving now in France . As she swerved into the driveway creating a cloud of dust, she noticed four faces, with stares of amazement at her rally style arrival. Olivier, Gino, Pierre and *Pascal*.

*Fuck! What am I going to say?*

Mel slowly got out of the car, wishing that the ground would somehow swallow her up. *Why are both Gino and Pascal here, shit shit shit.*

'Hi boys!'

A chorus of various greetings 'Bella, Mel, Madame'... came her way.

Gino stepped forward, 'Nice driving there, Bird killer.' He kissed her on both cheeks. She continued to look down trying to avoid his gaze, but could see through her sunglasses that Pascal wasn't happy.

The others greeted her as they started to walk into the villa, Pascal was bringing up the rear just behind Mel, 'so you like Gino too I hear.' he hissed.

'Pascal,' she turned to look at him, trying to think of something to say, 'it was just a meal, and I am helping James on this build, so I wanted to get to know the people in charge of the project.'

They walked on, she was trying to be brave, she didn't need this, she hadn't meant it to go this way. She liked Pascal, and Gino was just full of testosterone. The business should be her focus, she must keep her attention on the project.

    They moved through the large open plan kitchen, across the clay coloured flagstone floor, and continued on through to the dining area and living room. All the time discussing what work needed to be done against Mel's checklist. When they arrived upstairs, and stepped into the master bedroom Mel moved onto the small balcony and as she looked out over the incredible view. She thought that how, on a really clear day, you could probably see Corsica. She could picture herself sitting here, with a glass of wine in one hand and a book in the other, she smiled to herself.

'Madame?'

Mel stirred from her daydream.

'Yes, Olivier?'

'They are finished Madame, we wait for you downstairs.'

'Thank you, just coming.'

She took a last longing look at the vista before making her way back downstairs.

'Right, all good?' She mustered her most dominant and cheery voice.

The upshot was they had completed the appraisal and Gino would come back to Mel and James with a report in the next couple of days. Rather frustratingly, Mel noticed that Pascal and Gino were hanging back as the other two made for their respective cars, Olivier in a shiny new Audi and Pierre in a battered old blue Citroen 2Cv.

'Bella!'

*Oh Christ, here comes Gino, why was he so devastatingly handsome?*

Taking her sunglasses off and looking at Gino, 'Yes how can I help?'

'You could help me by letting me take you out again, very soon.'

'Gino, I need to focus on the project, I will text you, ok?'

'Ci Bella, but don't leave it too long.' he kissed her on the left cheek, a shudder of excitement went through her, she breathed in deeply, his warm scent lingered. 'Ciao Bella'.

He leapt into his sports car and, as was now his custom, sped off in a cloud of dust and squealing tyres.

Mel turned back to avoid dust going in her eyes and saw Pascal standing there, looking very forlorn.

'Did I misunderstand something from the other day?'

'No, you didn't, you know Gino, he is very excitable.'

'Hmmm, I do know.'

Pascal stood there, his arm muscles straining at the polo top fabric, this guy was a beefcake. A rugby player physique that Mel couldn't deny, made her feel weak at the knees and those huge hands! Mental images were popping up now, she looked at him.

'Pascal, I had a lovely day, and I am looking forward to tonight. That's if you still want to.' She did her best impression of a sad puppy.

'Well, you have an expression in England, don't you? 'Best man win'.

'Yes, may the best man win. Why?'

'I like you Mel, I want to see you tonight.'

He moved toward her, he was a good foot taller than Mel, he towered over her, he bent forward and kissed her on both cheeks, he pulled some hair away from her ear, 'Until tonight then.' he breathed.

He opened his car door, tossed the tape measure and paperwork on the passenger seat, wound his window down, 'Until tonight then, see you at 7pm,' and with that, he drove off.

Mel stood there, she was very excited, more than in a long time. Two men after her, a business starting and a new life, this is what this trip was about, her *rediscovery*. Having Pascal and Gino after her was a real kick, she hadn't had that since sixth form, and then it had just been Mark and harmless flirting with friends. Only one thing was bothering her, if anything was to happen, in a sexual way, she would have to tidy herself up bit particularly, her lady bush. It was currently resembling an overgrown thicket, not an inviting prospect for anyone.

She took her phone out of her bag and dialled.

'James, I need to see you!'

'Ok sure, why don't you swing by now'

Throwing her phone into her bag, she engaged first gear, spun the car's wheels on the gravel and shot off in the direction of Nice, and towards James' house, she needed a debrief on what just happened.

\*

Gino revved and squealed the tyres as he shot away from the house. What was Mel thinking? Why was she interested in Pascal?

He drove quickly and attacked every corner violently as he leaned into the bends. The road straightened out and a white van that had been blocking his path became easy pickings as he pressed the accelerator and roared past. Looking in the rear-view mirror, the van was already an irrelevant dot in the landscape. He caught his own reflection in the mirror, he was proud of his looks, he worked hard to keep fit and lean. Pascal was fat, that is what he thought, and doughy. If he was a prime lean fillet steak, Pascal was rump.

He had never had a woman spurn him, Mel had lapped up all he had given her that evening, she did look hot, he liked curvy women, and an English rose at that. She had something beguiling about her, a delicate femininity and vulnerability that got Gino hot under the collar. Not only that but she was clever and educated, Gino liked that, he liked the intelligent conversation and a challenge, and Mel was a challenge, as was pesky Pascal.

Looking at himself again in the mirror,

'Pascal will lose, Gino loses to no one!' He chuckled to himself.

*

*How did Gino do it?*

The question was running through Pascal's mind, as he lurched from one side of the twisting road to another, one hand behind him steadying the equipment that was liable to move about.

Pascal was annoyed, why didn't Mel tell him sooner. He felt like he had been made a fool of. How would he deal with Gino? He could see why Gino fancied her, the same way he did. She was intelligent, curvaceous and fun, what wasn't there to like? Pascal steered the car gingerly around the bends, he wanted to show Mel a good night, but how could he compete with Gino, the car, the money, everything!

Looking in his rear-view mirror, he pulled at his face. He needed to sort it out, he looked tired and unkempt. That was because of his work, but now he might have another reason to get up in the morning and someone to make an effort for. The only person he knew that could help was probably busy, he dialled anyway, and Mel was worth the effort he concluded.

'James, it's Pascal.'

'Hi Pascal, you ok mate?'

'Yes I need a favour, well two, can you keep a secret?'

'Sure.'

'I need the number and address of the place you go for massages and stuff.'

'You feeling ok? Haha.' James was slightly concerned as Pascal had never shown any inclination to have a facial!

Pascal wasn't laughing,

'I am doing it for Mel. I like her, James.'

'Sure, I will text you the number, she is a lovely person. Look after her.'

'Thank you.'

'What was the other favour?'

'Ahh oui, do you know what her favourite flowers are?'

'I see where this is going, you seeing her tonight?'

'Yes, I want to impress, and if you have any ideas of what I should wear…'

'Ok, well she is coming here now, let me try and find out for you and I will send over some clothing suggestions!'

'Ok please don't tell her!'

'Promise.'

He hung up, he wasn't going to let Gino just walk all over him and barge in on him and Mel. It had just started raining and as he joined the motorway, he saw a person struggling to raise the roof of their sports car, they had evidently had to pull onto the hard shoulder to do so.

\*

Gino had tried to dial James twice, eventually got through. He hadn't been helpful, but he was paying the bills at the moment, as the estate was losing money hand over fist. All James had said was not to take her to a place by the old port and he wasn't sure what Mel's intention was about staying in France. Useless!

Never mind, Gino would find a way! At that moment, he had just joined the motorway to head back to Italy, and it started to rain. He had to stop to get the roof up, he was getting soaked. He wasn't sure but he could have sworn he saw Pascal drive-by, through the torrential rain, and if his eyesight served him well, he could have sworn Pascal had a smirk across his face.

## Chapter 32 - Flashback - Empty Nest

September the 25th was not a date that Mel was relishing, the boys were off. 18 year old twins, both going down very different routes. Daniel was off to University to study for a business degree and Andrew was going to travel, he wanted to explore the Greek islands.

Leading up to the day, Mel had been very emotional, she did well to hide it from the rest of the family. She worried about the boys, their chosen paths and of course their happiness and safety. But there was a lingering concern, that suddenly it would just be her and Mark. What would life be like now once the boys had gone?

'You ok Mum?'

'Yes, all good you? Have you got everything you need Daniel?'

'Yes Mum, don't worry I am only going to Bristol, it's not a million miles away.'

It wasn't, thought Mel, but it would feel like it.

\*

'Now do you need anything?'

'Think I'm all good mum.'

'Now do you know what you need to get from Athens to Kefalonia?'

'Mum it's all planned, don't worry.' Andrew looked at his mum, 'Are you ok?'

'Yes, Ummm.' She turned away as her bottom lip started to wobble.

'Mum come on,' he put a comforting arm around her.

'What's going on?'

Mark stood there in the doorway of the bedroom, arms folded and his frame filling the gap. Mel wasn't sure what to say, was it silly that she was so upset that the boys were flying the nest? She was proud of them, both so different and doing such different things with their lives.

'Nothing, Mum is, Mum is just a bit upset I think.'

'Right well when you are ready darling, can you come downstairs?'

Mel turned to face him, her eyes all puffy.

'Yup, two minutes.'

Mark wasn't an overly emotional person. Mel contemplated that she had only seen him cry twice, once at the birth of the boys and once when his Mum had passed away. He wasn't really a hugger either, he usually rubbed the boy's hair, he did hug her, but not that much recently.

'Mum, you can always visit me, Greece isn't that far you know.'

'I know darling, Mummy is just being silly. You will have a wonderful time.'

She hugged all 6ft of him tightly, unlike his father the boys both enjoyed hugs, even at 18. Though these days they towered over her, and her head could only rest on their chest. The idea of the Aegean certainly appealed to her, and she could see why it would appeal to Andrew.

Later that evening, Mel was cooking the boys' favourite meal - steak and chips. Mark was off fiddling around in the outbuilding at the bottom of the garden, the boys were sitting at the big rectangular wooden dining table in the kitchen, chatting excitedly about their next adventures.

'Mum you've been to Greece, haven't you?'

'What was that?' as she slammed the oven door.

'Greece, have you been mum?'

Mel thought back to a very memorable trip, coincidently that had been to Kefalonia too. One September, many moons ago. A friend of hers at university had suggested they go after their second year, to celebrate getting that far! Mel had saved up. She had worked at the student union and had managed to scrape the cash together for the airline tickets and some spending money. Luckily her friend, God what was her name? Heather? Haley? *Andrea!* A petite velvety French girl she had bumped into whilst they both reached for the last slice of treacle tart in the canteen. She had persuaded Mel that a trip to Greece as two young girls was a good idea, what could possibly go wrong with that... Mel smiled to herself as she recalled the trip, suddenly vivid in her memory though the passing of time had eroded some of the details.

'Mum?'

'What?'

'We lost you there, what was it like?'

'It was a very long time ago boys, I mean there was no Easyjet then, we flew I think with Olympic Air, or BA, I was only 20.'

The garden door opened, and Mark trudged in, 'Smells good, what are the boys having?' he winked at them.

'Ok Dad, have you been to Greece? Mum has.'

'Have you?' Mark spun round to look at Mel who was shaking some frozen peas into a saucepan.

'Years ago, darling, I was just saying I was 20 and still at Uni, we hadn't even met!'

She snuggled into Mark and leaned her head on him, his old tatty jumper he wore for gardening smelt of him. She liked that reassuring scent, one she had known most of her adult life. There was something comforting about it, especially as tomorrow their 2 boys would be off. She began to cry, she turned into him to cover her face.

'Mum?'

'Come on darling, they will be back and asking for money no doubt!'

Looking up, 'Sorry, just feels strange, I'll be fine, Mark can you open some more wine?'

It had been a fun evening, they had chatted, reminisced and laughed. The kitchen, indeed, the whole house rang out with chatter and noise. The wine and beers had flowed.

Later that evening, Mel was brushing her teeth.

'Darling?'

'Yes?' Mark's voice came in from the bedroom.

'The outbuilding, do you think it's do-up-able?'

'Course, now come here.'

She rinsed her mouth and walked back into the bedroom. Mark was laid in his boxers on top of the bed. 'You need a cuddle.'

She climbed into bed and shuffled up to him and he put his arm around her and pulled her in tightly. Maybe she had been wrong, maybe this would be good for them, some 'us' time.

'The boys will be ok, won't they?' Mel couldn't shake off the worry.

'Of course, I suspect we will get texts and calls for urgent money. Look, Bristol isn't far and Greece is only a short flight, as soon as they start to miss their Mum's roast they will be back.' He kissed her on the head, she began to drift off into a deep sleep, dreaming...

*Kefalonia,* Mel was back there now. It had been a warm September when they had decided to go before the first term of the third year started. For 2 weeks, it would be bliss, to swim and enjoy the warmth, great Greek food and wine.

Andrea's distant cousin had an apartment, a 2 bedroom place in Fiskardo. While on their trip, Andrea had fallen for Christos, a big hearted, handsome Greek guy, the owner of one of the local tavernas and occasional renter of boats to tourists. Andrea went back, again and again, they married and Mel had lost touch. She considered to herself, *why did it always take someone else for her to do something new?*

## Chapter 33 - Dinner with Pascal

Pascal had managed to get an appointment at James' suggested salon and spa. The rain had begun earlier in the afternoon and by the time Pascal had reached the location he resembled a sopping wet bear, and his hair was flat against his head. He considered he had a good head of hair with very few greys, thick and brown with flecks of charcoal. He had rushed to get their only free appointment that day and using James' name they had squeezed him in.

The salon's manager greeted him and showed him upstairs, where he was given a quick refreshing facial. This was something alien to Pascal, so when the masseuse had entered the room to find him standing completely naked, as delicately as possible she'd instructed him to put his underwear back on and lay face up under the towel. Why was he doing this? All to prove a point to Gino or was there something more? He had enjoyed his picnic with Mel, even though she had covered him in food. It was evident she was hungover, though he didn't say anything as he assumed, being English, she would find it impolite of him to mention such a thing.

Now he was embarrassed, he had just stood there like a zombie, waiting for instruction, with everything on show. Once under the towel and face up as instructed, and in the brief pause between the lady leaving the room and coming back, he made a mental note that he should take more time for himself than he had been doing. With his face zinging from the peppermint moisturiser, he was ushered downstairs and into an awaiting leather chair. He looked at himself in the mirror, his face already looked better. The olive complexion from his father's Greek side, and the softer visage of his French mother he could see was visible in the reflection. His hair however needed attention. The lockdown of Covid had restricted his basic, grooming routine to say the least. Now restrictions were over, it needed some focus to get back into shape. He had kept up his gym sessions when time allowed, and his work kept him in decent physical shape. As he waited for the 'stylist' to return after washing his hair. He sat back and considered in more detail the situation he was in with Mel, in a vain attempt to move his thoughts on from the embarrassing episode upstairs.

He had assumed she liked him, she had been up for the picnic and clearly enjoyed herself, that much was evident. Mel had not recoiled when he had kissed her in the car, though he was out of practice. He was rusty, he'd had a very long dry spell when it came to dating, and unlike Gino. Gino! How dare he try to steal this woman from under his eyes.

Just then a cup of coffee arrived and was placed on the ledge under the vast mirror. Why did they do that? He was in the hairdressers equivalent to a straightjacket.

Why did he care so much about Mel? There was something, he felt chemistry, a passion, or was it just lust?

The issue was that James employed Gino, and maybe they were in cahoots? The fundamental point was he liked Mel, and he wasn't going to back down, not this time.

*

'Merda!'

Gino was soaked, bloody roof. He even deduced Mel perceived his car as silly, now he was thinking the same. Drenched, he drove, faster than he should back to Italy, pissed off, not only at the car but at James and that English rose, Mel. He liked her, she was fun, intelligent and not the airhead type he seemed to usually end up with. Even his ancient dad had said to him to find a nice *English girl,* he'd always frowned knowingly when Gino introduced him to his latest conquest, he liked voluptuous blondes, what was wrong with that? There was something about this British lady, older than he would usually consider but it felt like a challenge too, and Gino liked a challenge, though at the moment there seemed to be many challenges in his life.

He was wrestling daily with his father about the estate, what to do with it and how to make money. There was some family money and assets, but Gino was now trying to buy out his brothers, so the property would become his on the day of his fathers death, they had been willing to do this on the proviso that Gino stay and look after his father, while they had their careers and families. His brothers had no time for the property, or shared his vision of selling wine, selling bedrooms and starting a shop filled with local produce.

Simultaneously running the Bucci estate, the building firm and coupled with the added complication of his father's various illnesses, it was taking its toll on Gino and he knew it. If only he could get the last payment together for his brothers and get the Bucci estate filled with paying customers in the rooms and suites- something his father wouldn't hear of. The building firm he had started, and which he owned totally, was doing well - just a couple more big jobs and he would have the €50,000 for his brothers, and then the Bucci estate would be all his and he could finally live out his dream.

His elderly father was getting more frail and slowly was allowing Gino off the reins when it came to the family house, but there were many blocks to Gino's grand plans. The distraction of dating was welcome with everything else in such turmoil. Mel was an unusual attraction but one he would relish. Pascal? How dare he drive by and not help? He couldn't win over Mel, not against Gino, he was a mere carpenter. Mel deserved more, and he could give it to her.

*

Mel had swung by James' place to discuss the house and the romantic triangle she had managed to get herself into.

'What do I do?'

James soothed and raised his concerns about Gino, but rather suspiciously, seemed overly enthusiastic about Pascal.

'So, you don't like Gino?'

'What makes you say that?'

'I can tell James, you don't.'

'Honestly, I don't, I can't deny he is attractive in a typical bad boy playboy type way, but usually, it ends up all about Gino. He usually dates young blondes.'

'And I am a frumpy brunette!'

'Mel, I didn't say that. I am just telling you what I know. Look, can you keep a secret, I mean it.'

A smirk crept across her face, 'Of course.'

'Well, they both rang me before you got here, basically, both of them like you and want to know all about you.'

'And? What did you say?'

'I kept it very tight. I told Pascal a bit more than I told Gino, but that's it.'

'What did Gino want?'

'He wanted to know how long you were remaining in France and what you ate, drank, etc.'

A furrowed brow crept across her face, 'And Pascal?'

'Well, he was more worried he didn't impress you and wants to.'

'And you helped him?'

'I suggested a haircut and a facial.' he began to laugh.

'I can't imagine he's ever been to a spa! James, what have you done?'

'Nothing! Come on, I can tell you don't really like Gino. You avoid him and excuse me for saying this, but you *tolerate* him. Pascal, on the other hand, you blush when you say his name.'

'I do not.'

'Mel.'

'Ok, you are right, Gino's shouting about me being a *bird killer* irritates me, am I that obvious?'

'No, they clearly both think they are in with a chance.'

Mel looked up, 'Shit is that the time?'

'Ok be calm, you've got time, what time is Pascal picking you up?'

'He said 7 at mine.'

'Ok well, I will come with you, help you get ready and then leave you to enjoy yourself and make up your mind for yourself about Pascal, and whether you prefer him or Gino.'

'Deal, did Gino say anything about me?'

'He just said he liked you, but not much more.'

Mel was thinking, she must enjoy herself, that was the point of this trip! She needed to make up her mind. This was all part of rediscovering herself. That thought clung to her as she drove back to Theresa's apartment. She mustn't have a too sclerotic view of the situation and keep her options open. She had learnt that the hard way.

\*

Pascal was bang on time, and Mel was ready.

James had been more than helpful, and an outfit was selected, a confidence-boosting G&T drunk. Standing by the door to leave, she turned to face the full-length mirror that hung in the hallway.

They had opted for a navy-blue wrap dress, with brown leather sandals, and one of Theresa's slightly smaller than usual hessian bags with brown handles and tassel.

'You look fab, now go!'

James had stayed until she left, he would leave shortly after her, so Pascal wouldn't be doubtful of Mel's intentions.

The rain had eased, the mugginess had cleared and the coolness in the evening breeze was a welcome respite, as Mel greeted Pascal.

'Hello, how are you? Don't you look smart!'

Realising that he may be suspicious, she added, 'have you had a haircut?

They embraced, Pascal planting a stubble thick kiss on both of her softly made-up cheeks.

'Oui. I mean, yes, do you like it?'

Bloody hell, he looked hot as hell. A smart short back and sides and some length left on top made him look ten years younger, a fitted black shirt clung to his muscular body and some leg hugging dark indigo jeans showed off his stunning thick legs. He had matched it with a dark brown belt and some suede chestnut coloured Chelsea boots. He looked really good, Mel considered. Shaking herself from her dream-like state, she uttered. 'Umm yes suits you.'

She didn't want to give anything away, she had to pretend she knew nothing, and she must make up her mind soon, she didn't want to lead anyone on, well not for too long anyway.

Smiling broadly, she locked her arm into his and they strolled around the port. 'You look lovely tonight.'

'Thank you, where are we going?'

'Ahh, that is a surprise.'

Mel wasn't overly keen on surprises, she had enough to last her a lifetime, but she bravely went along with Pascal's. He began fumbling in his pocket for something, Mel was alarmed.

'What are you doing?'

'I need some keys, it is ok.'

He had read in Mel's eyes that she was nervous, he looked at her as they reached a door, 'here, we are here.'

'It doesn't look like a restaurant.'

The door in question faced over the port but in the opposite direction to Theresa's apartment.

'No restaurant then?' Mel tried to hide her nervousness and disappointment, she had fancied a night out, and she felt good and thanks to James looked good too.

'You will see.'

He took her by the hand, and gently held her right hand as they walked up a very familiar marble hallway he directed her into a lift.

'This is just like my apartment.'

'Well, I hope you like it.'

The lift juddered to a start, and they stood in awkward silence, Pascal was nervous, what if she didn't like his surprise? He felt a bead of sweat on his brow, as he went to wipe it, he dropped his keys. Instinctively he bent down as the lift jolted to a halt he stumbled backwards and ended up shoving his bottom into Mel's groin.

'Ouch!'

'Argh, I am so sorry.' the doors opened. 'Are you ok Mel?'

'Yes, I am fine, did you find the keys?'

'Yes, do not worry.'

She was worried, but what an arse, firm and round. Very masculine.

They walked to a door, which unveiled a set of stairs. 'Where are we going?' enquired Mel.

'Just up here, you will see.' A warm smile crept across his face, he was seriously worried now, and how had he managed to shove his rear into her?

She duly followed him up the stairs, and to her amazement, they exited onto the roof terrace, and at the far end was a table with two chairs. Next to the table was a bbq. Some candles in storm lanterns and fairy lights illuminated the scene.

'O wow, Pascal.'

She walked to the table, perched near the edge, it looked over the port and the view was a mirror of hers from the other side. The lights on the boats lit up the water and the stars dazzled like diamonds on a velvet cushion.

'Madame?'

He pulled a chair out and indicated to her to sit. At her place setting was a bunch of flowers, wrapped in brown paper and tied with string, they were stunning pale pink Peonies.

'These are lovely, I assume they are for me?' she smiled and winked at Pascal.

'Yes, they are for you, as beautiful as you are.'

Mel thought that was slightly creepy, but maybe it was lost in part in translation.

'Pascal, this is wonderful, won't other people come up?'

'Ahhh non, the owner is a friend.' a broad smile filled his face.

Adroitly he handled the BBQ, and the food was delicious. Mel sat munching on some rare charred steak. 'This is fantastique!' The French intonation wasn't intended as rude, it was just something she would say back home.

'Sorry, I meant yummy.' remembering the picnic.

'You and your "yummy", so you like the setting?'

'Yes, I like it, thank you, it is truly wonderful.' Mel meant what she had said, she felt special, but it didn't feel pretentious. 'Look Pascal, the other day, the picnic, I am very sorry, I spoiled it for you.'

He reached over and touched her hand, at the same time deftly topping her up with some smooth vanilla-scented red wine. The combination was perfect, a reassuring hand and the reassuring warmth of the red wine.

'You did not spoil it, I am, I think you say, *clumsy* also.'

'Ha! Yes, I am clumsy, what would you say?'

'In your case, Maladroite'

'Maladroite sounds much better! Where did you learn to cook like that?'

'My father was Greek and my mother French, we did a lot of cooking and alfresco soirees.'

'Funny I was just thinking....' she paused as she glanced at the view and wondered at her current situation.

'Yes, you were thinking?' prompted Pascal.

'I was thinking how much I am enjoying this. I only came out here because of that silly letter.'

'Silly?'

'Sorry yes, umm long story.

'And you did, are you glad you did?'

She looked into his big brown eyes, 'Yes I am glad.'

He took her hand and stood up, he pressed some buttons on a small Bluetooth speaker, and started to dance. They began to sway to Charles Aznavour. Mel was not going to deny, the whole experience was so romantic and, the sexual tension was palpable.

As the wine flowed and they ate Pascal's excellent food, she began to picture this as her life, her new life.

This could be her restart, but how did she know what she wanted? Was she just being carried along on a journey of longing? She had been here for such a short time? They continued to eat, drink and dance as the candles flickered in the now pitch black clear sky.

'You can see so many stars.'

'Yes, it's beautiful, are you having a nice time?'

'Yes, I am, it has been lovely, really lovely.' Mel could usually hold her drink pretty well, but the nervousness at the beginning of the evening coupled with the romantic setting seemed to propel her to sip her wine freely and in abundance. The upshot was she felt decidedly tipsy as she was led back down the ladder stairs, gripping tightly for balance.

'Careful there.' Pascal pointed to a particularly warn step. Said Pascal as he guided her down a particular tricky bit of the stairwell. He held out one of his massive brutish hands, and his hand and she clasped it. As if by magic a bolt of charged energy shot through her, excitement, nervousness and arousal. It was obvious from his face that Pascal had felt it too. As she took the last step down, he pulled her into him and kissed her passionately. They stood there for some time just savouring the moment, there on the landing of some friend of Pascal's apartment block. It was fun, it was spontaneous, and Mel was enjoying every minute. She felt safe with Pascal, and God he was a good kisser.

When they stopped, they pulled away and smiled at each other.

'I hope that was ok?' he asked.

'Very much so.' She took hold, and hand in hand they made their way out into the street and ambled along, chatting away.

*

Mel had left him there, James, he wanted to see a bit more of the apartment. He had a good nose around, he liked seeing what others had done, decoratively speaking.

Slurping the last of the G&T, he laid down on one of the large sofas in the living room, he felt sleepy. It had been a long couple of weeks, the project, then Darren and now the doer-upper with Mel. He shut his eyes and drifted off.

*

As they approached the apartment, they unhooked hands and Mel searched for her keys.

'Have you got them?'

'Yes, here they are, I have had a great evening Pascal.'

'I am glad, shall I call you tomorrow?'

'Would you like a nightcap?' she tentatively asked.

'A nightcap?'

'It means a drink before bed.'

'Oui, that would be good.'

They made their way up an almost identical hallway from the one they had just left and finally outside the door.

Rattling the key in the lock, they pushed the door open. Stop by the hallway table to continue the passionate kiss they had started earlier.

'James!'

With a start, a head poked up from the sofa. Rubbing his eyes and hair.

'O god what's happened?'

'Umm nothing James, why are you here?' Mel was annoyed she wanted to have this time with Pascal and now James was here clogging up her plans for the evening.

'God sorry I must have nodded off.' he stumbled to his feet, as Pascal looked on rather perplexed.

Realising that it might be odd that James was in her flat, Mel quickly suggested, 'James was here looking for one of those interior books, this is weak - weren't you?'

'Yes, I mean yeah I was, right well,' He grabbed his coat and made for the door, 'Sorry, see you soon.' the door slammed behind him. Pascal watched in bewilderment as Mel double-checked the door was closed and to make sure James had definitely gone. Turning round to face Pascal, 'Right so where were we?'

She motioned to the coffee machine, 'Would you like one?'

'First I would like you to explain why James was here?' He didn't look happy, why did James have to spoil the evening?

'As I said he was here to pick up a book.'

'Really?'

'Yes really, on interiors that Theresa has'.

Though this was a tiny lie, it was only a small little fib. She moved toward Pascal who was standing all rigid now by the dining table, Mel wanted to attempt to continue the line of seduction they had been on.

She put her arms round his neck and went in for a kiss. Pascal went along with it but there was certainly less passion than before.

'What's up?'

'It's just James being here, and Gino…'

'Ok, look I have been open with you, and James is a very old friend, I worked with him years ago.'

'I guess, maybe I am tired, I think I will make my way home.'

Mel was pissed off, she had thoroughly enjoyed her evening, the wine was now sloshing around inside her made it hard for her to make informed judgements or deal with this.

'Ok sure, well text me tomorrow.'

He kissed her on the mouth, his stubble rubbing her chin. She followed him to the door. 'Night then.'

'Bon Nuit.'

With that, he was gone, for someone so bulky he seemed to slink off very speedily. Mel reached into her bag to ring James. There were two messages unread.

*Hi M, transferred horse money today let me know you got it, and I want to catch up soon :) How's the dating? Work project with James? Love C xxx*

As it was now 11:30pm, she decided to text rather than call.

*Hi Cathy, you star, thank you for doing that. Work project is exciting, I will send pics, dating is complicated… What time are you free tomorrow? xxx*

She needed Cathy's advice, and she hoped that Cathy was ok. After she had mentioned the word *affair*, Mel's mind had spun around and tried to figure out why and how Chris would or could manage it.

The other text was from Theresa, the upshot was she was going to be another 4 weeks at least and would Mel mind staying on at the apartment. She was only just at the end of week 3, this meant another 5 weeks… *at least she could rinse her underwear,* she thought as her head hit the pillow.

## Chapter 34 – Too strong?

'Hullo'

James' voice had a certain nervous tension in it, Mel had rung him the next morning to remonstrate.

'What were you thinking? You knew he was suspicious!'

'Mel I am so sorry, I stayed to finish my G&T and then I nodded off. I am truly sorry.'

Mel knew that James would be and that he'd never mean to upset the apple cart.

'Look I am sorry too, it just took me by surprise.'

'No, I do understand, so how did it go?' his voice warmer.

'Honestly, it was great, he is very romantic, and the advice you gave him had certainly paid off!'

'You lucky thing, I can't seem to find a date anywhere!'

'Fair is fair I will help you now, you got me two, even though I don't really want one of them…'

'So, you've made your mind up then?'

'Well, I think so, I have a wacky idea to run by you.'

'Go for it, oh hold on…' Mel could hear what sounded like the noise of a pneumatic drill starting up in the background,… 'Sorry back now, last-minute work needed doing in the house.'

'Well, I am thinking of inviting both of them here, on my turf, so to speak, to help make my mind up. I'm going to cook them the same meal and serve the same wine, and it will consist of everything I particularly like. I want to gauge their reactions and see which one prefers it? Does that sound mad?'

'Mad, but I like it, just promise me one thing?'

'Go on…'

'Please don't serve me a super strength gin in the afternoon?'

Two identical texts were sent, one to Gino and one to Pascal. Invites for dinner, Gino tomorrow and Pascal the next day. Now what would she cook? Steak? That cote de boeuf had been amazing, followed by some cheese. These were all things Mel liked and the way to her heart and supposedly a man's was through their stomachs.

Her phone began to buzz, it was Cathy.

'Hi love, how are you?'

'I'm good, though I've been worrying about you since our last conversation.' Mel was concerned for her friend and confidant.

'Sorry, about all that last week, it was silly, everything with Chris is fine. In fact we've been thinking that maybe we could come out and spend some time with you.'

Mel didn't know what to say, on one hand, it would have been lovely to see a friend, well two friends, and spend some time with them, she would love to show them around! But on the other hand, it wasn't great timing with everything going on setting up the new business, not to mention her personal life. Mel had also wanted this trip to be, which sounded rather selfish, her time, an opportunity to shrug off the past, step away from everything, experience a new way of living and reinvigorate her life.

But she found herself saying, 'Yeh, ok, when are you thinking?'

'Nothing booked yet, just a thought.'

'Well, I need to check when Theresa is back as there are only two bedrooms.' Two little white lies there.

'Of course, well we wouldn't expect you to put us up, we would get a hotel or Airbnb of course.'

This made things easier, reflected Mel, she could still do her thing and spend time with them when it was convenient. Though the other downside was the fact that was coming as well. That would mean her, and Cathy would have little chance to spend time alone and catch up properly.

'I thought Chris had a lot on at work?'

'He did but the deal is done and while we, I mean, he, has some time we could come down, but if it's not ok then don't worry.'

'No, it would be lovely, let me just check in with Theresa and come back to you.'

'Of course, no worries, I am sure I can send Chris out for an afternoon on the beach so we can have a catch up.'

Phew, Mel was relieved she didn't have to suggest such a solution herself.

'Perfect, give me a day or two.'

'Of course, lots of love. Bye, Mel.'

'Bye Cathy.'

Cathy turned to her brunch partner, 'Bloody cheek, after all I have done, though I think it's a goer, book the tickets sweets.'

## Chapter 35 - How to solve a problem like Gino

She had told Gino to arrive around 7ish and checked that he was ok with beef. He'd said yes to both and seemed as keen as mustard, he was there at 7pm sharp. She tried to act casual. '7th floor, number 14.' she buzzed him in. Choosing what to wear was becoming an issue she hadn't planned on so many dates!

Tonight's outfit was a bright green summer dress, patterned with flowers. The candles were lit, the terrace lights were on, and the wine was chilling. She was ready, on her terms, she felt in control. It was a good feeling and it would be the moment of truth with Gino. Would he redeem himself or would it put him second billing?

She didn't heed James' advice and went ahead and had a cheeky gin while she was getting ready, so by the time Gino arrived she felt a small buzz that only the first drink of the day can give you.

'Bella, you look wonderful.'

She did a girlish sort of twirl in the doorway to swish her dress from side to side.

'Come in,' she noted he had a rather large bunch of red roses behind his back, and a bottle of red wine. Not bad she thought.

'These are for you.'

'Gino they are lovely', as she did the obligatory sniff at the roses and examination of the wine label, not that this made her any the wiser from doing so. Red roses, which Mel did feel was a bit of a cliché, but then Gino and the situation was a cliché to a certain extent.

'Please sit down, what would you like to drink?'

'Whatever you are having, and thanks, I didn't get to see much of the place on my last visit', he winked at her as he sat down, manspreading on one of the chairs on the terrace. She offered him a chilled glass of white wine, her knowledge of wine being limited, she hoped she had selected well.

'Gavi di Gavi!' he exclaimed.

'Yes, do you like it?'

'I do, the grapes are grown not far from where I was born.'

'Really, where is that?'

'Bra.'

Mel had to stop herself from spitting out her wine and laughing.

'Sorry where?'

'Why is that so funny?'

'Well, you will think me silly now, but *Bra* in English is the *bra* that a woman wears to keep things in place.' instinctively she clutched both breasts, maybe that large G&T wasn't such a good idea she thought to herself.

'Well not all of them work very well' he smirked and gestured at her chest.

Blushing and remembering that fateful night in the pool.

'Well, umm no, maybe not.' She looked down at her glass.

'Hey,' he moved towards her and placed his left hand under her chin to raise it back up. 'I didn't mean to upset you, Bella, now tell me all about you. Then if you are lucky, I will tell you all about me!'

She beamed back at him, noting that scent again, it was intoxicating.

More wine was poured, and the conversation was easy and casual. He talked about his father and the estate and how he was trying to turn it around, Mel talked about her life, the boys and home. It dawned on her, by the time they had finished the Cote de boeuf, that she was not missing her home, back in England.

'That was delicious Bella, so do you miss home?'

'Thank you, glad you liked it. Well, I thought I did, not so sure now.'

'Are you not working with James?'

'I will be yes, and hopefully, that will be a good investment. I haven't done anything like it before, and certainly nothing so spontaneous since Mark's death...' she paused, sipped some of the excellent Barolo that Gino had brought, and looked at her dining partner.

'Gino, can I ask a question?'

'Of course, Bella.'

The wine gave her Dutch courage and she couldn't let this go on much longer, stringing them along was unfair, so she decided to come out with it, 'Out of all the women on the Riviera, why me?'

He looked at her quizzically and then replied in a considered fashion,

'You are different, you are intelligent and funny, with a lovely body.'

'Not sure being *different* is a good thing but thank you!'

'It is Bella, it means you aren't like other girls.'

'Gino I am not a girl!'

'Good I don't want a girl. I want a woman.'

He moved aside the cutlery and put his hand on hers, his warm palm pressed into the top of her hand.

'Yes Gino?'

'I like you Mel, even if you do kill birdies…' at the moment he saw something over her shoulder. 'Those are lovely, where did you get them?' He gestured to the Peonies that were in a vase on the coffee table. Swivelling to take a look and without thinking, Mel answered. 'Pascal gave them to me.'

Turning back to face him, she realised her error. It was too late to cover up. 'Just a small thing…'

'I see,' his jaw clenched, she could see the muscles move below the ears. He looked annoyed. 'He is only a carpenter, his dad owned some restaurant, not much…'

Mel leapt to Pascal's defence, Pascal had been so warm and understanding the night before, she felt something that she hadn't felt for a long time. Passion. It was then that she realised that James was right, Gino was fine if it was all about Gino.

'That's not fair! He has done a lot. Not everyone can be born with an estate and vineyards!'

He recoiled. Women didn't usually speak to him this way. It burned. He went to say something,

'Bel...'

'Gino! How many children do I have?'

'Huh?'

'How many children?'

'I don't understand, I think three.'

'No Gino, two. I only mentioned my boys several times this evening.'

She glared at him, 'I think it's time we went back to where we were, Gino, you own a builders' firm, I am employing you and we remain friends and colleagues.'

Deflated didn't quite cover it, he knew he had messed up. But who was this English lady barking at him?

'I understand, I have learnt one thing..'

'Yes?'

'You are stronger willed than you look, a fighter.'

She took that as a compliment and topped up their wine glasses.

'Gino to us and the villa, friends!'

'Friends Bella.'

## Chapter 36 - Coq au vin

'Not to sound like a stuck tape recorder, but how did it go?'

'Well, it's Pascal or nothing, you were right unless it was all about Gino it wouldn't have worked.'

'What time is Pascal coming round?'

'7pm.'

'Blimey, you are keeping it the same! Are you free to meet up? I need to talk to you about the house project and next steps.'

'Ok where?'

'There is a cafe I like in the Place de Messina, meet you there at 12?'

'Perfect, see you then, text me the address.'

'Will do.'

The Place de Messina was beautiful. A wide-open space, surrounded by a mix of old and new four storey buildings. The upper parts were painted dusty pink with stone-coloured colonnades below that housed shops and bistros. Vibrant and bustling with trams slicing through the middle of the checkerboard piazza, it was a great place to people watch, Mel could see why James liked it here. As she arrived she got the distinct impression she was in a LGBT place.

'James, now don't tell me, feathers, a rainbow flag and hot waiters... '

'Haha, nothing past you! Look it's a great place and they do a good lunch, here take a look.' he handed her a menu.

'So, you wanted to talk about the house?'

'Well yes, the thing is we need to move quite quickly, I guess what I am saying is we need to put the money forward and I need to know if you are up for it.'

'Did they accept our offer?'

'They did, and for that price, they want a quick sale. No chain as I understand it.'

Two cafe au laits arrived and two large glasses of water. James was smiling at someone, but she couldn't make out whom.

'James, who are you looking at?'

Trying to be discreet, he leant in and whispered, 'that guy there with the suit and laptop, he comes here quite a bit, and I am trying to pluck up the courage to ask him out.'

'Right.' She stood up before James could stop her, and walked over to the tall guy in the blue suit, James could only watch and pretend to stir his coffee, he saw Mel point in their direction, James turned away to avoid the gaze. Within 30 seconds she was back.

Mel nonchalantly picked up the sugar sachet, tore it with her teeth and added the contents to her coffee. James watched as she did so. 'What just happened?'

Mel slid a small business car over to James, 'He said to text him later, and he would love a drink.'

James opened mouthed, turned to watch the guy stand up and collect up his belongings, walk towards the door, and wink at him.

'You have a date. Now shall we get on?'

'Umm, I don't know what to say,'

'Thank you?'

'Thank you! What a wing woman you are Mel! So about last night? Are you looking forward to Pascal coming round?'

Mel went into as much detail as she could remember about the evening, she also told James about Cathy wanting to come out and Theresa being delayed yet again.

'Well, I guess you will find out tonight. Can you delay Cathy?'

'Not sure, she has done so much for me.'

'Well maybe ask her to come in a few weeks, then Theresa should be back, and you have an excuse?'

'Good plan, right so the house?'

'Yes'

'Let's do it! I will call my bank later today and then transfer money to you. Did you bring the paperwork?'

While eating scrambled eggs they went through the formalities, this was it, she was going to sign. Take a big leap into the unknown and hope that it paid off.

*

It was just past 7pm when the doorbell went.

'Hi, come up to the 7th floor, flat 14.'

The sense of deja vu was not lost on Mel, she had changed the food, even she couldn't bring herself to eat the same meal twice, and had created her riff on a coq au vin, which was simmering away on the stove when Pascal reached the front door.

'Bonjour.' She opened the door enthusiastically and hugged him. He returned the hug and kissed her on the lips, his bristly chin rubbing hers, the musky scent and strong manly squeeze were definitely stirring some strong desires in Mel. She didn't want to fuck up like last night, so the red roses had been given to Annette downstairs, as a thank you – 'here is something to brighten up your day', Annette was bemused but grateful.

'Good to see you again.' as he released her, she guided him into the kitchen, the aroma of the food enveloped them as they passed through to the terrace. 'Smells good, I mean yummy.' he smiled at her.

'Well, I hope you like it, coq au vin with mushrooms.'

'Perfect, here.' He handed her a thin cylinder, gift wrapped in brown paper and placed a bottle of rosé on the table.

'What is it?'

'Open it.'

He sat forward to watch her, she duly did as she was told, sliding her hand inside the package to release the tape.

'It's amazing!'

An art deco style poster of Nice, a lady lying back on a balcony, with palm trees and the bay of Nice in the background.

'Do you like it?'

'Very much, thank you.' She kissed him on the cheek, and as she stood up, he grabbed her hand and pulled her back.

'That wasn't long enough.' He planted a big kiss on her lips and the moment made Mel weak at the knees. With the feel of his breath on her skin, his hands touching her body and the warm wet tongue exploring her mouth, she was in heaven.

Eventually, they pulled apart. 'Umm, shall I get some drinks?'

'Yes, that would be good, here pop this in the fridge.'

He had also brought her some Cote De Provence, her favourite.

'Here.' she handed him some chilled rosé, the sun was just about setting but the evening was warm.

'I love the poster, where did you…'

'You got James one similar, no? I saw it the other night, at the BBQ, and you seemed to like that wine, so there we are.' he beamed at her.

'It really is lovely, thank you, Pascal.'

    They sat outside until the timer on Mel's phone reminded her to check the chicken. 'Do you want to come in and we can talk in the kitchen?'

He followed her, holding the wine bottle in one hand and their 2 glasses in the other. The chicken was ready, and she just needed to finish the salad. She served and they sat with the sun setting outside with a candle flickering between them.

'This looks yummy.'

'Haha thank you, I hope so.'

They chatted about life and Mel told him about the boys and her home life, and he did the same.

'So, you don't live here?' asked Mel

'No, I live further north, I have a windmill near Bordeaux.'

'Really, that sounds amazing.'

Instinctively he said, 'You must come to stay.'

Mel was taken aback by this sudden offer, 'umm yes sounds good.'

'Sorry was that too forward?'

'No, not at all, I haven't been asked out, let alone for a stopover for a very long time.' She laughed

'No, I haven't asked either,' a warm smile crept over his face, mirrored by Mel's.

'So do you think your two boys would like France?'

She looked up, he had paid attention. That was very attractive. He poured some wine into their glasses. 'They would love it, one of them is exploring Greece as we speak.'

'Ahh lovely, my mother used to live in Greece.'

'Used too?'

'Sadly, she died, cancer, but she loved Greece.'

'Pascal I am sorry to hear that.' She got up to hug him, feeling a sudden pang of emotion. In doing so she jolted the table and some of his chicken landed squarely into his groin.

'She was old, and my sister…Owwwww!'

'O God hold on,' she moved to help him, but realised that wasn't going to be appropriate so landed up just standing there apologising.

'I am so clumsy, I am sorry.'

'Don't worry, I'll be right back, where is the toilet?'

She motioned to the hallway, 'First door on the right.'

'Thank you.'

What a fool you are she scolded herself, why did you need to get up? To try and take her mind off what had just happened, she began to tidy up the plates and prepare the cheese for later.

A warm hand pressed around her waist and a kiss touched the back of her neck.

'Hey, what are you doing? That's my job you cooked.'

'I am sorry. Don't know why I am clumsy, I think it's because I am nervous.'

'Why are you nervous?'

'You will think me silly.'

'I am sure I won't.'

'Ok well I haven't done this for over 20 years and I am worried I will make an idiot of myself, which I have just done very successfully.'

'Mel, you haven't and don't worry, I haven't dated in a very long time either and if it makes you feel better I can also be very clumsy.'

She rested her head on his solid chest and they stood there embraced for a few minutes before Pascal said.

'I don't want to do anything you don't want to do or rush anything with you.'

'Thank you, me neither.'

They sat outside under the stars and just talked. Presently cheese was brought out, with some red wine, and devoured. Mel felt much more relaxed and comfortable. They held hands while staring up at the sky.

'I think maybe I should go now, I saw you yawn.'

'Did I? I am sorry, what is the time?'

'Gone midnight. Don't be sorry. I had a wonderful evening.'

'Me too,' she blushed, and he kissed her.

'Let's get you to bed and I will walk back.'

'Can I get you a taxi?'

'No, I am fine thank you.'

He slid his coat on and kissed her as they reached the front door, 'now you get some sleep, and I will call you tomorrow.'

'Ok night night.'

He kissed her once more, and as he walked down the stairs he looked back and she waved. He blew a kiss right back at her. She hoped that he wasn't put off that she hadn't asked him to stay the night, but this was something she felt she didn't want to rush, plus she still had some personal grooming to attend to.

\*

'That spa you go to, is it for women too?'

'Yes, why do you ask?'

Mel wasn't about to divulge the more intimate beauty treatments she was in need of.

'I just fancied a facial, can you text me the number?'

'Sure, how was Pascal?'

'Really good, I will tell you all about it soon, now I have the money ready to transfer to you, shall we do it this afternoon?'

'Come to mine around 3pm.'

She rang the spa as a matter of urgency, and luckily the lady that answered spoke a small amount of English and Mel had googled the treatments list and could clearly explain what was required. She decided that her legs, armpits and pubic area all needed wax. They could fit her in later that morning, so armed with paracetamol she headed to the beauty parlour.

*

'Are you ok? You keep fidgeting?'

'Yes, I am fine' Mel tried to subtly grope at her groin area. The burn from the waxing was real and no amount of painkillers or balm seem to be easing it. Even walking was painful.

'Ok well, this is the account number and sort code, we should hear by the end of the week, and then it will take a couple more for all the paperwork and date to be agreed for exchange.'

She tapped her details in the laptop James had lent her, she peered and did as was instructed. The money was sorted. She shifted back in her chair. 'Ow!'

'Mel what's up?'

'O bloody hell, ok I have had a wax and it stings!'

'Right a swim...'

'No, I can't!'

'Yes, you can, in the sea, saltwater and then some Savlon.'

'Sounds like you have experience of this.'

'Maybe I do, now get your stuff - I'll drive.'

      Mel was wondering where James had been waxed and the mental image was not one she felt appropriate for a friend to have, so she quickly focussed on the issue at hand. They sped off in the direction of St Jean Cap Ferrat and parked where Mel had done so some weeks before. The bay was quiet, and she could slip into the salty cool waters almost unobserved. It stung, but felt cool and healing, relief spread over her face. James had remained with the beach stuff on the sand, she gingerly stepped out, James handed her a tube, 'Put some of that on.' Finding the public toilets at the back of the bay she applied the cream liberally and stood for a while just to let it all calm down. Feeling soothed and comfortable again, she returned.

'Mel!'

'O god what?' She assumed it was a bug or she had cream up her face or dribbling down her legs. Looking down she could see that there was a clump of loo paper trailing behind her that had got stuck to her shoe.

She kicked her leg up and managed to flick it off, but by doing this not only did it then land on James she managed to aggravate her inflamed groin all over again.

'ARGGGH'

She turned and walked in a rather ungainly way back to the loo to reapply the cream.

'Are you done now?'

'Yes, I think so, sorry about that.'

'It's ok, not sure anyone's ever kicked lavatory paper at me before!'

'James what am I like? Also how do you know all about waxing?

'Well, I once decided to get a full tidy, you might say.

'Enough!' I can't imagine that!'

'Haha has it calmed down?'

'Yes, I think so, thanks.'

They headed back to Mel's.

'So, is Pascal the one?' James asked tentatively.

'I don't know about the *one*, but he is certainly charming and...I forgot to tell you, you know that poster I bought you? Well, he bought me one very similar, I thought it was a very nice gesture.'

'That is very thoughtful, I wish someone would do that for me.' James looked slightly forlorn, maybe the Darren stuff had weighed heavily on him. Mel had after all instigated the split, though it was clear the relationship was rocky. Mel had just coaxed it along to its unequivocal end.

'Well, what about Marcus?'

'Who's Marcus?'

'Haven't you looked at the business card I got you?'

'Not yet no, we have been sorting out your lady garden issues!'

'OK, I thank you for your help, the guy at the cafe, he is Marcus. He's English, he is here teaching English.'

'Ok Miss Marple, I will give him a text. Right here we are.'

He had just pulled up outside the apartment.

'Do you want to come up for a cuppa? I have some proper English tea!'

James parked the Range Rover, and soon they were upstairs and outside sipping on a strong cup of builder's tea.

'One thing I miss,'

'Really nothing else?'

'Well might sound odd, but some green veg. Salad is great and green beans, but I miss all the veg you get with a roast.'

'Why did you mention it! I want a roast dinner now!'

'Sorry'

'Don't be, look what is today, Tuesday, why don't you come here Thursday afternoon, we can do a roast? All the trimmings, my treat to say thank you, it's the least I can do.'

'Thank you for what?'

'James, you have given me a new start, a job, a purpose and I am dating for the first time in god knows how long. That's worth a massive *thank you* in my book'

'Perfect, well let me know what I can bring.'

'We can discuss that later, now Pascal, he was very romantic James, I haven't felt like it in years, I felt 18 all over again.'

She told him all about the evening and the food-in-lap incident. 'Mrs clumsy, I will call you!'

She persuaded James to text Marcus, and she watched the text get sent.

'I do have a favour.'

'Ok sounds ominous..'

'Well, I have a friend from home coming down to visit, in a few weeks maybe, and I need some suggestions as to what to do and where to take them.'

'Easy, I will email you some ideas.'

At that moment James' phone began to ring, 'Sorry I better get it, it might be the estate agent.' He did a fingers-crossed symbol as he answered.

There were a lot of 'sures' and 'ok' 'sounds good', Mel mouthed 'Who is it?'

To Mel it looked like he was mouthing back 'Mother', then she twigged, James was asking 'where and what time?' - It was *Marcus*!

'He is keen. I will give him that! Tomorrow for lunch. Mel, it's my turn to be nervous!'

'Right, so I will come over and fall asleep on your sofa, yeh?' She smirked.

'I feel so bad for that, but can you come over and give me a pep talk before I go?'

'Of course, another cup of builders?'

'Maybe something stronger?'

*

'Hi Cathy, it's Mel, how are you?'

'Hi, yeh all good thanks, just in the supermarket, everything ok?'

'Yes, all good, I won't keep you, but I have just spoken to Theresa, and she is going to be delayed another few weeks, so thought maybe you'd like to come out at the end of June? In 2 or 3 weeks?'

'Yeh sure, you didn't seem keen the other day.'

'Sorry, I have a lot to update you on and I am dating this guy Pascal and the business with James…'

'OK you need to update me properly when I get down there, I will let Chris know and get the flights booked.'

'Perfect, keep me posted.'

'Really excited!'

'Me too, enjoy Waitrose!'

'Haha, Sainsbury's actually'

'Bye bye'

'Bye'

*

Pascal rang Mel, he was quite nervous. It had been a while since he had done this whole dating thing, losing his sister had upset him greatly and he'd lost interest and motivation in almost everything. He didn't want any more hurt or anguish. Mel, he considered to himself, was different, there had been years between his last romantic encounter, and now he was ready. She was a beauty, a real curvy English rose and on top of that someone he could talk to, he didn't feel awkward.

He just wanted to make damn sure that Gino Bucci didn't get his hands on the prize.

'Hi Mel, how are you?'

'I am good thanks, you?'

'All good, look I have to head back to my place for a few days, the windmill I told you about, and wondered if you would like to come.'

There was a hesitation at the other end he could sense it, 'it's ok I understand maybe another time.'

'No no', came the reply, 'I was just hanging up some washing sorry, when were you thinking?'

'Next week Tuesday to Friday, maybe Saturday.'

'OK well let me check with James that there is nothing I need to do paperwork wise, otherwise, I am good to go.'

'Are you sure?'

'I am yes, plus I have never stayed in a windmill!'

'Moulin'

'Moo... what?'

'Moulin, French for a windmill.'

'Why does everything sound better in French?'

'I don't know, 'yummy' is a good sounding word. Would you like to have breakfast with me on Thursday?'

'Lovely... no sorry, James is coming for a roast and lots to get, I can do Friday?'

'Why don't I help you on Thursday and then leave you in peace and we can do Friday?'

'Are you sure?'

'I will take you to the market.'

He hung up, he was pleased that it was going well. He was still dubious about James having such an influence, but after all, it was James that had helped him and recommended the spa, he certainly did feel better for it. He just hoped that his dating activities didn't cause any work issues, especially with Gino.

*

Gino sat bored, he was looking at paperwork spread out on his desk. The weather had suddenly turned and the usual warm inviting sun had become grey drizzle. He looked at his phone, no messages, no calls, nothing. Why when he had the Cote d'Azur at his fingertips did no one want him, well when he said no one, he was thinking of one person, Mel. Why hadn't she wanted him, as much as he wanted her? He didn't care that she was older than he was, she was a little plumper than he would usually go for, and her breasts, well one he had seen inadvertently, were not like the perky domes he usually admired. There was something there though, a palpable tension, he enjoyed the fight, he wanted to win her over.

That stupid dumb fuck wit Pascal had wooed her with his stocky fat body and rugby player physique. He was only good at carving and sawing wood, what would he be like with a woman? He was going to pursue her, he just had to come up with a plan, he waited long enough to get control of his own family, this would be a piece of piss.

*

Mel and Pascal ran, well jogged, to an awning. The rain had started, and neither were prepared for it. They had wandered around Nice together. It had been very romantic, he had bought her some flowers, she had purchased some Socca bread to share. Only the weather got in the way.

'Reminds me of home.'

'Il pleut!'

'Rain?' Mel queried, Pascal indeed, 'Yes it rains, but this is heavy even by British standards.'

They made a dash for the last shop on the list, the butchers or *Boucherie*. Pascal made easy work of ordering the meat.

'Here is your pork madam,' he playfully handed her the loin subserviently.

'Merci, Bon Choix.'

He kissed her quickly, it felt longer, his hairy manly lips stuck on to hers.

'I'm getting soaked, let's run.'

They trotted across the port back to the apartment, Pascal gallantly holding the bags, as Mel found the key and entered.

As they unpacked, 'This is a lot of vegetables.'

'I guess so though, we have a saying, 'meat and 2 veg back home', meaning lots of veg and meat.' She didn't explain the euphemism. 'Here, let's get you a towel, we can put your clothes in the dryer.'

Suddenly she felt all British and awkward, he can't just strip off here in the kitchen, 'umm maybe you want to go to the bathroom, I'll find you a robe.'

'Ok thanks, you need a towel too', and he playfully messed up her wet hair.

'Hey, you!' she pushed him in the direction of the bathroom, as they kissed.

Ten minutes later they were both sitting with mugs of coffee in bathrobes. Pascal was wearing one of Theresa's more unusually plain coloured robes, a dark navy one, and Mel in a grey and yellow one.

His hairy chest was poking out the top, and the length barely covered his thighs. He was obviously a bit uncomfortable as he kept tugging at the hem as they sat sipping coffee. They chatted away, Mel explained more about a British roast and the fact they had gravy and jelly with it.

'Will you let me help you make one when we go to the Windmill?'

'I would love to, these clothes shouldn't be much longer, do you mind if I start prepping?'

'Can I help?'

'Well, you could peel the potatoes.'

They stood, both in dressing gowns at the kitchen work surface, and every now and again they would kiss, or Pascal would touch Mel and she would get all gooey and girlish. The time had drifted, the roast was prepared when the doorbell went.

'Bloody hell, must be James. Will you stay? I feel so bad.'

'No no, you must have your catch up, the rain has stopped, can you throw me my clothes?'

She watched as he let the dressing gown fall to the ground, revealing a tight body, chunky and hairy, thick-set shoulders and prominent pecks. Just a small piece of material in the shape of briefs left covering his modesty. From the outline, Mel could see that everything was in proportion, or maybe it was good lighting.

'Am I interrupting again?' James couldn't help but have a good gawp at Pascal pulling on his jeans and socks.

'Blimey, it's meat and two veg.'

'Huh?' Pascal was none the wiser.

'James stop! Now don't we have work to go over? We are having pork.'

'Hmm I can see that.' he gestured to Pascal.

'Stop!'

'Right, I am off,' he kissed Mel, 'have a good evening. Nice to see you, James.'

'I will show you out.'

They stopped at the door, 'bye handsome man'.

'Goodbye beautiful lady, your food looks yummy.' he winked, kissed her and was gone. She looked on as he descended the stairs.

Turning back, she heard, 'Bloody hell Mel, this gin is strong.'

## Chapter 37 - Different shades of beige

'That was delicious, it reminds me of home!' exclaimed James.

They had eaten well, feasted on pork with crispy crackling, lots of veg and crunchy roast potatoes, Mel had made gravy too. James was wiping his plate as she topped up his glass with red wine.

'Thank you, I am glad you like it.'

'And I got to see Pascal in the flesh, he reminds me of that villain in Beauty and the Beast.'

'The beast?'

'No, he is the good one, umm Garcon, no Gaston! A big fella, brutish and smouldering.'

'James stop, now where are we with the house?'

'Well, the agent says the seller is happy, just waiting for the paperwork which might be next week.'

'Ok, so you don't need me for a bit?'

'Umm I guess not, why do you say it like that?'

'Pascal!'

'Oh here we go...' he jokingly nudged her

'Pascal' she continued trying to keep a straight face. 'Has asked me to his home, up in the umm…in the….near Bordeaux.' she waved her hand casually.

'And you are going?'

'Well, it's only for a few days, and I am keen to see where he lives. It's a Windmill!'

'Bloody hell good on you. So my turn, Mr Marcus was good fun.'

'Sorry, how'd it go?'

'Well, he's here teaching English, his parents are from Kenya and he moved to England when he was 4. Really nice guy, think he had a tough childhood, bullied for being black and gay was tough on him. Now he wants to settle and teach.'

'Do you think you will meet up again?'

'Yeh, as a matter of fact, I am using your technique!'

'My technique?'

'I am inviting him around for dinner and see how it goes, though it would be good if you could happen to be there before he arrives to accidentally meet him.'

'Sounds good to me!'

'Ok, so when are you off with Pascal?'

'Tuesday should be back by the end of the week. I just wanted to check with you that there was nothing to worry about - house project-wise?'

'Shouldn't be, when are you seeing him next?'

'Tomorrow for brunch, then was hoping we could catch up over the weekend?'

'Well Mr Marcus is coming round tomorrow evening, so maybe you could come to mine after your brunch date and bump into Marcus.'

'Plan.'

\*

Brunch was a typically French affair, linen-lined baskets with croissants and pain aux raisins nestled all warm and neatly inside. To accompany the pastries some strong smooth coffee and delicious apricot preserve. They sat chatting away and soaking up the scene. Mel was loving every minute of this. This was a true vision of France for her.

'This is lovely, thank you.'

'You are very welcome,' Pascal rested his hand on Mel's leg which sent a course of shivers through her. 'So how's the villa project going with James, can I borrow you for a few days?'

'Yes, yes you can, paperwork and dates won't be agreed upon until next week.'

She was happier than she had been in a long time, the sun was shining, she had a man by her side and the food was excellent. What more did a person need? Some sticking points did remain, she needed to make sure Gino understood he was nothing more than a friend and a colleague. She also had to navigate the visit from Cathy and Chris, but that, with James' help, should be a pleasant distraction until Theresa's return.

*

Back at James' things were not all as happy as they were in Mel's world.

'How could he!'

'How could he what?' Mel had literally just come through the door, and could see mayhem, paperwork all over the kitchen, two mobile phones thrown down and James at a bar stool with his head in his hands.

'James what's happened? Tell me please,'

'It's Darren, he's been kicked off that soap job, or been *written out*, as he says because he was caught doing a line of coke in the fucking bog of the set.'

'Shit, I didn't know he did that kind of thing?'

'Yeh it's one the many reasons it didn't work out, he would do any shit he could find to keep him chatting for hours, I was always worried about what he was buying and sticking up his fucking nose. Sorry I am so angry.'

'Don't apologise, look how can I help and what does he want from you?'

'He is now threatening to go back on his word, tear up the contract we had in, regards to this house and basically be a bloody pain in the arse. I could bloody well kill him.'

They sat and chatted, Mel helped James tidy up and told him to try and calm down.

'I can't go on my date, Mel, I really don't think it's a good idea.'

'You would tell me too, plus don't let Darren win.'

James looked very handsome, a fitted light blue linen shirt with smart Stone chino style shorts and some brown leather driving shoes.

'You have fab legs!'

'Haha thanks, you do too! We need to get them out for the boys!'

'Leave the house bits to me, will you? I will call my solicitor back home, he was amazing when Mark died, I am sure we can find a way to keep the project going. The key thing is not to panic.'

'Thanks, Mel, I owe you one…'

Interrupting, 'Umm after everything you have done for me? But I will keep it just in case,' she was joking and hugging as they had a glass of champagne by the pool.

'Right, so he will be here in a minute, get some magazines and paint charts out, at least that way it looks like we have been doing something business-like!'

Marcus, came through, Mel could hear them chatting as glasses chinked and they appeared on the terrace above where Mel was sitting.

'Marcus, this is Mel, my right hand woman, and Mel is a very dear friend and business partner.'

'Hello Mel, lovely to meet you again, James is very lucky to have such a resourceful friend as you.'

Marcus was about James' height, 6 foot ish Mel would have guessed, he wore a lemon-coloured polo top and dark navy shorts. He had a small black goatee and short black hair. He was a very handsome guy, even Mel had to admit that. He was leaner than Pascal, not a rugby build, maybe more swimmers.

'Marcus, lovely to meet you properly, don't worry I won't be staying.' She caught him looking at the magazines and paint charts, 'sorry move those.'

'What are they?'

'These are some ideas we are having for a villa we are doing up just outside Cannes. Just some bits for inspiration.'

'Looks like you have it all covered, I like a good kitchen myself.'

'Yes, me too, very important to a home.'

She was thinking back to her home, her home in England. The kitchen had been the focal point of many laughs, some arguments and lots of celebrations. A cooker under the old original chimney, a large cream butlers sink to the right and all her various pots, pans and utensils within easy reach. Suddenly she felt a pang of homesickness.

'More fizz?'

'Just a smidge, I must be getting back.'

They sat and chatted for a few more minutes then Mel left the boys to it and wandered back, via a little supermarche to grab some bits for dinner, a light Tuna salad, at least some greenery. She got back around 7:30ish, and as she unpacked her shopping her phone was vibrating.

'Theresa! Hi'

'Hi, how is it all going?'

'Well thanks, sorry I am just unpacking some shopping.'

'It was only to check in, see if you're ok? I want to know how the dating and business idea is coming on!'

'Well, the dating is going well, actually, I need to ask you something.'

''Not sure I am very good at dating! But fire away.'

'He, Pascal, has asked me to go with him to his house in the Dordogne for a few days, and I wanted to make sure you didn't mind me leaving the apartment....'

'Course not, you go have fun, be careful too! That's the mum coming out in me I'm afraid.'

Mel hadn't thought about it, for that matter she hadn't given a second thought to the sleeping arrangements when they got to his house…

'Would you mind calling me on Sunday?'

'Sure, just to check you are ok?'

'I know it sounds…'

'No, it doesn't, I will call you around this time on Sunday.'

'How's Chloe? Shop going ok?'

'Yes and no, we are getting there, just taking ages, but we have the stock arriving over the next few days, and then setting up, we have local press and stuff sorted for the opening in a few weeks. I will be glad to get back and chill out!'

'I bet. Well I shall keep your G&T cold.'

'Haha, thanks.'

'A friend of mine and her husband are coming down in a couple of weeks too, staying in a hotel, just to get some sun.'

'That's nice, hold on a tick…'

Mel could hear shouting and then mumbling.

'Mel, I have to dash, text me what's happening with umm what's his name.'

'James, he is the business guy and Pascal is the date.'

'Yes, well text me details, talk Sunday.'

'Ok good luck, byeee'

'Byeee…beep beep beep' with that she was gone.

Mel decided to email her solicitor back home and speak to him over the coming days to get things in motion. Pleased with her efforts and looking forward to her trip with Pascal she slept soundly.

## Chapter 38 - Trip to the Windmill

'What do you mean he is still there?'

'Just what I said, he is still here.'

'You mean he stayed over, James you dirty…'

'Hey! A man's gotta do what a man's gotta do.'

'I take it you had a good night?'

'Great, really great, such a nice guy. Thank you for the intro!'

'Haha, scaredy pants.'

'Enough about me, hold on? It's in the fridge door...what time you off with Pascal?'

'He's picking me up in about an hour, it's a good 7 to 8-hour drive apparently, and James there is something.'

'Well?'

'Sleeping arrangements, I am worried what if he only has one bedroom, do you think he expects…'

'Mel he is a lovely guy, if you don't want to, just say, though be honest with yourself with that hunky brute, you aren't going to want to go to bed alone, are you?'

It wasn't so much being in bed with someone, it was the expectation that comes with it. She hadn't been with anyone else for over 20 years, thank heavens the wax rash had gone, so that was one less thing to worry about.

*

Roughly an hour later the apartment doorbell sounded.

'Bonjour, are you ready?'

'I will be five mins, come up.'

She buzzed him in, she had rammed everything into a large overnight bag she had borrowed out of Theresa's wardrobe.

'Morning,' he kissed and held her close. She smelled coffee on his breath, she hoped that he couldn't smell hers.

'Right let me just get my bag and lock up.'

'I take it.'

'OK thanks.'

They climbed into Pascal's car and drove around the port and made for the autoroute heading for Montpellier and then Toulouse, the large estate, though old, soaked up the miles and before long they were heading north with signs indicating Bordeaux. They stopped a couple of times, once for a coffee and a pastry, which Mel had insisted she pay for. There was one other, for a wee, though this hadn't been as plain sailing as she had hoped. Relaxed and in holiday mode, she had ventured into the toilettes, not really paying much attention to the abstract symbols that denote 'men' and 'women'. She only discovered her mistake when a very fat, dirty clothed trucker, wearing a high vis, turned in surprise as he was using a urinal and splattered her shoes with piss.

'Not too much longer, are you ok?'

'Yes, I am fine, this countryside reminds me of home.'

'See I take you to a nice place, you will like it, I hope.'

'I am sure I will, so how many bedrooms has it got?'

Mel was convinced that this loaded question was particularly subtle, but back home it was a question you would ask about someone's house.

'Bedrooms?' he nodded 'two.'

Phew, she didn't want it to be awkward, she relaxed even more now. They were now winding their way through small mediaeval villages and twisting roads. They pulled in to pick up some provisions for dinner, and Pascal had suggested something simple, some large cooked prawns, a rustic baguette and a salad. 'Sounds yummy.' She said

They passed through a mediaeval village and wound around the ancient buildings and archways, turning off and along a yellow gravel path with a high dry-stone wall on one side and fields of sunflowers on the other. 'There'. Pascal pointed ahead and to the left.

'What, where?'

'There you see it?'

She struggled as the trees and hedges blocked her view then suddenly she got a peak of it , faded blue shutters, hove into view. She could only see the top half until they turned almost back on themselves into a meadow and there stood this amazing Windmill in the middle of a field with the most incredible views.

'Pascal, it's beautiful, really it is.'

'It's home for now, and I like it, away from everyone and everything.'

They parked right up against one side of the Windmill, 'so no blades anymore?'

'No, I removed them, but I have kept it special inside'.

A front door led straight into a round kitchen, with another door directly opposite, which Mel guessed led to the garden. As she looked up, she could see a wooden spiral staircase wind up and up to the very top.

'This is the kitchen, then you have the living room, then a bedroom, then a bathroom, then another bedroom right at the top.'

'It really is amazing, is that a pool?'

She looked out through the glass of the back door, to the left was a large tree and to one side was a small kidney-shaped pool. Surrounded by cream coloured large boulders and some metal loungers. Exploring the mill, Mel took in the tasteful decoration, and the attention to detail that Pascal had given it throughout. From the kitchen with its incredible handcrafted wooden cupboards on one side and a lovingly restored vintage range on the other. The bedrooms were light and airy with that slightly shabby chic feel. Mel got a real sense this had been a project of love. It was beautiful, a truly special place and she felt very touched he had asked her to stay.

'That was quite a climb,' Mel puffed as she reached the top.

'Yes, it keeps me fit, just look up there.' He pointed skyward.

The conical top of the mill housed all the woodwork from the original workings, it was lovely to look at, and was now a bedroom with a large bed, a small writing table, chair and a large old chest of drawers with a modern, Matisse style painting propped on top.

'Come here,' he held out his hand, she took hold, and he pushed the shutters open, 'what do you think?'

The view went on and on, fields and trees as far as the eye could see, the only giveaway that it was the 21st century was the telegraph poles and water storage towers.

'It's incredible, and you did all this?'

'Yes, I did, a "labour of love" I think you say? She had been right.

So this is your room, I hope you will be comfortable, I will let you get unpacked, and then we can have some wine and sit outside?'

'Right yes ok then.'

He made his way down the old creaky spiral staircase, Mel was pleased and not pleased that he had suggested this was her room, the view was amazing, though the wooden ceiling was slightly creepy. She also wondered what his intentions might be or not be? She had to stop overthinking everything, just unpack and then go and enjoy a very welcome glass of wine.

'Here you go' he handed her a small tumbler of rosé, 'Have you got everything you need?'

'Yes thanks'

She followed him out to a spot in the field, where he had set up some chairs, with cream cushions on and, a picnic-style wooden picnic table that was complete with a white table cloth thrown over it. Mel had to admit that not only was the setting perfect, it was very romantic.

\*

James was amazed at how he and Marcus had hit it off, in what was practically a blind date, he was only just getting ready to leave.

'Hey, you ok?'

'Sorry yeh I am good, I just have a lot to sort out work-wise.' James hadn't gone into detail about work or his relationship ending with Darren, he just wanted to forget all about it for a day or two. Mel the jammy thing had managed to get a trip away, James needed a trip away, this had not been as relaxing as he hoped.

'Do you want a drink before you head off?'

'Sure handsome, what are you having?'

'Gin and Tonic?'

'Eww no sorry, I can't stand the taste.'

Alarm bells went off in James' mind, what the hell? Who doesn't love a cool refreshing G&T?

'Umm well, I have some beers in the outside fridge or wine?'

'You know what, I am going to get going, it's nearly 7pm, and I need to be up bright for my run tomorrow.'

'Here let me show you out, have you got all your stuff?'

'Yeh, I do, and thanks for lending me some underwear.'

'Least I could do, thank you for a great couple of days.'

'We could do it again sometime?'

'You asking me on another date Mr Marcus?'

'Maybe I am, what would you say if I was?'

'Let me… it's a yes from me.'

'I have to go back to London the week after next, but only to pick up some stuff for work. I am all yours otherwise and will soon be a fully-fledged resident of the Cote d'Azur.'

'Sounds good, where in London did you say you would be staying?'

'Pretty central, my mate has a flat in Vauxhall.'

'Well, maybe I can drop you off at the airport?'

Perfect see you Monday then, it's the lunchtime flight.'

'Ok bye Mr.'

They kissed on the lips and James watched him depart down the steps to the driveway gate, which electronically slid open. Marcus waved and began his walk back into town, James watched and when he was out of sight closed the door and the gates closed. He went back into the kitchen, maybe there was something he could do to sort things out, he would need to run it by Mel. He began to formulate a plan.

*

Gino was out, he liked being out, he planned on a wild night. He had driven down into Monaco and in one of the bars bumped into an old friend who was down there doing some business. They'd got chatting and before long Gino was on the back of a superyacht sipping tequila, he couldn't believe his luck.

He wanted to get drunk. His brothers were asking him for the final €50,000 payment, which would make the Bucci estate belong solely to him, his father was on a ventilator in hospital and could pass away at any second. And Mel? She had really gotten under his skin, and he just couldn't shake her off. It wasn't going to plan for him!

He slid his hand further up the slim blonde's leg that he was sitting next to, he couldn't catch her name, except he knew she was Russian and he had to admit, smoking hot.

She had long smooth legs, petite features and long blonde hair. The revelry began to die down around 2am. He decided he would take this girl to bed, his friend had already offered a berth for him to stay the night.

They struggled in a tangle of arms and legs, pulling at each other's clothing within the confines of the cabin. They kissed passionately, he pushed her onto the bed, the tequila was strong and he knew it, he took off his shoes, stumbling as he did so, the shirt was next then the trousers. She laid there watching him, panting for his hot Italian body to be on hers very soon. He held on to the side of the bed to steady himself as he removed his left sock, and then the right.

At that moment he lost balance, smashing his arm into the wardrobe, the agony was excruciating, it ran up his arm and seemed to envelop his whole body.

'FUCK!'

'Are you ok honey? His date slurred

'No, I'm fucking not, just leave me alone Mel'. There was a pause as the blonde drunkenly computed what he had just said.

'Who, the fuck is Mel?'

'I mean, I mean…' stuttered Gino, realising his blunder. Unfortunately it was too late, the blond was now on full alert.

'You, arrogant arse hole…' with a slap across the face and a slamming of the door she bolted. He sat down on the bed, legs hanging over the side as he clutched his arm.

'What is wrong with you? You prick.' deflated, in pain and with too many tequilas to count in him, he passed out, hoping tomorrow would be a better day.

## Chapter 39 - Mothering Sunday

'Hello love, it's your Mother calling!'

'Hi you, give me 2 ticks…' Mel quickly moved out of the earshot of Pascal. 'Sorry just moving, don't worry I haven't been murdered or kidnapped.'

'I am very glad to hear it, how is it going?' Enquired Theresa.

'Well, I can't say much but we had a lovely evening last night, and he is being very gentlemanly'

'You mean he hasn't had his wicked way with you yet?'

'THERESA!'

A voice from by the pool 'Are you ok?'

Shouting back 'Yeh fine just speaking to Theresa, won't be a sec.'

Clasping the phone back to her ear, 'you are naughty you know I can't talk like that!'

'Haha look, as long as things are going well?'

'Honestly, I am all good, how are things with you?'

'Busy, but getting there, looks like I should be back in mid-July.'

Mel hadn't even thought about dates, bloody hell she had been here for nearly 4 weeks already and that added another 5 or 6 weeks.

'Well, that certainly works for me with everything going on. Hey, give my love to Chloe.'

'I will, now you have fun, you hear, *fun.*'

She walked back over the grass to the pool, and there he was striding around, he had a pair of navy blue swimming trunks on and nothing else bar some flip flops, he was skimming the pool for debris with a net. He looked even taller and bulkier, it reminded Mel of an American football player, he really was a gentle giant, and those hands... she must stop this nagging urge to leap on him.

Theresa, she ok?'

'Yes, yes all good, I told you her daughter is opening up a shop out in Canada,' he nodded, 'well there's further delays, so looks like you might have me for a while longer.'

'I am not complaining', he dashed over to her, and planted a kiss on her cheek. Suddenly, with the warmth of the sun and their closeness it all became overwhelming, they made for the bedroom. It was clear Pascal was very excited by the situation and Mel's nipples had gone like football studs. The arousal she felt was nothing like she'd felt before, he seemed to know where to press and where to probe. She writhed in pleasure and suddenly gasped as his full thickness and length found her. She clung to him as they moved around the bed, his rhythm building, the ease at which he could lift her and move her around was effortless. She gripped onto the sheet as he began to thrust harder and faster, 'don't stop' she cried as he whispered in her ear, 'I want you.' That was too much for Mel, the heat, the passion, the man, it all came to a breath-taking climax for both of them. Breathing heavily, they collapsed side by side, sweat pouring from both bodies.

'You are amazing.'

'I am? Thank you' Mel felt suddenly so embarrassed, she tried to subtly cover herself with the sheet.

'Hey what are you doing, it's only me.'

'I know, but you have now seen all my wobbly bits.'

'Now stop, I like you for you, I wouldn't have just done what we did if I didn't.'

He stroked her hair, watching her closely. He cupped one of her breasts in his hand and licked around the nipple. 'O stop.'

'Really?'

She groaned as he played with her erect bosom, 'What big hands you have!' she exclaimed as they wandered around her body.

'Haha, and what a lovely breast you have.'

'Only one?'

'Well, I have seen the other one before!'

'Right, that's it', she kicked out of the bed shouting 'you're not going to get away with that' then chased him down stairs into the garden, he dived into the pool, and she followed after him.

*

That evening she didn't go to bed alone; they shared the top bedroom together. He had made her feel so comfortable and desired that she was totally taken with Pascal. She just hoped she knew enough about him, surely, she did?

Waking up on Monday morning, Mel reached for Pascal. He wasn't there, she looked out of the window down towards the pool area, there he was with a coffee and some papers. 'Hey!'

He looked up, shielding his eyes from the sun with his hand, 'Morning Beautiful, you want coffee?'

'Yes, coming down.'

Grabbing her phone that lay by the side of her bed, she quickly scanned for any messages or important emails, only one stood out. A text from Gino. He wanted to see her. Christ! Thought Mel. This guy never gives up. She didn't reply.

There was a missed call from James, she would return it later, she needed coffee.

They lazed by the pool, read and chatted. Pascal had some bits to pick up in the next town, he said he wouldn't be long, and he would grab some supper. Mel picked up her phone and called James. He answered alarmingly quickly.

'Hi Mel, It's James.'

'Yes, I know, I called you.'

'Yeh yeh'

'James what's up?'

'I have had an idea about Darren, a way to get him out for good.'

'Ok' she took a swig of water. 'What's your plan.'

'Well, long story short, I am taking Marcus to the airport, so I could give him a letter to post when he gets to London. One that threatens him, not just this drug thing but exposure to end his career. I could do it typed. Use gloves.'

'Jesus! I mean it's a plan, is he really going for it now then?'

'He is saying that he wants his half of the house, even though it was all my money to start with and now the job has dried up he is struggling for work and needs help.'

'Hold on, this guy spent a fortune on clothes and drugs, that's not fair!'

'I know, I need some advice Mel, what should I do?'

Considering her options, and James'. She asked. 'What happens if he comes back?'

'I will be miserable, and you can forget about that villa doer-upper.'

*Fuck sake*, she had just started to get things rocking and rolling and this dick would bugger everything up.

'I would go with your gut instinct; I understand that this is tricky for you.'

'OK, I will get something typed.'

'Be careful, make sure it only alludes to stuff you two know about and doesn't mention anything incriminating.'

'Only thing is…'

'Yes?'

'Do you have a British stamp?'

'Bloody hell, yes I think so in my bag, but it's here.'

'That's ok, we have time.'

'True, now you go and relax, I think I hear Pascal coming back, I will text you when I am on my way back to Nice.'

'You're a star.'

Pascal strode over to Mel's sun lounger, 'Have you got sun cream on?' You look a bit warm.'

'No no, I am fine, I know what I do need though, another coffee!' She clapped her hands together and leapt up, and he followed back into the Mill, she wouldn't let him see the worried frown.

## Chapter 40 - Pizza 'dough'

They drove back to Nice later that week, the drive seemed to drag, the traffic built up around Toulouse and from then on it didn't seem to flow. A few days away had been lovely, Mel was relaxed, she and Pascal were getting on really well but at the back of her mind she was worried about James and his situation.

Gino kept texting asking to see her again, she had made her mind up this had to stop and the only way was to go and see him, and tell him to his face.

'Do you need to stop again?'

'No think I am ok, you can if you need to though.'

'Well, we could pull off for some food?'

'No seriously I'm really tired, and rather get back?'

'O yeah sure, sorry.'

She looked over to her handsome driver, bloody hell had she pissed him off. She was tired and really wanted to get back and catch up with what's been going on. Plus, this stop-start traffic was doing her head in.

'Sorry, I just have a headache and want to get an early night.' she forced a smile.

'It's ok I understand.'

The traffic eventually cleared, and they got back to Nice that evening.

'I will call you tomorrow, good night.' She kissed him, he held her in tight. He dropped her bag by the bedroom and bid his farewell.

She poured herself a very large glass of red wine and sunk into the large soft sofa. She decided to ring Gino.

'Bella!'

'You sound surprised.'

'I am, I didn't think…'

'Look Gino, I will come to see you tomorrow, we have to get a few things sorted, ok?'

'OK Bella, if you say so.'

'What's the address?'

She wrote the address down on a post-it and hung up, she wasn't in the mood for this Italian stallion. She drained her wine and got into bed, texted James to let him know she was back, and that she would touch base with him tomorrow.

\*

The next day she was on her way to Italy, this time she took the autoroute, she wanted to get this sorted once and for all, she didn't like Gino messing everything up. Exiting the dual carriageway she headed towards the coast, the sea looked so inviting, following the sat nav, she navigated the twisting country roads, and eventually turned off onto a light yellow gravel drive that was lined with cypress trees and eucalyptus. The driveway wound round to the right and after about half a kilometre she could see the sprawling, though slightly dilapidated Bucci estate.

The ochre and grey stone buildings were perched on the edge of the hillside overlooking the bay below, the windows were framed in light bright blue wood and the gardens, though somewhat neglected, were filled with olive trees, aloes and pines. The air was fresh and scented. Mel took some deep breaths as she pulled up alongside a grand stone staircase to the front door, Gino appeared.

He had some light beige chinos on, a white shirt, undone to the navel and some large black sunglasses on his head. He looked ravishing, but Mel had to focus, focus on the job in hand and that was to rid herself of this pest and move on.

'Bella!' he swung the car door open for her, 'Welcome, welcome.'

'Hello Gino,' Mel tried to be as frosty as she could without being too rude. As much as it pains her to say it, Gino was a nice guy at heart, he just wasn't her 'guy'.

'Follow me, I will show you my office and where I hide out.'

He led her round the first building, to stop and show her the view. From here you could see right down into the town of Ventimiglia and the Mediterranean Sea. The panoramic view was breath-taking. 'Gino, it's stunning.'

'I know, I love it here, it's as beautiful as you are.'

'Huh? I bet you say that to all the girls you bring here.'

'I don't bring anyone here.'

For a moment Mel stood still, why had he asked her here then? She felt sorry for him, though he was being cheerful, he didn't seem his usual bouncy self, something had deflated the Gino ego. Mel wanted to know what, and she was determined to find a chink in this Italian stallion's armour.

They continued round to a small outbuilding, that was more like a Gite, 'it was a sheep stable, now my office, where I run things.'

Inside was a large modern desk, a leather swivel chair and some modern art on the bare stone walls. Several Persian style rugs adorned the floor and a large bottle green velvet sofa in one corner with an olive wood oval coffee table in front of it. Gino made for his 'chief executive' style chair and Mel took one of the bucket leather seats on the other side of his enormous desk. She couldn't help wondering what such a massive desk said about the owner. Mel was nervous, she hated confrontation, he had offered her a drink, she declined and just had water.

'Gino, I wanted to see you face to face to get things clear once and for all!'

'Bella! Why do you insist on being so business-like?'

'Because I am tired, and I want to know what is going on?'

'I like you, and I want you, and that Pascal is not for you.'

'How could you possibly know?'

He stood up, the swivel spun slightly on its own, he moved around the large piece of furniture and perched on the desk on the same side as Mel. His lean body was on full show for Mel, his figure-hugging trousers left little to the imagination, and the shirt revealed a tanned ripple of torso.

She gulped, suddenly feeling very flushed. He moved to stroke her hair, she blushed. 'You are gorgeous when you are angry.'

'Gino, stop please!'

'Bella, ever since that incident on the Grand Corniche there has been a chemistry between us, you must have felt it.'

'Gino, I don't know what you're talking about.' she looked down into her water glass, she could feel her palms beginning to perspire.

He moved closer, shifting his position closer to her.

'OK Gino, you've seen me, now I really must go.' Steadying herself on the desk as she went to leave, he held out his hand which she gratefully took, however, he pulled her in close and whispered, 'I will have you, Mel.' His musky sweet scent, his warm breath brushed her cheek, she couldn't fight it. 'Bella.'

He stroked his hands up her back, and they kissed. She deeply wanted this not to happen, but a burning desire rose up from within, due in part because she wanted to know, wanted to know what this man was really like. They moved to the sofa and the kissing continued, he gingerly slid a hand in her blouse and caressed her breasts, he began to unbutton her top. *Phew,* she had a decent bra on, she thought to herself. The unbridled passion continued, and before they knew it they were down to their underwear, touching and exploring each other's bodies, she played with the bulge in his pants, he unclipped her bra, revealing her milky white breasts. 'Bella, now I get to see both of these.' He went in with his tongue, the feeling of a wet slipperiness on her delicate nipples was one of ecstasy. She reached down to pull at his pants, he stood up and in front of Mel, he pulled them down to his ankles, a long throbbing cock was presented before her, he stood there gorgeous, tanned and glistening. As he moved closer to her, his prick at her eye level, the door handle began to rattle, then the phone began to ring.

'Gino, who is it?'

'I don't know!'

Both scrambled to put some clothes on, he dashed to the door, 'Ci.' He pulled the door ajar, and in what can only be described as a diatribe of Italian, Mel not understanding a word. Eventually, the door was shut and with shoulders slumped and head hanging, he sat in his chair, banged his elbows down and placed his head in his hands.

'No no no!'

Managing to grapple her clothes on speedily, and slipping her feet back in her shoes, she went over to him and put an arm around him. 'What on earth is it? Gino?'

'My father is dead. He died this morning in a hospital in Milan.'

'Oh my god, Gino, I am so sorry.'

'You don't understand, it's not him dying, we were never that close, it is the fact that my brothers will now want their last instalment for this, the estate. The only thing stopping them before was because papa lived. I don't have the money ready.'

'Shit. What will you do?'

'I will have to sell. I was so close Bella.' Mel could feel his shoulders and body shaking, he was crying. Mel had only seen a grown man cry a couple of times, and though it was good for a man to let out his emotions, it was nevertheless still a harrowing sight.

'How much?'

'Huh?'

'How much do they need, or do you need to pay them off?'

'€50,000, not much I know, but until I can open this place up I have no money, and James has delayed the build of his house, and your villa project is on hold.'

'Is it?'

'James said he didn't have the cash, something to do with some paperwork delay.'

That must be the Darren thing, which was worse than Mel thought, suddenly everything she had set her heart on would be crashing down. She had to act, but what could she do? Every time there had been a crisis she had been at home, and someone was there to guide her and sort things out. Even after Mark died, Cathy had been there or her solicitor... *her solicitor.*

'Gino, where is the phone, what's the dial code for the UK?'

'Bella what are you doing?'

'Just tell me, and can I have a drink, a large one, anything, please.'

She took the number for a solicitor off her mobile and keyed it into the phone on Gino's desk, once he was out of the way she could get planning.

'Mr Davies please and tell him it's urgent, Mrs Melissa Baker, his goddaughter. Yes, I'll hold.'

## Chapter 41 - Money for your life

Mel had a plan, she just needed it to take shape. She wasn't going to let something stop her from living, not this time.

'Here, Bella.'

'Thanks,' She gulped it down, 'Jesus Christ, what on earth.'

'Grappa'

'Right Gino, you need €50,000, how soon do you need it?' She had now become the chief exec and he sat opposite her. He had to admit that watching this woman at work was horny, he loved the power. 'Gino?'

'Sorry, I need it by the end of the week.'

'Ok, I can give it to you, on three conditions.'

'Bella, I can't...'

'You want this place?'

'Ci.'

'Well...'

'OK, what do I have to do?'

'You don't have to do anything, I will lend you the money, all €50,000. First, you must promise never to mention what happened here today and second, we must only be friends and business partners.'

His face looked forlorn, what was he to do? He wanted this place more than anything.

'Ok and the other?'

Mel was getting a massive buzz out of this. She was in control, she was commanding someone's attention in a way she never thought possible. She had watched Dragon's den. She knew what to do and how to behave, she had seen it her entire life, men with power.

'The third is, 10% of the Bucci estates profits, once you are up and running.'

He looked at her in amazement, this little English rose was suddenly calling the shots, he found it very attractive. 10% of the Bucci profits though, was a big ask.

'Will you help?'

'Help? I am already lending you the cash.'

'I mean can you help with the design? Interiors? I saw how good you were the other day.'

'OK deal. Now you need to get some paperwork sorted before the end of the week, Gino.'

'Ci Bella.' he beamed.

She sauntered out, turned and kissed him on the cheek, 'Ciao'.

She jumped in the car and skidded down the drive, she flung the car into the bends and headed back for Nice, and to James, who needed a bloody postage stamp of all things!

The car buzzed and a warning on the dashboard came up, she needed petrol, as she headed along the Grand Corniche in her haste she took a wrong turn, and was now battling with small traffic-filled roads back to the apartment. Eventually, she eased the car into a petrol station and filled up. With her confidence and tank brimming she strolled into the petrol station to pay.

'Oui, Madame?'

'Number two, merci.'

'Madame..' the boy behind the counter was looking at her chest, she looked down.

'Crap'

In her haste to get ready and out of Gino's lair, she had done her blouse up incorrectly, she had a button lower than she was supposed to. The effect was a lopsided front to her blouse and her left bra cup on display for all to see.

'Merci!' She threw down some cash and arms folded ran back to the car, roof up, she adjusted her buttoning. She drove on a bit further, pulled in and rang James.

'James?'

'Hi, you ok?'

'Yes, look I can get you that stamp and some good news, I will be 30 mins max.' Mel was in a hurry, she was not to be deflected from her course.

'Ok see you soon.'

She ran upstairs rifled through her purse and found what she was looking for, back down at street level her phone rang.

'Hi, Mel, it's Cathy.'

Mel was marching back to the car, 'Hi how are you?'

'All good, look I have made a balls-up with the dates, we are coming next week, sorry.'

*Next week! Stupid woman, how did she get it so wrong?*

'OK that's fine, text me your flight times, do you want picking up?

'Oh no, Chris is driving, he's got a new car and we fancy a bit of booze cruise on the way home.'

*Course you do,* thought Mel. 'How lovely, well where are you staying?'

'Near the sea, umm the rue de Anglais?'

'Promenade de Anglais?'

'Yes, that's it'

'I am really excited.'

'Me too, well lots to catch up on, I will call you later in the week, we can make a plan!.'

'Lovely, see you soon, Au Revoir.'

'Au revoir.'

Cathy ended the call and turned to Chris, 'She seems distant, maybe it's the sun, you don't think she knows about the money, do you?'

The man turned, Chris was a handsome guy, chiselled jaw and designer stubble, 'Of course not, it's not like she's here or been in touch with anyone back home except you.'

\*

'I'm outside, can you buzz me in?'

'Sure, come on in.'

They sat around the kitchen island on stools, making pleasant conversation, remarking on the weather and how bad the traffic could be around Toulouse.

'So did you bring the stamp?'

'Yes, I did, now James are you sure…'

'I need to get him gone Mel, I can't let him spoil it all.'

'OK I think I understand, so what is the plan?'

'The plan, right yeh, well Marcus is coming round in about an hour for his flight and I am taking him to the airport…'

'And then?'

James slid a piece of paper that was in a plastic document wallet, 'Don't take it out.' He said rather menacingly. The inscription was made up of cut out letters from magazines and newspapers.

> *I know your secrets, photos have been obtained.*

'That's it?'

'Yeh well, what else can I say?'

'I guess not much, do you really think this will work, the last letter clearly didn't.'

'Last time he hadn't been kicked off the show, this time he has his career to fight for, one scandal you can survive just look at tv stars today, but two, as Oscar Wilde would put it, looks like carelessness.'

'James, I like that, could you add that to the letter, it gives it a dramatic twist don't you think?'

'OK will do, let's see, here are some gloves, we need to cut out the letters'

He handed her a wodge of newspapers, British ones, 'Where did you get these?'

'A vendor near the flower market sells them.'

They began the cutting process, the updated letter read,

> *1 scandal may be regarded as a Misfortune, 2 looks like carelessness. I know your secrets, photos have been obtained.*

There was silence as they sat back and peered through the plastic cover at their handy work. 'I hope this makes him think Mel.'

'I am sure it will,'

The stamp was applied to the envelope using a sponge to dampen it rather than using their tongues and the letter was sealed in a plain envelope with a typed address on the front.

Suddenly the buzzer of the door went and they both jumped.

'Bloody hell, we are on edge!'

'It's only a letter and probably won't work!'

'Hey, come in'

'Hey,' Marcus pecked James on the cheek.

'Come through, Mel is here.'

'Don't you travel light Marcus,' Mel ventured as she saw the small holdall he was carrying.

'I guess so, I am staying with friends, so I only need the essentials. How are you?'

'I am well, we were just ironing out some of the details on the next project.'

'Sounds good, look we better go, Mel why don't you stay here and swim? I won't be long.'

    Mel didn't need to be persuaded, the day was a warm one and already wished she hadn't worn jeans. Once the guys had left, she ventured into the inviting pool and began doing some breaststroke. She ideally wanted to keep her hair dry, so she looked more like an old lady bobbing around rather than any kind of athlete. She mulled over her newfound business acumen, *had it always been there?* The main thing was she had put Gino in his place, and hopefully would see a return on her investment into the Bucci estate. Mr Davies, her solicitor had advised against it, though he had been more than willing to help facilitate the transaction and release some of her capital, he had always been a mine of information and a supportive godparent. Mel considered she hadn't seen enough of him. She must pop up to Oxfordshire when she went back to the UK.

## Chapter 42 - Cathy falls for the Cote d'Azur

The week passed quickly, in a blizzard of paperwork. She had asked Theresa for advice and Theresa had been very helpful in all matters concerning business in France. Mel had also been making use of Theresa's scanner, printer and laptop. Most of the paperwork on Mel's side for the purchase of the villa had been completed and the money was ready for transferring. James had been unusually nervous and quiet, Mel supposed it was the plan to get rid of Darren that was the cause, she had tried reassuring him that going with his gut instinct was the best option.

It was now Sunday, and the day before Cathy and Chris arrived. Mel wasn't sure why, but she wasn't overly excited by the prospect of having to show them around and with so much else going on her mind wasn't fully engaged, or maybe it might be a welcome distraction, she considered her situation as she opened the oven door and slid a tray with two croissants in.

*I'm starving! Now tea.*

The croissants were warm and delicious and flaked everywhere as she munched on them. She took a deep breath as she savoured the flavour and the view. Another sunny day, she just loved how the terracotta roof tiles were bright against the light clear blue sky.

She flicked absentmindedly through one of the magazines she had laying on the coffee table. By coincidence she happened to come across the article about James again. *I wonder if we could get a nice piece of editorial in one of these for the villa project?* As she considered this her phone began to ring. She had purposefully not checked it, having decided to give herself digital detox, at least for the morning. Last week had been non-stop emails, phone calls and staring at a screen reading the small print in all the legal documents required for all the projects she was now involved in.

It was Gino…

'Hi Gino, you ok?'

'Hi Bella, I mean Mel, yes I am good. You?'

'Fine thanks, how can I help?'

'Help? You have already helped me greatly.'

'Yes, I hope you are putting the money to good use.'

'I am I am, I want to show you the website soon, then we should get our first paying guests.'

'Sounds good, when are you thinking?'

Mel was keeping it cool with a slight air of aloofness, he was, after all, a business partner now. She wanted this to work and her investment to provide an income she could live off.

'Next week Bella, if that works for you?'

'Yes it does.' any excuse not to be a tourist guide for Cathy and Chris thought Mel.

'You come here?'

'No, you can come here, maybe we could go out for lunch?'

'Perfect, I also have some paperwork for you to sign.'

'Is this the copy I have already seen and sent back home?'

'Yes, I just need you to sign.'

'Ok, well see you next week.'

'Bye Bella, I mean Mel.'

'By Gino.'

She hung up feeling pleased that one of her plans was working out. There was also another plan formulating in her head, but she needed to give it more time and think it over.

*

'Darling, you look amazing!'

'You are very kind! But hey, you both look like you could do with a drink!'

'Well, it was a long drive, though great to be away.' Chris beamed as he went on to extoll the virtues of his car, how well it had handled the roads, fuel consumption, navigation system and so on. Mel tried to stop herself from drifting into a daydream, when she broke the conversation with 'Here is good, you both like seafood?'

Over lunch it was clear that the two of them were fine, she didn't know what Cathy was worried about, the two of them chatted and smiled and it all looked very rosy. I guess people would have thought the same about her and Mark, from the outside that is.

'What are your plans?' Mel hoped that it wasn't going to include her too much or fall on her shoulders to come up with a six-day agenda.

'Well, I would like to go to the beach you told me about and do some shopping, maybe a trip to Grasse for the perfume.'

'I want to check out the cars, I hear Monaco is the place to go.' Chimed in Chris.

'Well yes, it is, you'll love the drive too, it's, up and over the Grande Corniche.'

'I've always wanted to drive that.' Mark looked excited, Cathy less so.

'Really Mark? What about exploring Nice?'

'Well, you two can do some of that without me, Yes?'

'Come on Cathy, we can have a girly day, maybe two if Mark wants to get to Monte Carlo more than once.'

After lunch, Mel showed them the apartment where she was house sitting. There were the usual 'oohs' and 'ahhs' over the view and design of the space, along with general chat about home and the weather.

'I hope you don't mind, but I think we will head back to the hotel?'

'Of course, do take a stroll around the port on your way back, it is really lovely this time of day. Text me tomorrow, but don't worry if you just want to chill, I quite understand.'

'Thank you, see you tomorrow.'

She showed them out and picked up her phone to fire a text to Pascal, she had told him about her friends arriving and he was very understanding. However, they were clearly knackered from their journey and Mel wanted to see Pascal, ever since the windmill, he had become her overriding thought day and night. He was still staying at his friend's apartment where he had been working too so they had met up a couple of times since the trip, but tonight she thought about inviting him over for dinner, and secretly hoped he would stay over.

      Pascal replied, saying he would be round later, and could he pick up anything? Mel had decided she would go into town and grab some food for dinner herself.

'No thanks, maybe some wine?'

Before she left to go shopping, she sent another text.

      *Hi Gino, how is the plan coming along? Can we meet on Wednesday?*

She strolled around town, picked up some flowers and decided on duck breasts for dinner. When she'd got everything she needed she decided to call James to see how he was.

'Hi James, how are you?'

'Hi Mel, yes all good, Marcus is heading back to Nice soon and hoping the damn letter does the trick, how's umm it's Cathy and Charles?'

'Cathy and Chris, yeh all good, tired from the journey, so seeing Pascal tonight and then maybe seeing them later in the week. I know this might sound like an odd question but is there any car related stuff going on this week around here?'

'You mean like a rally or formula 1?'

'Yeh Chris is into cars and…'

'There's Top Marques.'

'What's that?'

'It's a collection of the world's supercars in Monte Carlo.'

'O god perfect, can you…'

'Mel it's seriously exclusive, let me see if I can wangle some from a friend of mine.'

'You are a star, when is Marcus back?'

'Wednesday, I will pick him up from the airport.'

'Sounds good, now I hate to ask, but anything from Darren?'

'Hmm nothing really, just demands from his solicitor for information, but I am delaying it until next week.'

'Well, why don't we catch up on Friday?'

'Ok cool and I will try to get tickets now.'

James hung up and sat back in his lounger by the pool. He couldn't lose all this, not because he got tangled up with that drug addict boyfriend, ex-boyfriend now. He was now demanding 50% of the house and cash, which apparently, he had contributed to during the relationship. If he hadn't been so high-profile James would have told him to fuck off, but he needed to handle it carefully, he didn't want lenders or friends doubting his kudos and reputation. The letter had been a risk, but one worth taking, he had a life here now, and he wasn't going to let anyone spoil it.

Mel was a cheeky one, asking for tickets to that event. There was something about her James thought, a vulnerability and openness that he could see why people would find her endearing and want to help her out. She was helping him, but at this rate, he wouldn't be able to get all the cash together

He picked up the phone again, raised up his sunglasses and perched them on his head in time and the deal on the villa would fall through. He needed to get Darren off his back and let him get on with his life. He took a sip of his drink and picked up his phone.

'Hello, Charlotte, it's James. Look I need a favour…'

\*

Wednesday came round with alarming speed, it was a bright day, and the sun was strong. Mel was up and wafting around in a borrowed kaftan of Theresa's.

Chris was going to drop Cathy off in about an hour, and then he was heading off to Monaco. Cathy and Mel were going to have a girly day, shopping, sunbathing and swimming.

The buzzer went,

'Come on up.'

She opened the front door, 'Hi, how are you?'

'Really good thanks, a bit warm though!'

'Yes, it's going to be a hot one today, now have you got everything you need?'

'Yes, and thank you for getting the ticket, Chris is so excited, he couldn't wait to get there.'

'He's welcome, maybe he will buy me a drink.' she winked at Cathy.

'Don't worry, he is under a three-line whip to thank you in a special way.'

Mel couldn't help but inwardly cringe, the way Cathy had phrased that had created a mental image she didn't want to think about. He had always been an accountant, pretty safe and had no real enthusiasm for anything besides his career, Cathy and now seemingly cars.

'Right, let me grab my bag and we will be off.'

Mel drove them to Cap Ferrat, a place she had revisited since her first excursion. She loved the covered bays and the little shops in the town.

'Right I think we'll stop here?' As Mel laid her towel down on the beach, the view stretched over to Nice and in the foreground a rather large yacht, which was presently offloading some passengers into small tenders.

'It's perfect. I can see why you like it here. Do you think you will come back?'

Mel had not gone into any detail over her newfound business dealings or her inner thoughts on where to live. It didn't seem appropriate and she wanted to keep her cards close to her chest until all the deals were signed and sealed.

'Yes, I do like it here, though I do miss home.'

They lay chatting away, flicking through magazines and pointing out items of interest and sharing news about Pascal and Chris.

'So, you really like him?'

'Yes, I do, I didn't think I would after Mark.' Mel looked out to sea and paused, 'but I think I need to find a new life Cathy.'

'You poor thing, look I understand…'

Mel's mobile went off, 'Shit'.

'Who is it?'

'Um my Italian business partner.'

'Wow, you do move quickly. What happened to Gino?'

'This is Gino, I have invested, but only money.' She smiled. 'Do you mind if I take it?'

'Course not.'

'Hi, Gino.'

'Hi Mel, look what time are we meeting?'

'Crap, is that today? Gino I am sorry I am Saint-Jean Cap Ferrat with Cathy.'

'I could bring it there?'

'Ok let me just check with Cathy.' She placed a hand over the speaker and turned to Cathy, who was now lying on her back, oversized sunglasses on and a black figure-hugging swimsuit, matched with the right amount of gold jewellery.

'Cathy look, do you mind if Gino pops by, I just need to sign one silly document, it will take three mins max.'

'Don't be silly, of course, be good to meet the infamous Gino!'

She took her hand away and spoke again, 'Yes Gino we are at Passable Bay, I am wearing a big sunhat.'

Within the hour Gino arrived, a slim file under his arm. Cathy was in the sea swimming when he arrived.

'Bella!'

'Gino, hello, now what do you need me to sign?'

'Here,' he flicked through the papers and pointed to a dotted line.

'OK, let me just double-check.'

'Where is your friend?'

'There,' she pointed vaguely in the direction of the water. 'Swimming.'

He gazed in Cathy's direction and sat down by Mel.

Cathy walked out of the sea, pulled her hair back with both hands as she walked out of the cool sea and onto the sand. 'Bella!'

'Gino, I told you to call me Mel!'

'No, her, Bella!'

'Who?' She followed the direction of travel of his eyes, which were fixed on Cathy. 'Gino, has anyone ever told you that you are fickle?'

The question went unanswered as Gino stood up, and greeted Cathy very enthusiastically.

'Bella, you must be Cathy, Mel didn't tell me how beautiful you were.'

Cathy flushed and quickly gathered her towel and dabbed herself down.

'Thank you, umm Gino.' She held out a hand ready for Gino to shake it, he took it and kissed it instead. Mel just watched on as the Italian stallion rolled out all the tricks in the book, all the ones he had used on her. Cathy cooed and smiled and like an excited puppy, she flashed her round doe-like eyes and flirted using all the techniques she clearly had acquired over time.

Mel read and then signed the document while Gino chatted up Cathy, she occasionally dropped the odd word or two into the conversation.

\*

  Gino had got up early, he usually did, he wasn't one for wasting a day. Today was a beautiful day even by his standards. The sea was crystal clear and the bathe he had taken that morning had invigorated him even more than usual. He stood wiping down his body with a grey towel, his lean body glistening in the early morning sun. He slipped his feet into a pair of flip flops and made his way back to the house. As he walked, he considered the option laid before him, a cool €50,000 just handed to him. He had to keep his mouth shut but that wasn't an issue, she had fallen for the Bucci charm, nearly, until someone interrupted him. He had nearly won, he had nearly beat Pascal. That stuck up English lady, Mel, he had nearly bedded her, but now she wanted some of his estate. He would allow her that, he would keep her close, and when Pascal fucked up, which people like him inevitably do, he would pounce.

As he made his way to his lair, the phone was ringing, he answered with a click,

'Yes? When? OK next week, thank you.'

The funeral was confirmed for next week, he had every wailing Italian matron coming it would seem. And his brothers were off busy with work, and he was left to sort it all out. However, he was in the clear with the money and the estate was all his, all he had ever wanted. Today that English girl would sign the papers, she was a smart biscuit or was it cookie, anyway, he would make this work, he had to - in order to survive. He didn't want to have to sell the Ferrari, he was a Bucci, he had the family honour to upkeep.

     He picked up his mobile and rang Mel, silly cow had forgotten all about the paperwork! So now he was summoned like a schoolboy to her, he would find a way to make her see him, he wanted her. He threw some stuff in the tiny boot of his car and sped off towards Nice, pulling off the main road, as he got to St Jean Cap Ferrat.

He revved the engine as he got near, the bay was pretty quiet, he could just make out a big straw hat, which must be Mel. As he sauntered toward her he could see another woman splashing in the sea, and Mel looked as if she was waving to her and shouting something.

'Bella, I mean Mel.'

He had greeted her, she was frosty, maybe hungover, he couldn't tell. She had snatched the paperwork from him and began to read, he had enquired about the friends that were staying and she pointed to a curvaceous beauty bobbing in the sea. She had come out like some film star, a round girl with round brown eyes and a curvy Marilyn Monroe type figure, though squatter in height.

He ramped up the Bucci charm, and he hoped it was having the effect he desired, jealousy. He wanted Mel to get jealous.

*

Chris had only meant to pop to Monte Carlo for a few hours, though the buzz of the place was amazing, he had managed to park his car in a multi-storey which seemed a long walk from everywhere. Though the car spotting was off the scale! Ferraris, Rolls and a Bugatti Veyron, they were all here, just parked, no one taking any notice.

The exhibition had been amazing, the ultimate in luxury and cars were just the start, there were watch brands, super-yachts and jewellery, his couldn't believe his eyes with some of the stuff there, including the incredibly glamourous women wearing all the latest designer fashions were also really rather appealing.

*Sod it! I am going to have a drink,* he thought to himself.

He found a bar, there was some sort of commotion as HSH Prince Albert made his way through the crowd, smiling as he shook hands graciously greeting guests, VIPs and sponsors.

'Hey, you English?'

Swivelling on his barstool, he saw a leggy blonde before him. Wearing a tight silver dress that was just long enough not to be perceived as too hookerish. 'Umm yes I am.'

'I adore English men…'

They sat and chatted, he ordered some drinks, for her champagne and for him another beer.

\*

'Mel, are you sure you don't mind?'

Cathy was in the arms of Gino, he smiled at her, a beaming Bucci flash of white teeth, and he winked at Mel.

'Of course not, now Gino not too fast!'

Cathy and Gino practically skipped to the car. He was going to take her for a spin. Coolly Mel sat back, watched them roar off and found her phone.

'Hi it's me, how's work?'

'Hi pretty lady, well actually I am nearly done here, where are you?'

'Cap Ferrat, Passable Bay.'

'Well, I can come to join you, if that's ok?'

'Yes, that would be great, see you soon.'

Smiling to herself, she decided to go for a swim. Sliding off her sarong she made for the water's edge, she wasn't the only one who could flaunt it.

*

Gino turned the wheel hard and the tyres squealed as they shot across the junction into Monte Carlo harbour.

'You enjoy?'

'Yes, very much,' Cathy was clinging onto her straw hat for dear life. This man really knew how to drive, to think she had been stuck in that dreary car that Chris had bought for over 9 hours yesterday! This, *this* was fun.

'Weeeeeee' she shouted as she waved her hat at passers-by.

Gino beamed on, this Bella was enthusiastic, he wasn't sure if his plan had worked, but he liked entertaining, and this was fun for him too. He had to stop at a pedestrian crossing, he blasted the car horn as a daft blonde bimbo tugged at some drunken middle-aged guy by the tie to lure him across the road.

'CHRIS!' exclaimed Cathy

The middle-aged guy stopped and stared,

'Cathy?' questioned Chris.

'Honey what's wrong?' asked the Russian blonde.

'You!' cried Gino.

*

'Gino is driving me back to the hotel', sobbed Cathy.

'Ok ok, as long as you are safe, call me when you get back.'

She turned to her sunbathing partner, 'what a mess.'

'You don't seem that concerned.'

Mel was flicking through a magazine, 'Well how would you feel if you knew your supposedly *closest* friend had stolen £3,000 off you?'

*

There was lots of damage control required and James was roped in to help, 'Look can you just be here, I need help.'

'Of course, what a nightmare.'

Eventually, things were calmer, the situation was brought as under control as could be, Chris stayed at the hotel and Cathy was with Mel in the apartment.

'I can't even look at him, let alone share a bed with him!'

The next morning the pair of them met in public, in a small cafe to discuss what was to be done.

Mel waited anxiously. Pascal had been brilliant, helping with a sobbing Cathy and with a confused Gino, who apparently had known the Russian blonde from some sordid escapade on a yacht.

Pascal had found a good breakfast spot for him and Mel to meet at, and chat.

'Thank you, I am so sorry to drag you into this.' said Mel.

Pascal looked into her eyes, 'it's ok, I want to help. Plus, I get to be with you.' he held out his hand and she took it and kissed it. She smiled up at him and he back at her.

'What about the money?'

Mel had forgotten all about that, what should she do? Maybe talk to Cathy when things had settled, maybe there was a completely rational explanation.

'Nothing, for now, I will talk to Cathy soon.'

Chris and Cathy's breakfast seemed to go on for ages, Mel was beginning to wonder what the outcome would be and how Chris would explain being dragged, by the tie, across the main road in Monte Carlo by another woman. Finally, Cathy was back, she was collecting her stuff and going back to the hotel. The whole episode had been a dreadful mistake by both parties. They were to continue the holiday as if nothing had happened, *such a British thing to do*, thought Mel.

'Have lunch with me tomorrow?' invited Mel.

'OK but what about Chris?'

'Cathy just let him go to the beach, we have to catch up properly and I am sure he will do anything you ask, after what happened.'

'Don't remind me!'

Pascal had gone off to work early that morning to finish his latest project, installing a wooden spiral staircase into a gite up in the hills above Nice. It had been a nice change to wake up with someone next to her in the morning, to chat over a coffee and watch him go off to work. She hadn't done that for a long time, and it felt good, reassuring, a comfort.

'Morning!'

'You are cheery!' Mel responded to James as he had rung her before she'd had a chance to finish her coffee and have anything to eat.

'How's it all going with Cathy and Chris.'

'Pretending nothing has happened…'

'Really?'

'Yes really, very English to bottle it all up.'

'As you say, I am off to get Marcus from the airport later, do you fancy lunch before?'

'I am meeting Cathy, why don't you join us?'

'Sounds good to me, cheer her up I guess.'

'Yes, that's the plan, invite Marcus, more the merrier and it may dilute any tension!'

'Ok good plan, I will get him to meet us in town.'

'James before you go, I have one more favour…'

## Chapter 43 - Death comes as the end

'Are you enjoying yourself?'

'Yes it's lovely, very French, am I allowed to say that?'

'Haha yes it's fine, so you are having a good time Cathy?'

Cathy had been putting a very brave face on things, ever since she had seen Chris with the blonde. Mel had arranged a lunch with Cathy, James and possibly Marcus. She hoped that some time together would take Cathy's mind off what had happened. She knew that James needed perking up too, so she'd decided to take them to the restaurant James had taken her when she first arrived in Nice, that was over a month ago. Wow how time had flown by.

'Monsieur, en bouteille de Côte de Provence rosé, merci.'

Music to Mel's ears, at least this wasn't going to be a dry lunch. As much as she was sorry for Cathy and James, she was starting to feel a pang of annoyance, she knew that Cathy's trip wasn't going to match up to her expectations and she had been proved right, as for James, his silly ex-boyfriend was now going to bugger up her new business venture, but she couldn't blame James for that.

'So, shopping later ladies?' ventured James.

'Yes please, I want to spoil myself, I would love a Longchamp bag.' chimed Cathy.

'Well, this is the place, isn't it James? There's a huge boutique here, just next to Hermés.' Mel remembered from her many walking jaunts around the city, and though in recent times she hadn't really bothered with what was considered 'smart' dressing she knew all the high-end brands and had a few lingering in her wardrobe. Maybe she might treat herself too.

'I think we should all treat ourselves to today, cheers.'

'Fab thank you, you're such a good friend. Oh and you of course James.' Cathy suddenly looked embarrassed.

'Salut.' James subtly checked his watch under the table.

The wine flowed and they all enjoyed a lovely long lunch. It was a good couple of hours before coffee was served and the bill requested. As is customary the bill was handed to the man.

'No no, I am getting this.' Cathy snatched the small silver tray from James.

James, always the gentleman, 'No you can't, please let me get mine at least.'

'No, Cathy, let's split it'. Added Mel, though she wasn't going to lie, it would be nice if she did, especially after the short notice and all the kerfuffle.

'No really I want to, I would have been lost without you two yesterday…' she began to well up.

'Now come on, think of all the shopping we're going to do, have your coffee and we will get out into the lovely sun.'

From the front of the restaurant, Mel could see a tall lean chap asking the waiter a question and then walking toward their table.

'Bellas! And Bello of course', he smiled at James as if to imply - *don't worry, you are included.*

Cathy's mouth was agog, as she turned wildly in her chair and saw who it was. He stooped down and kissed her on both cheeks. Mel was the first to speak.

'Gino! What are you doing here?'

'Well I needed James to sign some paperwork and I found out from my guys he was out to lunch, and as none of you have answered your phones…' which is true they hadn't, they had been so engrossed in lunch and chatting, 'I thought I would just come find you myself.'

James shifted in his chair, 'Well ok, have you got what needs signing?'

Gino suddenly looked slightly alarmed, fumbling.

'Ci, here it is.'

He whisked a folded piece of paper from his back pocket. Handed it to James and sat in the empty chair next to Cathy.

'Umm, I understood you were back in Italy Gino…'

'Can't stay away from my Bellas, and I needed James to sign.'

James handed the paper back to Gino, and Cathy looked down. This was an awkward situation.

'Sorry Gino we are off shopping,' Mel tried to deflect the eager Italian.

'I love shopping, let's go.' and Gino was up helping Cathy out of her chair.

As he led her out of the restaurant, she turned and mouthed 'help' to Mel. Mel mouthed back 'don't worry.'

As they made their way along the road and across the Jardin Albert, Gino wasted no time in putting his arm through Cathy's, she turned back to Mel and mouthed again, 'What do I do?'

Mel mouthed back, 'Make him pay.'

'You go ahead' said Mel, 'We are just going to pop in here.' Mel grabbed James by the arm and led him to the next shop along, as they strode in she asked, 'What the hell did he give you to sign?'

'A bloody receipt, just glad Cathy didn't see it.'

'Well looks like it's done the trick.'

They smiled at each other, moved some of the neatly folded jumpers, unfolded them and walked out, and joined Gino and Cathy in Longchamp.

'Mel, what do you think of this?' Cathy held aloft one of the massive shopper style bags with leather handles.

'Love it, Cathy.'

'Here.' Gino held out a credit card.

'No, I can't possibly.'

'Ci Bella, you can,' he planted a kiss on Cathy's left cheek.

The assistant then for some reason made a beeline for Mel, 'Madame?'

He unfurled a large shopper, grey with yellow detailing, which Mel had to admit she loved. 'That is beautiful.'

'My turn.'

'Huh.'

Cathy held out a rather glitzy platinum card and flashed it at the server. Mel leaned into Cathy, 'Well it's a start.'

Cathy looked startled, 'What do you mean?'

'Well, you did skim a nice profit off the sale of my horse. Oh, don't look so surprised, I have been in touch with my solicitor, you remember? My godfather who lives in Oxfordshire.'

'But how could you…'

'Madame. Carte?'

Cathy looked very unsettled, red in the face. She dropped the card, and then picked it up, Mel just watched smiling to herself. The payment was made. Gino and James had wandered outside as Mel and Cathy joined them, Mel beamed, 'Look what Cathy bought me, so sweet.'

Cathy didn't know where to look, she practically threw herself at Gino and quickly marched him off down the street. Mel and James hung back, 'I told her I know about the money they cheated me out of from the sale of my horse.'

'But how did you find out?'

'I have my spies.'

'Now where are we with Marcus, I thought he was joining us?'

'He got delayed, won't be back until Saturday, hold on let me check if he's texted.' He got out his iPhone.

'Hold on guys.' Mel shouted ahead at Cathy and Gino.

'FUCK!'

James had stopped walking and held out his phone.

'Mel…' he steadied himself on the wall outside Hermés.

'What is it, are you ok?'

'He's dead!'

## Chapter 44 - Cash rich

They were all back at Mel's residence, a bottle of wine had been opened, and none the wiser Gino and Cathy were out on the terrace dancing slowly to Cafe del Mar style music and James who had feigned some sort of sudden headache, was sitting with Mel inside. Though Mel wasn't sure the rest of the party had been convinced by the onset of James' feigned illness.

'What does it say?'

'Here' James handed his phone to Mel.

*Ex Soap star found dead in hotel. At this stage the police are not treating it as suspicious.*

'OK let's stay calm. Here have a drink?'

Mel poured a very large glass of wine out.

'It doesn't say anything about a letter', Mel soothed.

'Shall I ring them?'

'No!' then thinking quickly. 'Yes, the police, you should, concerned boyfriend, they won't know you have split. Ask how he was found, and in what state and if you can offer any help'

James did as was instructed, and it turned out that Darren had been found with traces of cocaine, some prescription sleeping pills and two empty bottles of whisky by his side. The police, so swamped with the backlog from Covid, were not treating it in any other way than 'accidental death by misadventure or suicide.'

'Did they mention any letter?' Mel asked.

'No nothing, maybe he binned it?'

'I suppose it means we can crack on with the build, but what if they do discover the letter?'

'Don't worry, there is no way they can trace it back to you, yes James it means we can get on with our lives.' Mel, her eyes were bright and sparkling.

They cheered each other's glasses and moved out to the terrace, 'What will you do with these two?'

'Well, I know more than she thought, I know now that Gino has bought her an expensive bag, I am sure Chris wouldn't like that, would you, if you were him?'

*

'Why?'

'I am not sure, but there is a delay in getting all the paperwork, plus I need to go to the funeral.'

'When is that?' Mel was fuming, the build plans on the villa were on hold again as James had to wait for more paperwork before he could rightfully claim the house as his own.

'Everyone is blaming the Covid backlog, but it might be a few weeks, I am worried we might lose the house.'

'Ok well let me know how you get on when you speak to your people in London. Cathy has asked to see me.'

'Well, good luck with that.'

It was 2pm-ish by the time Mel had made it to the cafe that she and Cathy had agreed to meet in.

'Nice day?' Cathy forced a smile.

'Yes lovely, au café au lait, merci.'

'The same.'

The waiter moved off with his pad to another table, and Cathy looked out at the view over the square.

'I can see why you love it here.'

'The weather, the food and now a business idea of sorts, are all very compelling.'

Cathy turned to look straight at Mel, she pulled her glasses off, to reveal puffy dark eyes, 'Ok, what do you want from me?'

'Cathy, I just want to know why, why you stole the money from the horse sale.'

She sighed and put her glasses back on. 'I don't know what came over me, I was mucking out the damn horses, you had just told me how lovely it was down here, and I wanted a bit of that.' the waiter returned with the coffees 'Sucre?' 'Non merci' Mel waved him away. Cathy continued.

'Chris spends all his time working, I have no money of my own, I am completely reliant on him,' she took a deep breath. 'I suddenly saw how I could get some…'

'By lying to me Cathy? Surely you knew if you had just asked I would have agreed a commission?' Mel added.

'If you like to put it that way then yes, I am not proud of it, and to do it to you of all people…'

'Cathy, are you happy?'

She looked down at the untouched coffee, the foam was beginning to dissipate 'No, I don't think I am.'

'You can keep the money.'

'What no I can't…'

'Yes you can, but loyalty comes at a price! Before Mark died I was just like you, unhappy and rudderless. Now I have found a new start, rediscovered myself. What if I can help you do the same?'

'Really?'

'Really.'

They spoke animatedly for a good hour, and the tension eased. Cathy was a good friend.

'What about Chris?'

'Well, I assume the £3,000 went into his account?'

Cathy nodded.

'It wouldn't look good if an accountant was skimming clients' funds now would it?'

A broad smirk crept across Mel's face. She sipped the remnants of her coffee. They got up, hugged and Cathy went back to the hotel, with lots on her mind, and some decisions to make.

Mel grappled with some euros, threw them down on the table and strutted off, she was enjoying being in control. She delved into her bag for her phone and rang James.

'Hullo, how are you?'

'Good, you?'

'Where are you? Sounds like you're driving.'

'I am, Marcus is finally back, and I am picking him up from the airport. Why don't you head to mine, and we can all catch up over a drink?'

'Ok see you shortly.'

Hanging up, she dialled another number.

'Mr Davies please, Yes, Mrs Baker his goddaughter. Yes, I'll hold.'

\*

Mel reached James's house, just as she saw the large 4x4 pull up to the electric gates, 'Mel!'

'Hi, you two, how are you Marcus, good trip?'

Mel followed as the car moved into the driveway and Mel walked behind.

'I'm dying for a cuppa,'

'Yes me too.'

They sat around the kitchen island, chatting and finding out about how Marcus's trip had gone, turns out paperwork is being delayed everywhere. James was oddly jittery, and Mel knew why.

'So, any washing I can do for you?' James asked.

'Umm yeah sure,' Marcus clearly didn't really fancy doing it himself.

James found Marcus's bag out in the hall, 'Do you want me to do all of what's in here?'

'Yeh that would be amazing, here let me help.'

They brought the bag into the kitchen, Mel watched as James helped sort out the washing. Then all of a sudden, Marcus let out, 'Oh god I am so so sorry.'

'Why? What's up?'

      Marcus pulled out an envelope from one of the side pockets in his bag, 'I totally forgot, James I am so sorry, let me post it now, I will pay for next day delivery…'

'No don't be silly,' Mel interrupted.

James looked quizzically on,

'It was only a silly update for my solicitor, here let me.' Mel interjected.

'Are you sure? I had so much on my mind and…'

'Honestly Marcus, I know the feeling.' She popped the envelope in her bag and smiled.

James shovelled the clothes into the washing machine with newfound vigour. He clapped his hands together, 'Right who wants some fizz?'

Mel left the boys to it after a couple of glasses and made her way back to the apartment, she needed to eat. She made a sandwich and sat overlooking the pastel-coloured buildings, down to the masts of the yachts below. An alert on her phone made her jump, *Bloody email*. Another spam one no doubt, however, the subject grabbed her attention '*2nd instalment of funds*'. This she had to read straight away.

## Chapter 45 – Theresa returns

Cathy and Chris had gone home, it was evident that Cathy needed more time and Mel needed someone she could rely on to keep an eye on her house. Apparently though Cathy had seen Gino once more before she'd left.

Mel could now spend some time with Pascal, and they had spent the whole weekend together. Which she had thoroughly enjoyed. As a lover, he was attentive and passionate, warm and gentle and made her feel very special.

'I can't believe how the time has flown by.'

'How do you mean?' He kissed her on the back of the head as he leant over her to grab a piece of her croissant.

'I mean, I have been here nearly two months and Theresa's gets back tomorrow, well I think it's tomorrow. The line wasn't very good and with the time difference I'm not sure.'

'Maybe ask her for her flight number, and we can track it?'

'Aren't you clever one!' She stood up and went over to sit on his lap feeding him more croissant.

'Merci,' he mumbled

'You are welcome,' they kissed, and he ran his hand up her dressing gown and cupped her breast. He tweaked her nipple. She moaned. Then wriggling away, she said, 'Not now handsome, I have to get the flat sorted, and Simone will be here in a minute to help.'

'Ok you are the boss.' he winked and smacked her bottom playfully as they walked to the shower together.

'So, when will I see you next, and have you made up your mind to stay?'

'I will stay on as long as Theresa doesn't mind, then, well, I just have a couple of things to sort out.'

As they stepped into the shower together, Pascal looked downbeat. 'Hey, chin up, I am only one flight away, and I thought you might like to come to England with me for a trip?'

*

'Bloody hell, another one?' James shouted down the phone as he got off the plane back in Nice.

He couldn't believe it, the whole process had been painful, he had gone back to London for Darren's funeral and booked in appointments to try and get things moving regarding the money and paperwork. The lawyers have said they were waiting on some documentation from the police... the list went on.

Back at his home, he sat, his flip-flopped feet resting on the footstool, gazing at the pool, and pondered.

*If this doesn't hurry up, we will lose the villa to do up, I will have let Mel down.*

The mobile next to him began to vibrate,

'Hullo.'

'Yes speaking.'

'Ah bonjour Monsieur estate agent.'

'Oui, oui'

'TO WHOM?'

'How the fuck?' He threw the phone down next to him.

*

'Mel what a rollercoaster of a time you have had!' To think I nearly didn't send that letter!'

Theresa was full of energy as always. The jet lag didn't seem to affect her in the slightest. In her usual floaty, brightly coloured regalia she flamboyantly dashed around unpacking and commenting on how clean the place was.

'Well, Simone is a star.' Mel added.

'I am so glad you have had a good time, so do you think you will come back?'

'Oh yes, I think so,' she turned and walked into the kitchen to make a drink for Theresa...'and sooner than you think.'

'Darling, did you use the car?'

'Yes I did' Mel shouted back, 'It's full'

'You star, I need to pop out later, do you want to come?'

'I would love to, but I need to see James, he is in a bind about that villa I said we were going to do up together.'

'Of course, we can catch up over dinner?'

'Yes, of course, I am going to walk to his place now.'

'Ok see you soon, I might have a lie-down.'

Mel had become very used to the area now, the bustling streets around the college and university, and the small cobbled tracks up to James' house. She pressed the buzzer firmly, 'It's me'. The gates moved aside and she made her way up the steps to the front door. James was waiting for her.

'Hello you, you look well.'

Mel had to admit she couldn't say the same for James, he looked knackered and clearly needed a good night's sleep.

'Thanks.' She said as he

Kissed her on both cheeks. 'Come in.'

'OK so what's up?' Quite unexpectedly James burst into tears. Mel went to console and comfort him, 'What is it?'

'I am so tired Mel, I think it's release, it's been years of trying and working so hard and now I might lose it.' He pushed his face into her shoulder.

'Now come on James, you won't, you're a fighter like me.'

'Mel you are stronger than you think, I am just tired of always having to fight, all my life. Now I am free from one thing, that horrid man Darren. I am now stuck in a financial bind.' he paused and looked up at her, 'and there is something else…'

'Something else?' Mel went stiff, what the hell was he going to say? What on earth has happened now!

'I'm so sorry,' he took a deep breath, 'an anonymous buyer has bought the villa, we have lost it.'

Mel calmly held him tightly. He had been through the mill. He had told her about the bullying at school for being gay, the macho men in the office giving him grief, then to lose his father and mother, which might have given him financial independence, but that horror Darren had brought new pain.

'James, can I tell you something?

## Chapter 46 - Flashback – Mel and the police

'And you got home at about 12:20?' asked the Sergeant.

'Yes that's right, it seems so silly now to think I was just out shopping! If I've been home earlier I could have helped.' Mel's eyes began to well up.

'It's ok, there there, I'm sorry I had to ask but it's just routine.'

'I, I understand. Can I go home now?'

'Of course, that's fine, I don't think we will need any further assistance with your husband's death, a tragic accident.'

Mel was led out of the police station Cathy was waiting in the car.

'God are you ok?'

'No, not really, I just want to get home.'

'Of course.'

They drove back to Mel's house in silence. The traffic was busy, but they got back in just over 20 minutes.

Later that evening Mel was alone, all alone in the house, she sat looking at her reflection, in the worn and slightly shabby bedroom mirror, she spoke to herself or at least her reflection.

'Well, that was that, lying about 20 minutes isn't a crime surely? Living a humdrum life for 20-years might be considered one though.'

She recalled having to go and identify the body.

'If he'd been found 15-20 minutes sooner…'

'I know, I know I'm so sorry.' wept Mel.

'Now now, you couldn't have done anything.' consoled the doctor.

Mel had known that the roof had been a death trap. She'd known her life was dull, she knew that something had to be done, she just hoped she covered her tracks. An extra 20 minutes to get home hadn't been noted. Anyway, it was polite to be 20 minutes late.

## Chapter 47 – All mine

'So, it's yours?'

'YES!'

'And you plan to live here?'

Mel was brimming with pride and power, she had bought the villa, and she planned to make it hers. The Bucci estate was also starting to pay dividends, and Gino was expanding his plans for more B&B's and shops.

Pascal was dishing out the drinks, 'Did you know?' Theresa asked Pascal.

'No idea!'

'You absolute treasure Mel,' Theresa hugged her. 'I am so excited to have you here, and close by.'

'It will be fun,' James added.

Pascal stood behind Mel and put his arms around her waist, 'It's an exciting next chapter.'

The sun was beginning to set, the wispy clouds had started to turn a golden yellow with hints of red and orange appearing. 'What will you do about the house in England?'

'No rush, I will keep it, I have someone I can trust to run things when I'm away and I will want to go back regularly.' Mel knew Cathy's secrets now and Chris', she had them where she wanted them.

'Plus, there are a few people who I know want to go and stay in England so when I'm not there I will rent it out.' Sweet little Annette had reminded Mel so much of her life before Mark had died, she was going to encourage Annette to break free. Maybe she would rediscover herself.

'Do you still want me to help?'

'Of course, I do James, this is our project. I just fell in love with it the first time I saw it and when things weren't going as fast as we hoped I just couldn't dream of letting it go.' she looked out to the sunset.

James was a good friend, there was something there, a calculating mind, he had been very willing to bump Darren out the way. Anyway, that was covered, she had not destroyed the letter James had meant to send, she had it stashed away somewhere safe, just in case things got rocky she could subtly remind him. It was the same thing with Gino, he had been very fickle and stupid, how dare he try it on with her and then later get off with her friend Cathy? Now she had him under control too. Mel was in control, she had power. All her life it had been the men with power, and now it was her turn.

'You didn't say what's next?' Pascal kissed her on the cheek.

He was amazing, she really was in love. For the first time in years, she felt passion for someone, and it felt good, really good.

'Next? Well, I have always dreamt about having a place in Kefalonia, one of my boys is there now, and ever since a trip some years ago I have wanted to go back.'

'Well, I am in.' James chipped in.

'Me too' said Pascal.

'What? Oh yes make that three!' laughed Theresa.

They watched the sunset and drank champagne. What could be more perfect than this?

## Epilogue – A year ahead

'James, what time are we due to land?'

'In about 15-20 minutes.'

Pascal, Mel and James sat together on the plane to Kefalonia, the flight's progress had been hampered by a small storm that had now passed and they were coming in for a bumpy landing. They went as fast as they could through passport control and baggage reclaim. The estate agent was now ringing Mel.

'Yes, yes we are on our way.' She shouted into the phone. As she passed the various car hire vendors and men with signs waiting for their pickup.

They jumped in a taxi and sped across the island. Mel made a note, once the house viewing was over, that they would go sightseeing.

They squealed off the main road onto a narrow track which became very steep and wound their way carefully down. They started to get glimpses of Ithaca an island that stood proudly just off Kefalonia in the gin-clear Aegean Sea. Just like in Greek mythology, the whole place had an aura, one that felt special, magical in fact.

They pulled into a steep cobbled driveway and drove through an avenue of tall trees, before coming out into the sun. A wonderful stone house stood before them, with balconies overlooking the view of Ithaca.

'Perfect.' Mel said as she scrambled to get out of the damn taxi.

'Kalí méra.' She shook hands with the agent, he didn't look very happy, but it wasn't anger but surprise that was spread across his face.

'This is James and Pascal, can we go in?'

'No.'

'What do you mean?'

'You are 20 minutes late, the sale has happened.' He shrugged.

'HOW IS THIS POSSIBLE?' Mel was fuming, they had dashed across from Athens, missed seeing the wonders it had to offer in order for this little man to tell her the house had sold within minutes of them disembarking the aircraft and arriving!

Pascal stepped forward, 'This is Madame Baker, she has an appointment.'

Mel loved how he fought for her corner, like a knight in shining armour, gallant and fearless.

'I know, it has been sold over the phone.'

'Without a viewing?' Mel questioned.

'He saw the pictures online.'

'He? He? That isn't enough to go on, you have to look over a place, that man is stupid who is he?' asked James

'It's a group I believe, the Bucci estate.'

'I could bloody well kill him!' gasped Mel.

## **Acknowledgements**

Thanks to everyone who helped me so much, thanks go to Angie Beeston and Michael Heppell for helping me build the confidence to write a book. Special thanks to Edward King for the moral and emotional support over the past two years (or should I say 14 years and counting!). Last but definitely not least, an enormous thanks to the most amazing mother and editor I could ask for, Tracy Hastain - Thank you. Here's to the next one! C x

Twitter @CharlieHastain

Instagram @charlie_writesbooks


Copyright

Rediscovery on the French Riviera © 2022, Charlie Hastain

All rights reserved.          **ISBN:** 9798359260183

No part of this publication may be reproduced, stored in a retrieval system, stored in a database and / or published in any form or by any means, electronic, mechanical, photocopying, recording or otherwise, without the prior written permission of the publisher.

Printed in Great Britain
by Amazon